# PRAISE FOR
## *THE ROAD TOWARDS HOME*

"Corinne Demas is amazing! *The Road Towards Home* is about two opinionated, rigid, and, yes, curmudgeonly septuagenarians who will have you falling in love and rooting for them as they negotiate and argue their way to a last run at happiness. Noah and Cassandra are so believable that I'm certain I've been over at their house for dinner—and the dialogue between them made me laugh out loud and also shake my head at their stubbornness. I utterly adored this novel, which is filled with wisdom and generosity and heart, qualities that readers of all ages will appreciate."
    —Maddie Dawson, bestselling author of *Matchmaking for Beginners*

"When Noah (saved the world with a boat) meets Cassandra (sees the future way too clearly) at the aptly named Clarion retirement home, they are both seriously not getting with the program. Though barely acquainted, they agree to escape together. As they break free from the planned trajectory and plunge into the uncharted territory of each other, you'll be rooting for the oldsters all the way. *The Road Towards Home* is a wonderful novel—engaging, wry, and genuinely touching."
    —Valerie Martin, author of *Property* and *I Give It To You*

"How welcome and true: late love, beautifully and wryly rendered. Both light hearted and insightful, with age-defying charm and wit, *The Road Towards Home* is a totally satisfying (and identifiable!) read."
    —Elinor Lipman, author of *Ms. Demeanor* and *Rachel to the Rescue*

"This latest novel by the always wonderful Corinne Demas is about a growing relationship through the hiccups of aging. The two main characters are both fascinating and thoughtful people. He an English professor emeritus, she a bug-and-spider scientist plus bird-watcher. The 'home' of the title is rather two homes: the first where they remeet (they knew one another in college some fifty years in the past), and the second Noah's rather charming but broken-down cottage on a Cape Cod marsh, a great metaphor for the two of them. They are both wise and wisecrackers, both loving and snarky. And I, at eighty-three, sat up half the night finishing the book. It's *that* good."

—Jane Yolen, author of *The Devil's Arithmetic* and the short story collection *The Scarlet Circus*

"In the novel *The Road Towards Home*, feisty entomologist Cassandra Joyce, who has been married multiple times, moves to a senior-living community. Quickly, she finds Clarion Court is not her clarion call. So, too, does widower Professor Noah Shilling, whose son and daughter-in-law are behind his relocation. When Cassandra drives Noah to his summer cottage on Cape Cod, there's a lifetime of baggage to be unpacked. Kudos to Corinne Demas—heralded author of thirty books for children, teens, and adults—for this late-in-life romance: a story that shows both love and friendship can be found where and when least expected . . . and most necessary. Cassandra and Noah will open your mind—and your heart—to finding love at any stage of life. Uniquely uplifting."

—Marilyn Simon Rothstein, author of *Crazy to Leave You*

# The Road Towards Home

# The Road Towards Home

## CORINNE DEMAS

LAKE UNION
PUBLISHING

Published by Lake Union Publishing, Seattle

www.apub.com

Amazon, the Amazon logo, and Lake Union Publishing are trademarks of Amazon.com, Inc., or its affiliates.

ISBN-13: 9781662511905 (paperback)
ISBN-13: 9781662511899 (digital)

Cover design and illustration by Philip Pascuzzo

Printed in the United States of America

*For Matt*

*They forgave each other for what they were ashamed of in their past, they forgave everything in the present, and felt that this love of theirs had changed them both.*

"The Lady with the Dog," by Anton Chekhov

# I

There was a new resident at Clarion Court. Noah normally didn't pay attention to the arrival of newcomers, but he couldn't miss this one because she was accompanied by one of the biggest dogs he'd ever seen. Dog owners could live only in first-floor apartments, which had french doors opening straight outside so they could take their beasts for walks without menacing the other tenants. Cat owners—Noah was one—and the petless could live on the second and third floors. The downside of an upper floor was getting stuck making small talk if someone joined you in the elevator. The upside was you got a balcony. High enough so you had a view over the conservation land with a meandering river— polluted, perhaps, but scenic nevertheless, from the distance. (If you had the misfortune to be on the east side, you looked out over the parking lot.) The west-facing balconies also had the sunsets, though Noah feared they encouraged residents who had decided to spend their dotage doing watercolors, and who were not embarrassed, as they should have been, to have their framed work on display in the hallway that Clarion Court—equally without embarrassment, or was it cynically?—called "The Gallery."

Noah watched the woman being dragged along by her dog on the overly-groomed trail that led towards the marshland. Surely the Clarion Corporation, when deciding on a pet-friendly environment, had something in mind more like a cat or a goldfish. Nowhere in the brochure did it mention livestock, and this hairy Goliath was black and white, like a Holstein. Noah recalled someone had been forbidden to bring in a rooster. No, must have been a chicken.

Noah went inside his apartment and found his binoculars. They had been a present from his son, Larry, along with a bird identification book. Birdwatching from his balcony was one of the hobbies Larry's wife, the Intrepid Elizabeth, had decided Noah should pursue now that she'd managed to have him incarcerated at Clarion Court. The binoculars were top of the line, a feeble attempt of Larry's to assuage his guilt in going along with Elizabeth.

"So, Dad, how are you feeling? Settling in OK?" Larry had asked after they'd moved him in.

"It feels as if I stepped into my own coffin and someone shut the lid."

"Your father has always been overdramatic," said Elizabeth, to Larry, as though Noah was not present.

"Quite the contrary," said Noah. "His father has always expressed his reaction to a crisis with the mildest verbiage possible."

Elizabeth, consistently humorless, merely scowled.

Noah had no desire to identify birds, so he'd off-loaded the book on a shelf in the Clarion "library"—a room that would have been a pleasant retreat for a booklover like him if it weren't for the tables covered with jigsaw puzzles—and used his binoculars to watch more interesting things. Like the new resident having to stand around acting nonchalant while her dog squatted in an ungainly way to defecate on the wood-chipped path. Residents were expected to clean up after their pets, but this woman had failed to produce a doggy-poop bag, which must come in jumbo sizes to accommodate the manure pile her dog had produced. Noah refocused his binoculars. Yup! A scofflaw for sure. She found a stick by a tree and started to prod the pile, but the stick was defeated quickly by the volume, and the woman tossed it and started back to the building, leaving the pile where it had been deposited. This was promising.

That night in "The Terrace" dining room, Noah heard a laugh that was disquietingly familiar. Everything at Clarion Court was given a name. It was like a theme park. "The Terrace" dining room was for "gracious dining" (as described in the brochure). The more informal dining room was called "The Garden," and the snack bar was "The Nook," which sounded like a time-out corner in a progressive preschool.

In "The Terrace" tables were arranged in clusters separated by chest-high dividers, many of them planters where philodendrons were replaced the moment they started drooping. The aging residents might be drooping, but the philodendrons were perennially youthful.

There were no tables for one, but Noah had slung a sweater over the other chair. It was a navy-blue sweater, given to him by Larry, selected, no doubt, by the Intrepid Elizabeth, which had a little insignia on the chest of someone on horseback playing—what was it, lacrosse? No, polo. He disliked insignias on clothing, and the idea of advertising such an elite sport was particularly ridiculous. It was a sweater he'd never wear (even when his son and family came for their Dutiful Visit), but he brought it to dinner.

"Shall I put your wine away in the cellar, Dr. Shilling?" Residents at Clarion were able to import their own wine, which was stored for them somewhere in the back of the kitchen and brought to them at dinner. The waitress tonight, Adele, was one Noah particularly liked. She looked almost old enough to be a resident herself—though Noah thought sadly that on what she made, she'd never be able to afford to live here. Unless that was one of the perks?

Noah squinted at the bottle. It was close enough to half-empty to count. "Thank you, Adele," he said. "I may as well finish it." He would have liked to have called her by her last name, too, but the staff at Clarion went by first names, and the residents all by their last. A reversal of elementary school.

"Dessert, sir?"

Noah shook his head.

"There's a special blueberry cobbler tonight."

"Tempting, I'm sure," said Noah, "but I don't eat cobblers as a matter of principle."

"Ice-cream?"

"Thank you, no. I'm happy with just this." Noah touched the neck of the wine bottle. He wished there was a way to tip individual servers, but monthly gratuities went into a common pool.

Noah filled his wineglass, took a sip, and leaned back in his chair, his eyes shut. Once he had been interested in wine and had spent an unforgivable portion of his salary on Burgundies and Bordeaux, but now he was indifferent to them. It wasn't that his taste buds failed to distinguish the subtle distinctions between vintages and châteaux but that he no longer cared. What he liked was wine itself, and unless it was particularly bad, he was content.

Noah tuned out the chatter at the table on the opposite side of the planter. Several women's voices, and occasionally one male's. David Sussman, he guessed, who talked little and grunted much. Women outnumbered men at Clarion Court eight to one. In spite of presenting the most disagreeable facade he could muster, Noah was still besieged by the ladies.

"How flattering," Elizabeth had said when he reported this.

"Hardly," said Noah. "The paucity of male specimens contributes to the situation. And I am one of the few eligible men still on my feet with my faculties more or less intact." This was not an exaggeration. The few younger men who were relatively hardy were there with their wives. The single men—predominantly widowers—were more often confined to wheelchairs or straddling walkers.

"I need to beat them off with a stick," he continued, knowing this would rankle Elizabeth, who, when convenient, was an outspoken feminist.

Then there was that distinct laugh again. It went up the scale, descended a few notes, halted tantalizingly, then rose again. It wasn't a laugh he'd heard recently—he was fairly sure of that—but it stirred something in him. It annoyed him that he couldn't place it, but he'd gotten resigned to the fact that his brain was inundated with trivia, a great swarming mass of untethered sights and sounds and smells that no longer connected to anything solid.

Noah drank his wine and refilled his glass. The party of ladies at the nearby table was departing, and before Noah could grab what was left of his bottle and escape, a gaggle of ladies had descended upon him.

"There's someone new we'd like you to meet." Obviously pretending to be dozing hadn't been sufficiently successful. Noah opened his eyes and looked up into the overeager face of Jennifer DeMatteo, whose skill as a top-selling real estate agent made her a natural ringleader of social life at the Clarion. The woman she had in tow was the Lady with the Dog. Behind them, three smiling ladies—whose names Noah had never bothered to try to remember—bobbed like plastic dashboard figures. And behind them, David Sussman grunted.

"This is Cassandra Joyce," said Jennifer. "She moved here last week. She's in the Waskawiczes' old apartment."

Noah had no idea who the Waskawiczes were, nor did he care. He pulled himself to his feet and held out his hand.

"Noah," he said.

"Noah Shilling," said Jennifer.

"My apologies. I'd thought it was a hyphenated first name, Cassandra-Joyce."

"No, Joyce is my last name," said the Lady with the Dog. "As with James."

"Ah," Noah said.

David Sussman grunted more audibly. "I thought we were going to play a round of Scrabble."

"We are!" said Jennifer brightly. "Why don't you join us, Noah?"

"Thank you," he said. "I'll take a pass tonight."

"That's what you always say!"

"For good reason," said Noah, and then because there was no point in ruffling Jennifer DeMatteo, he smiled and added, "But I will someday. So be on your guard!"

"We'll all look forward to it," said Jennifer, and she took Cassandra's arm.

"You know, I think I'll take a pass, too, this evening," said Cassandra.

"But everyone's so eager to get to know you better!"

"There will be plenty of opportunities for that," said Cassandra. She extricated her arm from Jennifer's grasp, pushed aside the sweater on the chair across from Noah, and sat down.

Jennifer, outflanked and momentarily perplexed, took a breath, then looked at Cassandra, eyebrows up, as if to suggest she knew what Cassandra was up to. But Cassandra smiled innocently, as if oblivious to the hint.

Jennifer took a second to recover her cheerfulness. She slid her disengaged arm through poor David Sussman's. "Scrabble time!" she announced to her entourage. "See you later, then," she said, and she waved to Noah and Cassandra with her free hand.

Cassandra said not a word until the entire entourage had made their slow way out of "The Terrace" dining room. Then she leaned across the table and in a loud stage whisper said, "That was a narrow escape."

"You're not a fan of Scrabble?"

"I have nothing against Scrabble. It's all those well-meaning people."

"They can be exhausting, can't they? They descended upon me when I arrived, and I've been trying to fend them off ever since."

"With success?"

"Modest. Hence the sweater." He pointed. "I bring it with me for the purpose of warding off anyone who might want to join me for dinner."

"I guess it didn't work this time!"

"It's not foolproof."

"So I'm a fool?"

"I don't think so," said Noah. He looked around the dining room, and when he spotted Adele, he held his finger in the air until she noticed him and came over.

"Can I get you something, Dr. Shilling?" she asked.

"Another glass, please." Noah tapped the stem of his wineglass.

"Let me guess," Cassandra said when Adele had left. "Orthopedic surgeon? Orthodontist?"

"No," said Noah. "A mere professor. They like their formalities here."

"They didn't refer to me as Dr. Joyce."

"Sexist holdover, no doubt. Let me guess. Pediatrician? Shrink?"

"Entomologist."

"Shall I inform them?"

Cassandra laughed. And there it was. It was *her* laugh.

There was not enough wine left in the bottle to fill Cassandra's glass. He held his own up and began to tilt it but first asked, "You're not a germaphobe, are you?"

"Hardly!"

Noah managed to pour some without spilling too much. "So," he began, "we might as well get the basics out of the way. How did you end up here?"

"That's easy. There aren't that many senior communities in this area that are pet friendly, and I have a dog."

"I know."

"Word gets around."

"It's a dog that's not easy to miss."

"So I'm told!" The laugh, again!

"But why a senior community?"

"Why not?"

"Why not! Where shall I begin?"

"You're not happy to be here?"

"What!"

"Then why are you here?"

"My daughter-in-law convinced my son, who is easily convinced by anything his wife espouses, that it was no longer in my best interest for me to be living on my own in my old house. And in a rare moment of weakness, I allowed him to convince me. Granted, it *was* an old house—1792, to be exact—but I was quite used to navigating the uneven floorboards—beautiful wide-board pine, I might mention—without tripping. Mind you, she was not truly concerned about my welfare as much as thinking of it as an inconvenience to herself because my son would be obliged to cart me to the ER if I required his help."

"I gather you are not fond of your daughter-in-law."

"She is a woman of modest intelligence, excellent bearing, and an instinct for self-preservation. She is tone-deaf to irony. Does that suffice?"

"Oh, yes!"

"Now you have to explain why on earth you've chosen to be here."

"I was tired of the hassles of owning a house. I didn't want to have to shovel in the winter and water the lawn in the summer. And I don't have to clean or cook for myself here—I hate cooking. And there's lots to do here."

"Like what? Scrabble?"

"No! There's a pool. And I love to swim. And there are walking trails. I needed a place where I could walk my dog."

Noah realized both of their glasses were nearly empty. "Willing to have another?"

"Why not?"

"Red?"

"Sure."

Adele was nowhere in sight, but another, younger server appeared. "Would you please fetch me a bottle of my wine. Any red wine will be fine." He turned back to Cassandra. "I have a confession to make to you."

"Maybe you should wait until our glasses are full again."

"I watched you walking that dog of yours earlier today."

"I didn't see you out there," said Cassandra.

"From my balcony."

"And?"

"You didn't pick up after him."

"Oh, that! I'd run out of poop bags. But don't worry. I went back later, fresh rolls in hand, and took care of it."

"I wasn't worried. Since I avoid walking on trails if I can possibly help it, I'm unlikely to benefit from your conscientiousness. But they have their rules here."

"The thing about rules is that too often they exist just to slow things down."

"I like that," he said.

"Does Clarion give you a discount for spying?"

"I wish."

When the bottle was delivered, he took the opener from the server and told her he'd do it himself. Being waited on was one thing; he liked to uncork his own wine. He filled each of their glasses and was about to take a sip, but Cassandra held up her hand.

"I think we should toast first."

"What should we toast?"

"Old friends," she said.

"What?"

"I have a confession for you, but first—" She clinked her glass against his.

"I'm all ears."

"Hearing aids in?"

"My eyesight may have diminished, but my hearing, I thank you, is just fine."

"And other organs?"

"Still operating, though perhaps rusty with disuse." He took a long sip of wine and set his glass down firmly on the table. "Confession?"

"We know each other."

"We do?"

"Well, we knew each other once, about fifty years ago."

"We did?"

"I'd seen the list of residents and recognized your name. Then I spotted you at dinner."

"You recognized me?"

"Not exactly. It was more a process of elimination. And now that we're face to face and talking, I can connect you with the person I knew."

"But where do we know each other from?"

"You went to Amherst, didn't you? I went to Mount Holyoke. Second semester, junior year, I dated your roommate, Charlie Gustafson."

"Oh!" That laugh! He hadn't been crazy. "But I don't remember a Cassandra Joyce."

"Joyce is my married name. And I was Sandy back then. Sandy Karras."

He stared at her.

"Same eyes! Same nose! Same teeth!" She spread her lips wide to reveal what was in fact still a perfect set.

"I do remember you. You had really long dark hair, didn't you?" Her hair was shoulder length now, scraggly, but still quite dark. His was nearly white. At least he hadn't gone bald, in spite of the fact that his mother's father had been bald. A genetic anomaly. He and Charlie Gustafson had been friendly roommates, but they hung out with different crowds.

"You were a member of SDS or something, weren't you?"

"Not exactly. But I was always protesting something. And you were a clean-cut, boring old jock."

"Guess so. But I was always curious about you hippies. All that free love!"

"For your information, I was a virgin when I graduated."

"I'm not sure I need to know that."

"I made up for it in grad school."

"I'm not sure I need to know that either."

"On that happy note, I'll say good night. There's a dog waiting for his dinner. But we can continue this conversation another time."

"That would be nice," said Noah.

"One more thing, for your information. I am not in the market for a new husband. I've had more than my share."

"That's a relief."

Cassandra got up from the chair and replaced the sweater over the back of it. "Just in case they return." She did not wave goodbye or turn back again.

# II

Melville had been sleeping on the sofa when Cassandra got back to her apartment. He lumbered to his feet as quickly as he could manage, but even if he'd been at the door to greet her, the dog hair on the sofa would have given him away. He looked too tired to wag his tail, but wag his tail he did, and he trotted over, nuzzled her fondly, and drooled on her neck when she crouched to hug him.

"Hello, you big, sweet goofus," she said.

She lugged out the bag of dog food that took up most of the space in the small kitchen pantry. She'd moved in more than a week before but still hadn't found a place to store the food she'd carted from her old house, let alone big, useless things like the pressure cooker and the lobster pot. The dog dish wasn't exactly clean, but she gathered Melville wouldn't care, and he didn't. She'd walk him before she went to bed.

Melville would have liked to sleep in Cassandra's bed at night, but even when Rob was dead and unable to protest as he'd done when alive, Cassandra made Melville sleep on the floor. It was not merely his size, his shedding, and his drool but the fact that he was rarely what you would call clean. He loved to swim, and when he had no access to lake, pond, or ocean, he'd waddle in ditches and puddles, collecting not just water but mud, sticks, and a variety of debris. And he smelled. Having him next to the bed, but not on it, was sufficiently comforting. He was an early riser—unlike Cassandra—and he was more effective than an alarm clock because his approach was multifold: nudging her, whining, drooling, and wafting great clouds of doggy breath over her face so she woke batting it away.

Cassandra staggered to the kitchen and fed Melville, then sliced an orange and took it to the bathroom to eat while she showered. Both bathrooms in the apartment were uniformly, deadly white. White towels had been fine in her old house, where the bathrooms were painted vivid colors, but not here. While she ate more breakfast (three slices of cheese, a piece of french bread that was unfortunately already stale, and a glass of milk), she ordered new ones online: two forest-green and two purple bath towels, and an orange bath sheet for Melville. She held the screen of her iPad up to show him. "You'll like this, won't you?" she asked, but Melville was unimpressed.

Her friend Mallory had extracted a promise from her that she'd come for a visit that day, and it was too late to get out of it now. She gave Melville a short walk and fetched her car from the parking lot. He could have ridden in the back of the station wagon, but he preferred the back seat. She opened the window for him, but he stuck his head forward towards her and drooled on her shoulder. It was an hour's drive to Mallory's house—she must have been crazy when she made the date!—and if she went out of her way a little, she could have driven by her old house, but she forced herself to speed past the highway exit. Maybe on the way back.

Cassandra and Mallory had been friends in college, and their friendship had been reignited years later when they'd ended up living near each other. They'd become better friends when they'd campaigned for the new library, and their despair over the narrowly-defeated, failed referendum had brought them even closer. They'd known each other now, Cassandra realized, for more than five decades.

Mallory's house had always been disturbingly immaculate, and because it was warm enough for them to sit outside, Cassandra had been able to bring Melville with her, which would have been impossible if John were home. Mallory's obsession with cleanliness stopped at the back door, but John's encompassed all two acres: patio, garden, and lawn, down to the shore of the small pond in back. He could be undone by a fleck of white bird poop on the armrest of an outdoor chair. The pond, gloriously untamed, was out of his jurisdiction, since it was conservation land the developers had been forced to set aside in exchange for being allowed to install septic systems in wetlands.

Cassandra let Melville off his leash.

"He's not going to take off somewhere?" asked Mallory.

"No worry. There's only one place he'll go." And he did.

The pond was too murky for swimming, unless you were a dog, but an ideal habitat for dragonflies and damselflies. Cassandra planned to come when the weather was warm enough for them to be out, but without Melville, since it was impossible to observe odonates with him splashing around. When the girls were young, she used to bring them here in the winter to skate with Mallory's kids, a boy and a girl. Both of them were perfect children who had grown up to be accomplished adults who had produced grandchildren who were not only perfect, but accessible. Mallory never bragged about them, but she didn't need to—the facts were all there. The Christmas card photo of the family gathering in Maine—the pyramid with smiling grandparents, children, grandchildren, in matching red sweatshirts—was not a staged display but an honest representation of harmony and affection. If Cassandra wasn't so fond of Mallory, it would have made her sick.

"Well, you don't look the worse for wear!" said Mallory after they'd embraced.

"Was I supposed to?"

"Moving into a senior community accelerates the aging process."

"An urban legend. And it's a retirement community, not assisted living. A critical distinction. Here I am, the same me. No walker, no cane!" Cassandra did a little circle dance, waving her arms in the air, and Mallory smiled at her indulgently and shook her head.

Cassandra plopped down on the faux-wicker chair. She'd sounded upbeat when she'd prattled on to Noah Shilling about her decision to move to Clarion Court, but though she may have convinced him she was entirely on board, she hadn't yet convinced herself. There was a certain dishonesty, she realized, when you tried to simplify something that had in fact been rather complex, and there had certainly been emotionally treacherous moments as she'd navigated her way from house to apartment. There still were.

"I know you've got your prejudices against places like Clarion," she said, "but let me ask you this—what would you do if John suddenly dropped dead? Would you stay in this big house alone? Or would you move in with your kids?"

"I'd stay here, of course. My kids love me, but who wants to be underfoot? I don't worry about John dropping dead, though. He'd never do anything that dramatic. He'll just peter out slowly. In fact he's already begun. And he's hardly essential around here—he's already been replaced by a handyman, a gardening service, and an exterminating service."

"If you lived at Clarion, you wouldn't need an exterminating service. There are no mice. It's written in the contract."

"As long as John's still working, I have the house to myself. So I'm happy here." Mallory had retired as a school administrator a decade before and filled her days with the kind of projects that Cassandra found boring, and said so.

John, who'd already ventured across that scary threshold to the next decade—eighty!—was a psychiatrist and still trotted off to his office every day. Some of his patients had been seeing him for more than forty years—without being cured—and he'd vowed to continue his practice until they no longer needed him. Or were dead.

"You never told me: How did the girls feel about your move?"

"Oh, well, it's not been exactly easy." Whatever small competitiveness Cassandra and Mallory had once felt when they were students had evaporated, and they talked now with an honesty that would have been unimaginable when they were young. Perhaps, thought Cassandra, it was because now there was nothing to lose.

"I was thinking especially of Maggie."

"When I said I was selling the house and moving to Clarion, she immediately asked 'Are you doing this to punish me?'"

"Why would she think you'd want to punish her?"

"For moving to New Zealand. Which is about as far away as Maggie could possibly have moved if it were *she* punishing *me*."

"What did you say to her?"

"I wasn't going to waste our phone time with me bawling—which sometimes happens when I'm talking to Maggie—so I pulled myself together and told her I missed her and I'd give anything to have her closer. It stinks to get to see my grandchildren only once a year."

"I can imagine," said Mallory.

"She asked me if I understood why she was there."

"Do you?"

"Ostensibly it's because Kathryn's family and job are there, and that's where they met. But Maggie's family is here, and both she and Kathryn could get jobs here. So I don't really understand."

"Is that what you told her?"

"What I said was: 'I'm trying.'"

"You're getting more tactful in your old age."

"Yeah, well—some things change for the worse."

"How did she feel about you selling the house?"

"She was surprised, since she'd thought I loved it. But I told her I loved it less than I used to, and I was tired of having to take care of it. There were other things I'd rather be doing."

"Perfectly reasonable."

"What I couldn't tell her was that I'd been hanging on to the house since Rob died only because of a reckless hope my grandchildren would come for long visits. But now it's clear that's never going to happen. Maggie and family are on the other side of the world, and Laurel and her husband had no intention of having children. So there went my dream!"

"People change their minds."

"Maggie?"

"Well, maybe not."

"The house just seemed to reproach me, Mallory. One woman and nine rooms, eleven if you count the bedrooms on the third floor, seemed ridiculous, even with the addition of a large dog. I put it on the market on impulse, and then it was snapped right up before I could really think about it."

They both looked out at the pond where the large dog in question was paddling happily in brown water.

"What was Laurel's response to it all?"

"Actually I didn't tell her until the house was already sold and the moving van was scheduled."

"Cassandra!" said Mallory, dragging out the middle syllable in exasperation, just as she used to do when they were young.

Cassandra held up her hands. "OK, you're right, you're right! But I kept putting it off because I was afraid of her reaction. Or maybe I was afraid she wouldn't care at all."

"Did she?"

"You know how it is. I've never been very good at predicting anything about Laurel. It turned out she was more upset than I would have ever expected. 'You could have at least consulted me first, Mom,'" said Cassandra, perfectly capturing Laurel's injured tone. "'Did you consult Maggie?'"

Mallory sighed. "There's still that?"

"Yup! Laurel's nearly fifty years old, and she still feels aggrieved anytime she fears her sister has been shown preference."

"So what did you say to her?"

"I told her the truth. I said, 'I did not consult Maggie. I informed her, as I am informing you.'"

"But you didn't let her know you'd told Maggie about the move weeks before?"

"OK," said Cassandra, getting to her feet. "So I didn't."

Mallory got up, too, and they watched Melville emerge close to shore, decorated by pond guck. He stood chest deep in the water and panted in the sunlight.

They were quiet for a while, then Mallory was the first to speak. "Jay and Adriana decided to come back early from their sabbatical in France."

Cassandra turned to look at her. "How come?"

"Adriana never wanted to go abroad in the first place. She said she wanted to come back because the children were having difficulty socializing, but I think it's because she misses the comforts of home. King-size bed, the right sort of milk. She doesn't adapt easily. She wants everything to be just so. She's her father's daughter."

"And Jay?"

"He's used to Adriana. I think he was surprised she lasted that long. I'm worried they won't be able to get a refund on their house rental there. Not to mention they'll have to oust Jay's brother, who's been living in their house for a low rent in exchange for taking care of their cats."

"You do put more energy into worrying than most people."

Mallory sighed. "I wish I could be like you. You manage to weather everything without suffering a lot of stress."

"Not exactly."

"I'm sorry, Sweetheart. What I should have said is you deal with it better than I do."

"Not always."

Mallory studied her for a moment, then reached a hand out and laid it softly on Cassandra's forearm. "You know, you don't have to stay at Clarion Court if it doesn't seem right for you."

"I can't get my old house back."

"No, but there are other houses. You're not stuck at that place forever."

"But I can't just bail!"

"Why not?"

"I don't like seeing myself as the kind of person who can't stick with something."

"Are you referring to Denny?"

"Well—"

"Leaving a destructive, unsuitable marriage bears no resemblance whatsoever to moving out of a senior living community to live someplace that's more—that's more *you*."

"It's the indecision. I don't do well with it—consult my internal organs for confirmation."

"Indecision is a temporary state."

"OK, then let's say I do end up deciding I've made a horrible mistake. How do you think I should go about extricating myself?"

"You'll come up with something. You always do."

They were quiet for a moment, then Mallory smiled and started getting to her feet. "Come, let me show you what we've done in the basement since you've been here. We've set up a gym."

"A gym?"

"John's doctor told him he needed to exercise if he cared about his longevity. Which, as you know, he does. Excessively so. And this way we can work out together. I could certainly lose a few pounds, too."

"You could have joined a gym."

"Do you think John would want to share equipment with sweaty strangers?"

They both laughed.

Cassandra followed Mallory inside the house and took off her shoes in the back hallway.

"Would you like some slippers?"

"Stocking feet OK?"

"Of course! Oh, before we go downstairs, I want you to see how I've reorganized the pantry."

Mallory opened the folding doors to an array of shiny wire shelving units packed with cans, jars, matching plastic containers, and bins.

"New shelves?"

"Yes," said Mallory, "and they're on casters so you can clean behind them." She rolled one section back and forth.

"I prefer the kind you *can't* clean behind," said Cassandra, but Mallory wasn't really listening.

"Everything's arranged alphabetically," she said, "but I had trouble deciding about some of them. Where would you put the garbanzo beans, 'b' or 'g'? Or 'c' for 'chickpeas'?"

"I've never owned garbanzo beans," said Cassandra. "What are they for?"

"Making hummus."

"Why not just buy it?"

"It's never as good."

The house was built on a hillside, and the gym had been set up in the part of the basement that had sliding glass doors to the backyard. Twin exercise bikes, an elliptical, and a treadmill were stationed so they faced the view. The equipment looked brand new. The floor was covered with black matting that gave off a faint rubbery smell.

"What do you charge for a membership?"

"Friends are free."

"How's it going?"

Mallory sighed. "We started off ambitiously, but we've slacked off."

"That's the way it always is," said Cassandra.

"Are you using the gym at Clarion?"

"I've been using the pool every day, but I hate gyms." Cassandra waved at the exercise equipment. "Instruments of torture. And I have a dog, which means I necessarily get exercise walking him. You can't slack off with dogs."

As they went back out to sit in the garden, Cassandra asked, "Do you remember Charlie Gustafson?"

"That guy you dated junior year? Tried to grow a beard but it always looked like—like something you'd scrub pots with. I never knew how you could kiss him. Did he die?"

"Not that I know of, but by coincidence, his roommate—Noah Shilling—is living at Clarion now. I ran into him at dinner."

"You recognized him?"

"I'd checked over the list of residents when I moved in, and his name popped out at me, and then we were introduced last night at dinner."

"How does he look?"

"Not as decrepit as you might expect. I remember he was ironic back then, and he's a cynical curmudgeon now. But I rather like him."

"Cassandra!"

"No, no, don't get any ideas. I'm not interested in nabbing a new husband. And if I were, I'd choose one two decades younger rather than one over seventy."

"You already tried that. And how did that work out?"

"The sex was great."

"And?"

"You're right." Her marriage to Denny had nearly destroyed her relationship with her daughters.

"How about as a lover?"

Cassandra laughed. "When we were in college, I went out only with guys with scruffy beards, but I'm going to confess something now: I harbored a fantasy about seducing one of the fraternity boys. Noah Shilling was the quintessential clean-cut jock, but I'd found him attractive. Not that I would have admitted it then."

"Did you admit it to him now?"

"Not yet!"

"Oooooo! This sounds promising."

Cassandra laughed again. "I think he has potential as a friend, but certainly nothing more. To begin with, I'm not interested in him, and even if I were, I'm sure he wouldn't be interested in me. I'm an old lady with wrinkles and floppy boobs."

"You still have great legs!"

Cassandra held her legs straight out in front of her. "Yeah, well, some parts of the body hold up better than others." Melville staggered up to them from the pond, and as soon as he was close to Cassandra, he shook himself, leaving the still-great legs slimy, icky, and trailing a piece of algae.

On the way back to Clarion, Cassandra couldn't resist passing by her old house. She drove by quickly first, backed around in a neighbor's driveway, then approached the house slowly and stopped just at the end of the property. The new owners, whom she had come to hate through no fault of their own, had already installed an elaborate climbing structure in the side yard. There was a castle-like platform at one end, with a slide on one side and three swings, a trapeze, and a climbing rope, but there were no children playing on it. Her daughters had had a modest two-swing affair that had eventually rotted. Cassandra sat in her car and allowed herself a moment to picture them swinging on it, both girls pumping hard to see who could get higher. Then she drove quickly back to the highway.

The bathrooms in Clarion apartments were all handicapped accessible—mildly useful, and not so as to be disfiguring. It was a feature Cassandra had found attractive since the handheld shower made the bathtub ideal for washing Melville. At her old house, she'd hosed him down before he came inside, but at Clarion that was not an option. Strawberry-scented shampoo did not entirely mitigate the aroma of Mallory's pond. You were supposed to comb Newfies out first, but Cassandra had long ago decided she did not have a show-quality dog and what Melville lacked in grooming, she'd make up to him in affection. She couldn't find the old beach towels she always dried him with—she thought she'd used them to pack dishes with, but maybe not—so she took two white ones from the bathroom. Her new towels should be arriving in a day or so.

At dinner she didn't see Noah Shilling, and so she allowed herself to be corralled by Jennifer DeMatteo and her crowd. There were complaints about the filet of sole almondine—complaining about the food at Clarion seemed to be an honored conversational topic—but so far she'd liked everything the dining room offered. Maybe she was less critical because she was so relieved not to have to think about cooking for herself.

"I heard through a reputable source that there's a merger afoot, and Clarion Court will soon be part of Oakdale Living," said Jennifer. "So there may be improvements in the menu in the future."

David Sussman grunted.

A tiny woman with curly, unnaturally red hair joined them at the table.

"I thought you'd left already, Carole!" cried Jennifer.

Carole took a chair and caught her breath. "I decided this morning at the last minute not to go. My suitcases were packed, and I was all ready for my ride to the airport, but I suddenly thought, 'Oh, no, this isn't a good idea.' I was this close to leaving," said Carole, and she held up her hand, forefinger pressed to thumb. "But then I thought, 'What if something happened and my daughter's baby was born early and I wasn't here.' My sister was going to meet me at the boat, and I called her just in time before she caught her flight to Florida."

Jennifer turned to Cassandra. "Carole was going on a two-week cruise in the Caribbean."

"My sister told me I was being ridiculous. There was no reason the baby would be coming a month early. And I should enjoy this trip and having a chance to relax before I was helping out with a new baby all the time. But how could I relax when there was a chance that my daughter would go into early labor? I told my sister if she still wanted to go, she should go without me. She could have the cabin to herself."

"Is she going?"

"Maybe. She'll blame me either way. She hates traveling alone, but she hates changing plans at the last minute."

"It's a good thing you decided to stay," said Jennifer. "I can't imagine being stuck on a cruise ship worrying about not being able to get back for the birth of your first grandchild." She turned to Cassandra. "Could you?"

"I'm someone who wouldn't choose to be on a cruise ship in any case," she said. And then, realizing that might be considered tactless in this company, she added quickly, "I get seasick."

There was a documentary film showing and discussion after dinner that people were trooping off to, but Cassandra begged off. She was walking back towards her apartment when she spotted Noah Shilling getting off the elevator. He noticed her when she waved.

"I didn't see you at dinner."

"I'm eating late. I wanted to grab some time in the pool when it wasn't taken over by a water-aerobics class." His hair looked wet still around the ears.

"You don't believe in water aerobics?"

He pumped his arms feebly in the air. "You call this aerobic?"

"You swim laps?"

He nodded. "Easier on the knees than jogging."

"I'd join you for dinner, except I already ate." That was forward of her!

"A drink after dinner, then?"

"I need to feed and walk my dog first. But why not? Actually, I have a question for you."

"Can it wait?"

"Oh, it's nothing important. Why don't you stop by when you're done eating. I'm 124 West."

"Shall I bring a bottle of wine?"

She thought she'd brought some wine when she moved, but the liquor-store boxes she'd unpacked so far had all been books.

"That might not be a bad idea."


Cassandra had done what she'd thought was a heroic job in culling her possessions before she sold her house, but perhaps it had been insufficiently heroic. The small second bedroom, which she'd planned to use as a study, was stuffed with boxes and odd furniture she hadn't been able to part with. There was an island of liquor-store boxes packed with books in the middle of the living room that might be there for a long time. No matter; she could walk around them. She'd already filled the built-in bookcases that flanked the fireplace (electric, not wood-burning—this was a senior living community, after all). The lower and upper shelves held books; the middle shelves were devoted to living creatures—two tarantulas in terrariums, a cage of stick insects, and a cage of crickets. Cassandra had hung a long net cage from a ceiling hook (left from a previous tenant) in anticipation of chrysalises of painted-lady butterflies she planned on ordering. She sprayed water in each of the terrariums, fed a cricket to each tarantula, and gave the stick insects some fresh lettuce. Since the coffee table was piled high with boxes, she put two wineglasses and a corkscrew on a stack of boxes on the floor. Then she made a futile effort to brush some of the dog hair off the sofa and sat down in the spot prewarmed by Melville.

Melville had been lying with his back against the french doors, where it was cooler, when Noah came in, and he lumbered to his feet.

"Stay, beast!" commanded Noah. He gripped his wine bottle with one hand and held up the other, palm towards dog.

"He's quite harmless," Cassandra assured him.

"That's what all dog owners claim."

"He just needs to make sure you're not a threat, and he'll be fine. Just let him sniff you." Cassandra grabbed Melville by the collar as he circled Noah, then settled down again. "See?"

"This was not what I had in mind when I agreed to stop by here," said Noah. He looked around the living room with a critical eye, and Cassandra pointed to a chair that was free of dog hair. He sat down cautiously.

"I gather you don't like dogs. I hope you aren't a cat fancier."

"I happen to have a cat, but I am not fond of cats either."

"Then why have a cat?"

"My daughter-in-law decided a cat would be a good companion for me. So they presented me with one when I moved here. It was a fait accompli."

"That's a pathetic reason for owning an animal. You should donate him to someone who would appreciate him."

"It's a her. And yes, I've considered that." The wine bottle had already been opened. Noah poured them each a glass without asking.

"What do we toast now?"

"Sleeping leviathans," he said, and he gestured towards Melville, who was curled up by the french doors.

"You missed the drama at dinner," said Cassandra.

"Drama? Here at Clarion Court?"

"Apparently a woman named Carole was all ready to set off for a cruise and came to her senses at the last second."

"Carole?"

"Short. Curly red hair that looks like a wig for an amateur production of *Annie*."

"Ah, yes," said Noah.

"Her daughter is going to be having a baby sometime in the next few months, and she was afraid it would arrive while she was stuck on a ship on the high seas. She's opted to be stuck here instead, on this cruise ship that doesn't go anywhere."

"Not exactly a cruise ship, since there's no shuffleboard."

"It might be coming. The rumor mill says that Clarion is about to be taken over by some conglomerate called Oakdale Living and we should expect some changes."

"I have made it a practice to ignore the Clarion rumor mill, and you would be wise to do so as well. And now for the question you had for me?"

"It was actually posed by a Mount Holyoke friend of mine I visited today. Is Charlie Gustafson dead?"

"Dead? What made her think he might be dead?"

"No reason, except lots of people our age are dead."

"Is this friend of yours particularly morbid?"

"No, merely curious. His name came up when I told her about running into you here."

"I'm afraid I'm unable to satisfy her curiosity."

"So I guess you don't keep up with him, then."

"I don't keep up with anybody," said Noah. "And would you mind telling me what that is, in that tank over there?" He pointed to one of the terrariums, where a tarantula was making its way along the side.

"That's Marigold. A Chilean rose, *Grammostola rosea*. I hope you're not an arachnophobe."

"I may not be fond of zoos"—he waved his hand from dog to spiders—"but the only phobia I have is of ladies who try to lure me into Scrabble games."

"She means well."

"Do you?"

"Not always."

"That's good," he said.

# III

It would be the last time Noah would see all of them there at Clarion for what would be a long time—but none of them knew it then. Not even the Intrepid Elizabeth, who, Noah remembered, once claimed that if there was anything she didn't know, she at least knew a way to find out about it.

"Daddy and I have something we need to discuss with your grandfather," Elizabeth said to Cammie and Richard, and she dispatched the children to the Clarion game room. Noah feared this did not bode well.

Tall and wiry, Elizabeth had a patrician nose and eyes that were a color you wouldn't remember. Her personality—quick, imperious, heartless—so matched her looks that Noah wondered how it was possible. She was a caricature of herself. One look at her face and her posture and you would correctly imagine what her voice (brisk, definite, every word clearly enunciated) would sound like too. She was no "Betty," "Liz," or "Lizzie." Noah, in his secret thoughts, called her "Lizard," and that suited her well: an ectomorph married into a family of mesomorphs. Noah wasn't sure if Elizabeth had married his son because he was a project so much in need of improvement or because she'd realized her good fortune in finding a man who'd tolerate her nervous energy and her overriding sense that the world was simply not up to snuff. Noah might have felt sorry for her once.

"There's nothing to do there," whined Richard, but Cammie, more than a year older, leaned close to Noah. "Can we go to the greenhouse?" she asked. "It's kind of hot, but there's that little waterfall thing."

"Of course you can," said Noah, without consulting Elizabeth. "And then how about I take you to lunch afterwards. Just you and me?"

Elizabeth's disapproving intake of breath was so predictable Noah smiled. He looked up at Larry. "You take your wife and son out to lunch, and I'll take Cammie to the dining room downstairs."

"I think it would be better if Camilla—" Elizabeth began.

But Larry cut her off. "I don't see why not," he said. Some kind of nonverbal dealing was going on between him and Elizabeth, something he was promising her in exchange. Noah didn't have to look.

"Well, all right, then," said Elizabeth. "Run off now, and be back by twelve noon."

Cammie consulted her new watch. "That's when both hands point up," she said.

"Correct," said Noah. "And they also both point straight up when it's twelve midnight."

"But everyone is asleep then, so nobody knows."

"I know," said Noah. "I'm often up late, and I check it out."

The children were barely out of the room before Larry began the clearing of throat that Noah knew preceded an uncomfortable conversation, something initiated by Elizabeth, no doubt, with Larry appointed as executioner.

"Elizabeth and I were talking about this coming summer and thought—"

It was always like that: "Elizabeth and I." "I" for "inconsequential," since the thought was entirely Elizabeth's. Because things had worked out so he would be able to take Cammie to lunch, Noah just smiled and waited. He guessed he would not like what was coming next, and he was not proved wrong. Elizabeth's "thought," parroted dutifully by Larry, was that since Noah was so comfortable at Clarion Court, he should consider staying here for the summer and renting out the cottage on the Cape.

"Why would I want to do that?" Noah asked.

"You have a whole community here, and there are so many amenities," said Elizabeth. Was she quoting the Clarion brochure? She looked at Larry, who remembered his lines and added, "Since you're not driving anymore, Dad, we thought a whole summer stuck in the cottage might be lonely for you."

"You are gravely mistaken," said Noah. "The solitude of the cottage suits me perfectly."

Elizabeth didn't wait for Larry to reply. "But the past two summers were so hard for you. You couldn't get anywhere!"

What she meant, of course, was that it was hard for *her*, because Larry had to use one of his vacation days driving Noah down there and helping him get things set up and another day at the end of the summer helping him close up the house and driving him back to Clarion.

"There's nowhere I need to get."

"But you do need to go to the store. You need to buy food!" Elizabeth had taken over Larry's part of the conversation, as she so often did.

"It worked out last summer. Artie and Bernice took me with them when they went shopping."

"You can't impose on them forever!"

"I'm sure if they feel I'm an imposition, they'll inform me of the fact."

There was a moment when all three of them were quiet, and Noah hoped the discussion was at an end, but Larry's renewed throat clearing alerted him that the worst might be yet to come.

"Dad, Elizabeth and I have been considering the possibility that maybe it's time for you to sell the cottage, since you're not using it much anymore, and—"

"Not using it? I intend to use it every summer," said Noah. "And as for selling it, that's out of the question."

"It's a good time to be selling right now," said Elizabeth. Hadn't she heard him? "The cottage is in terrible shape and would probably be a tear-down, but the land is valuable."

"You're right," said Noah, and he enjoyed a second as this unexpected admission sank in. Then he went on. "The land is valuable. It's valuable to me. And the cottage is valuable to me too. It was built by my grandparents, and it's been an integral part of my life ever since I can remember. If Cammie doesn't want the place when she grows up, I'll donate it all to the conservation trust."

That was a cruel blow. But he couldn't resist. Elizabeth brought out the worst in him.

"I still think it's worth considering—" began Elizabeth, but in a rare moment of spousal rebellion, Larry cut her off.

"I think Dad's done talking about it," he said. And as if in response to their father's cue, Cammie and Richard returned, ready for lunch.

"Don't you lock your door?" Elizabeth asked as they left the apartment.

"Nothing much worth stealing," said Noah. "No one's in the market for a cat."

"You have some very good art," said Elizabeth, and Noah wondered if she was aware of the resentment in her tone. She no doubt expected he'd pass some of the paintings on to them when he'd sold his house, but instead he'd brought them all here. There was insufficient wall space to hang them all, so some of them were on the floor, leaning against the wall.

"No one with the strength to steal it," said Noah.

"What about the staff? The maintenance people?"

"I don't think Dad needs to worry about them," said Larry.

"You never know," said Elizabeth, and the arrival of the elevator allowed her to have the last word.

"Lemme push!" cried Richard as they got into the elevator, and he shoved his sister from the panel of buttons.

"You can both push," said Noah. "Richard, you push 'L' for 'lobby'; Cammie, you push 'close' for the door." Richard pushed the "L," and when Cammie had pushed the "close" button, he took a jab at it, too. His finger was stubby, like those "baby" carrots ubiquitous on crudités platters, but Cammie's was so slender Noah feared it could be snapped right off.

"That's my button!" cried Cammie.

"You can push them both when we come back after lunch," Noah told her. "You know, when I was a kid, I lived in an apartment building and rode the elevator all the time," he said as they walked through the lobby. "But I still loved pushing the buttons. Larry, you should get an elevator for that house of yours, so your kids won't grow up deprived."

"Can we get our own elevator, Daddy?" asked Cammie.

"Sure," said Larry. "Why not?" He did not look at Elizabeth.

"You're taking her there?" Elizabeth asked when Noah stopped by the doors to "The Terrace" dining room. "I thought you'd be going to the luncheonette."

"Only the best for my granddaughter," said Noah.

"Why can't I go with them too?" asked Richard.

"You're coming with us," said Larry.

"But it's not fair!" cried Richard, who had inherited his mother's inherent sense of injustice. Noah realized that in this case, at least, Richard was correct. He was flattered that Richard would prefer eating with him than with his parents, but he didn't want to include Richard, not just because he didn't feel up to having lunch with his grandson, but because he knew Cammie would appreciate spending time with him alone. If he were a kinder grandfather, he acknowledged, he would have promised Richard that he'd take him the next time. But he didn't.

"Remember to tuck in your napkin so you don't get anything on your dress," said Elizabeth as they started to go off on their own way.

"We'll just eat invisible food," said Noah, "so the spills won't show."

Cammie giggled and squeezed Noah's arm. "I'm not going to spill anything, Poppy."

Richard, left out, took off noisily (justifiably) for the front entrance, so his parents had to go after him.

In "The Terrace" dining room, Noah glanced around quickly, then sat at his accustomed table for two. Cammie took the seat usually guarded by his sweater. She unfolded the upright triangle of white napkin and spread it assiduously on her lap. The luncheon choices were listed on the menu sheet on their plates.

"What's this say?" she asked.

"I thought you were a great reader."

"This is cursive, Poppy. We don't do cursive in first grade."

"I hope they're still teaching it," said Noah. He lifted the menu and read the choices aloud in a formal voice with a pseudo-British accent that made Cammie giggle so hard she almost toppled her glass of water.

"What's 'poached'?" she asked.

"Cooked in a simmering liquid. The word sounds awful, but the fish is no doubt excellent. I think, however, the quesadilla might be a safer choice. It's what I am going to have."

"Then I will too," said Cammie.

Adele was on lunch duty that day. Noah introduced her to Cammie and ordered the quesadillas and a chocolate milkshake for Cammie.

"I'm not supposed to have that for lunch," she said.

"Then we won't tell," said Noah. "And how about strawberry shortcake for dessert afterwards?" he asked.

"Yum!"

He looked up as Cassandra entered the dining room. As he'd hoped, she came right over to them. She pulled over a chair from the neighboring table and sat on the edge of it. "Hello," she said, "you must be Camilla. Your grandfather told me you were coming. I'm Cassandra, but you can call me Sandy."

"Everybody calls me Cammie. Almost everybody," Cammie added.

"You're seven, right?"

"Yup! I had my birthday in February. I had twelve friends at my party. Remember, Poppy?"

"I do," said Noah. Though the kids running around had been a blur. He would have guessed a hundred kids, at least.

"Second grade?"

"Next year."

"So almost second grade. Right?"

Cammie smiled. "I don't live here. I'm just visiting Poppy."

"That's what I imagined," said Cassandra. "And I hope you'll come again soon."

"I have to wait till Daddy drives me, because it's too far for me to walk. But I'll come every day, when I'm grown up and have my own car."

"Is your grandfather buying you a car?" Cassandra looked over at Noah.

"Why not?" said Noah. "What color would you like?"

"Pink."

"A wise choice," said Cassandra. "Then it will match your dress."

Cammie laughed. "This won't still fit me when I'm grown up."

"Then we'll have to invest in a new pink dress, when the time comes," said Noah.

Adele arrived with the lunch. "I'll be right over with another place setting," she told Cassandra.

"Thank you, but I'm just stopping here for a moment. I'll be sitting over there." Cassandra pointed to a table over the planter. "I don't want to intrude."

"You won't be intruding," said Noah.

"This is a special lunch for just you and Cammie," said Cassandra. "Maybe another time." And when Noah looked at Cammie's face, he could tell Cassandra was right. Women's intuition.

"Should I order the quesadilla?" Cassandra asked.

"Have a taste," said Noah. He slid his plate towards her, but she held her face up like a baby bird, so he cut a piece and held the fork out to her.

"Not bad," she said. "What do you think?" she asked Cammie.

Cammie took a bite of hers. "Not bad!"

"Melville would love this," said Cassandra.

"Who's Melville?"

"My dog."

"He eats quesadillas?!"

"He eats everything."

"He eats a lot," said Noah. "He's big as a horse."

Cammie giggled. "Poppy has a cat. She's a picky eater."

"Sandy not only has a dog, but has a menagerie of tarantulas and stick insects."

"Really?"

"They're called stick insects because they look just like . . ." Cassandra waited.

"Sticks?" asked Cammie.

"That's right!" said Cassandra. "Come see them next time you're here, OK? You're not afraid of insects, are you?"

"No," said Cammie. "I'm not afraid of insects or arachnids." She pronounced the word perfectly.

"I didn't think so."

"Do they come out, or do they stay in their cages?"

"They stay in their cages, but they can come out if you want to hold them."

Cammie looked uncertain.

"They may take a little getting used to." She looked over at Noah. "Poppy hasn't quite warmed to them yet."

"And it's unlikely he ever will," said Noah. Surprisingly, her calling him "Poppy" had seemed OK.

"Do they have names?"

"Of course. The tarantulas are Marigold and Petunia—"

"Petunia!" Cammie broke into giggles.

"The stick insects are nameless, I'm afraid, but you're welcome to name them for me."

"What do they eat?" asked Cammie.

"The tarantulas eat crickets, and the stick insects eat lettuce. Which reminds me—it's time for me to go have my own lunch," said Cassandra, "but let me show you something first. I bet you Poppy knows how to do this, too." She picked up the straw that had come with Cammie's milkshake and made a wiggly worm with the wrapper. It was a trick Noah remembered from sixty years before.

It was amazing what one remembered. And what one forgot.

"Enjoy your lunch," Cassandra said. "And remember, you have a date with Marigold and Petunia when you come here next."

"And Melville too."

"Of course, Melville."

"And all the stick insects who don't have names yet, and I'll give them all names."

"They will be most appreciative."

"Dinner tonight?" asked Noah.

"Sure thing," said Cassandra.

"Is she a new friend?" asked Cammie when Cassandra was barely out of earshot.

"An old friend, actually," said Noah. "We knew each other many years ago."

"When you were kids?"

"When we were in college."

"I like her," said Cammie.

"I'm glad to hear that," said Noah. "I hoped you would."

Cammie had dissected her quesadilla with her fork but not eaten much of it, but she had no trouble devouring the strawberry shortcake. Noah signed his room number on the slip Adele brought and took a last sip from his water glass.

"You know, Cammie," he began, "since your Grammy's been dead, I've been feeling kind of lonely. Now, if you lived with me, that would be one thing, but—"

"I'll come live with you!" cried Cammie.

"No, Honey, your parents would miss you too much. Even that brother of yours would miss you. And besides, you wouldn't want to live here with a bunch of old people."

"You're not that old, Poppy," said Cammie.

"Thank you, Darling. I may not be that old yet, but I imagine I'll be getting old eventually. So I thought it would be nice for me to find someone to keep me company while I'm doing this getting old thing. Maybe get married again. There are lots of ladies living here who would like me as a husband. Not many guys my age who still have their teeth and their marbles."

"Marbles?"

Noah tapped his head. "Brains. So the ladies here are all wild about me. The one you just met, Cassandra, seems like the best of the bunch. So that's why I'm happy you liked her. I think she might be the one."

"And she has a dog and tarantulas."

"A definite plus."


Larry, Elizabeth, and Richard were waiting for them back in his apartment.

"We walked right in," said Elizabeth. "Anyone could walk right in."

"Did you have a nice lunch?" asked Noah.

"You were right about the deli down the road," said Larry. "Good sandwiches." He turned to Cammie. "How about you, Honey? What did you have?"

"We had quesadillas," said Cammie. A smile spread over her face. "And we had strawberry shortcake."

"How come she got cake and I didn't?" wailed Richard. No one answered him.

They didn't stay much longer after that. Cammie hugged Noah tightly.

"Goodbye, my darling," he said. He brushed his palm over her head and stroked the soft upper ridge of her ear.

After they'd left, the room seemed no larger. He looked around at the paintings in the room—the landscapes and especially the seascapes. They were not so much arranged as just crowded on the walls. But he didn't care. He liked being surrounded by these remnants of his old life. He settled in his old leather reclining chair and imagined it back where it belonged, in the reading corner of his study in his old house: the bookcases with books two deep—books he'd taught, books he'd read at least once but didn't remember well—the fireplace with a log charred on the underbelly and the bellows propped against the brick.

His plan had gone off even better than he had hoped. Cammie would do all the work for him now. Perhaps he should feel bad for using his granddaughter this way, but he was sure it wouldn't harm her. He could picture the alarm on Elizabeth's face as she pumped Cammie for details about Cassandra. He could imagine the discussion between Elizabeth and Larry, Larry saying, "You're the one who wanted him to move there. A hotbed of eager widows."

And Elizabeth, tight lipped, saying, "We wanted him to move there because it didn't seem safe for him to live alone in that old house anymore—uneven floorboards, narrow stairs."

And Larry saying, "It's a good thing you didn't persuade him to give up the cottage. If he's away all summer, maybe this whole affair will cool down."

"As long as he doesn't marry her first!"

They wouldn't ask him outright about Cassandra, wouldn't admit they pushed Cammie to disclose whatever she could. But they'd be more solicitous of him, and the Intrepid Elizabeth would have to be more cautious about saying or doing anything that might displease him. She would willingly allow Larry to chauffeur him to and from the cottage on the Cape.

At dinner that night, Noah told Cassandra about Elizabeth's complaint that he didn't lock the door to his apartment when they went to lunch. "I don't suppose you have to think about locking," he said, "not with that guard beast of yours."

"Oh, Melville would be quite useless if someone entered my apartment when I was out. And if they gave him something that resembled food, he'd become fast friends."

"You also have those terrifying tarantulas."

"I was about to say that Marigold and Petunia wouldn't hurt a fly, but that of course is not accurate. They might well devour it. The truth is, I have nothing much anyone would care to steal. If a thief did get into my apartment, perhaps they'd take pity on me and help me reduce the quantity of stuff. What do you have worth stealing?"

"Nothing much of value except some paintings that Elizabeth has had her eye on since she first entrapped my son. She already has the picture hooks in place on her living room walls, awaiting my demise."

"You really don't like her, do you?"

"That is a fairly accurate assessment. And I have yet to be presented with a reason to revise my opinion."

"Well, here's one: Cammie's a truly delightful little person, and Cammie's her daughter, so at least she's done a good job parenting."

"Or Cammie is delightful in spite of her."

"There's something else at work here."

"And you expect to ferret it out?"

"I do," said Cassandra, "but not tonight, and not until we know each other a little better." And then she got up from the table.

"I was going to invite you to my apartment for an after-dinner drink."

"Another time. I enjoy the verbal scrimmage, but I don't want us to get tired of each other. We may be stuck at Clarion together for a long time."

# IV

There were ribs for dinner. Cassandra was a confirmed omnivore, but meat with the bones still intact gave her pause. When Maggie had embraced vegetarianism as a teenager, she'd actually thrown up at the sight of a standing rib roast, and Cassandra hadn't been able to face one since. Maggie had been dogmatic, pugnacious, and self-righteous (in spite of the fact that she was not a true vegetarian, since she was heartless when it came to invertebrates), and though Cassandra had found this trying, she'd tried to be equitable and cater to all eating choices at dinner—a particular challenge for someone who didn't like to cook at all. Maggie's revulsion at the consumption of dead mammals had made Cassandra less able to enjoy dinners that required gnawing on bones. If meat was on the plate on its own without adhering to anything skeletal—or better yet, ground up and rolled into balls or flattened into patties—it was easy to disassociate it from a creature who had once mooed, baaed, or oinked.

Cassandra had ordered the fettuccini alfredo, a cholesterol-boosting road to the grave, but at least guiltless when it came to what Maggie described as "murder."

"David's not joining us for dinner tonight," reported Jennifer. "He's come down with the flu. We'll need you at Scrabble." She pointed at Cassandra.

"I don't think—" Cassandra began, but Jennifer cut her off.

"I've managed to persuade Barbara. She's been putting me off forever, but she agreed to join us tonight." She turned to smile at Barbara Enfield, who looked up from her dinner, a strand of fettuccini dangling from her impatient fork.

"Jennifer is pretty persistent," said Barbara. "Scrabble is not exactly my choice of how to spend an evening, but I decided to play tonight and hope I'll have paid my dues for the year." This was one of the longest speeches Cassandra had ever heard from Barbara. Barbara, like quite a number of residents at the Clarion, was a retired professor, but unlike most of the breed, she was anything but loquacious. Cassandra ascribed this to her being both a mathematician and a Midwesterner, two disqualifiers. But maybe it was also because when Jennifer was at the table, no one else got much airtime.

"You'll love it!" crowed Jennifer, and Barbara looked at Cassandra and shook her head.

"I hope it's the flu David has and not something worse," said Barbara.

"What's worse?" asked Jennifer.

"Pneumonia," said Barbara. "They call it 'the old man's friend,' but that's only if the old man is eager to check out."

"No one said anything about pneumonia," insisted Jennifer. She smiled at Barbara. "I'm so happy you'll be coming to Scrabble tonight!" Barbara was one of the few people of color who lived at Clarion Court, and Cassandra noted that Jennifer was especially solicitous of her, as if in demonstration of her own open-mindedness.

"So you'll join us, too, won't you?" Jennifer *was* persistent.

"I'd love to, sometime," said Cassandra—she was a skilled practitioner of this kind of innocuous lie—"but I have a project I'm working on tonight."

The word "project" was useful, since it covered just about anything, including her work as an entomologist, which Jennifer had laughingly admitted she was intimidated by when they'd first met.

"Oh," said Jennifer. She deflated quickly but also had a remarkably quick recovery period. "Another time then!"

"Sure," said Cassandra, and to further demonstrate her geniality, she continued. "I wanted to ask you about something. Last night when I was walking Melville before going to bed, I was coming back up to the building and saw an ambulance had pulled up by the rear entrance. Two EMTs wheeled out someone on a stretcher and drove off. I was surprised they weren't using the main entrance in front."

"It's what they always do," said Jennifer. "It must be because it's easier to maneuver a stretcher out that way."

"I wondered if it might be because it's not good for community morale, as well as Clarion PR, to have residents carted off to a hospital. They like to portray this as a place of health and eternal youth. People don't really notice what happens at the back of the building."

"You did," said Barbara.

Jennifer scowled. "There's nothing wrong with the rear entrance."

"There's something rather depressing about being carried out past the garbage dumpster and the recycling bins."

Barbara laughed, but Jennifer said, "If you're sick enough to have to go to the hospital, I'm sure you wouldn't notice the recycling bins."

"I might," said Cassandra, and Barbara laughed again.


Noah had not come to dinner, but he'd called Cassandra and invited her to join him for an after-dinner drink. "I'm 324 West. Two stories right above you."

"You're inviting me to your apartment?"

"I am."

Cassandra waited a moment, then asked, "Shall I bring a chaperone?"

"If you are referring to that beast of yours, the answer is an unequivocal no."

"Melville will be disappointed."

"Melville will have to learn to bear disappointment."

It was strange to be in an apartment that had the same floor plan as hers but felt so entirely different. The living room looked as if two interior designers with antithetical taste had fought a turf war. An assortment of old bookcases, a leather chair and ottoman with the buttons popped off, and a brown velvet sofa that was balding on the arms vied with an austere beige loveseat (though Cassandra thought "beige" and "love" was an oxymoron) flanked by matching chairs, a glass coffee table, and a sleek lamp. Whatever walls weren't covered by bookcases were covered head to toe with paintings. Cassandra looked them over.

"I'm not fond of art in general, but these are rather pleasant."

"'Pleasant' is a cruel adjective when it comes to art."

Cassandra looked through some of the paintings stacked against the wall. A few pieces of gilt molding that had broken off the frames rested on top. She picked up a piece and held it up to Noah.

"I intend to repair them, once I get the proper kind of glue."

Cassandra laughed. "Right. One more project to add to the to-do list for when you're retired. Or you can leave the project to your daughter-in-law when she finally inherits the lot."

"Fortunately I am not yet cremated remains dissolving in the sea, and I may still choose to bequeath them all to a museum or historical society."

"What about your son?"

"What about him?"

"It sounds as if you're considering denying him his birthright because you're not fond of his wife."

"Birthright?"

"OK, that's unquestionably hyperbolic. I just think it causes a lot less stress if you simply leave everything to your kids and not go around flapping a will and threatening to disown them if they don't measure up."

"It's not a question of just measuring up."

"Something more hurtful, then?"

Noah looked at her without speaking.

43

"Sorry," said Cassandra. "I'm afraid I have a tendency to just plunge right in."

"Do you do this with everyone?"

"No, only with someone who has potential for—"

Noah raised his eyebrows.

"Not *that*. I was thinking of friendship."

"I stand corrected," said Noah, and he smiled.

Cassandra turned back to the art on the wall and leaned close to study a small, rather dim oil painting of a harbor with sailboats in the distance.

"I gather you like the sea."

"My true home. I'm happiest in a boat."

"I remember now," said Cassandra. "You were on crew, weren't you?"

She squatted down and rowed in the air.

"You're circling the wrong way," said Noah, and without squatting, he demonstrated the proper direction for the oars. "And that was on the river. I'm talking about sailing. No rowing necessary."

"Sailboats tip," said Cassandra, and she stood up and leaned sideways, eyes closed, and let out an "eek!"

"Sailboats are *designed* to tip," said Noah. "That's how you get speed."

"I prefer slow."

"My sailboat is named *Sarabande*, which is a slow, stately dance, so I think you'll approve of it."

"You have a sailboat?"

"Not here. I keep it at my place on the Cape."

"If you have a place on the Cape, and you hate Clarion, then why not live there?"

"It's just a rough cottage. Not properly winterized. No central heat."

"Electricity?"

"Well, yes."

"Then not technically *rough*."

"Even if the electricity is prone to outages?"

"Internet?"

"Yes, but temperamental."

"Definitely not rough." Cassandra looked around the room. "I thought you had a cat."

"I do."

"I don't see it."

"You won't. It doesn't like people."

"A not-uncommon characteristic of cats. Which is why I fail to understand why anyone would want to own one."

"You prefer dogs, who bark without provocation, knock you over, and slobber on your face."

"Who wouldn't?" There was a cello propped against the wall. Cassandra plucked a string. "You play?"

"Yes. It's not a decorative element, if that's what you were asking."

"Any good?"

"Good enough to keep myself entertained. I'm working on some Bach. It's both strenuous and relaxing. I find him—well, sympathetic."

"Bach? Te-di-ous. My mother made me take piano lessons as a kid, and the height of my career was a little Bach minuet that I had to play in a recital. I practiced it so much it got ingrained in my fingers." Cassandra drummed out the melody on the arm of the sofa and hummed the tune. "Not that I played it flawlessly at my great, traumatic moment on stage." She smiled at Noah. "I know I'm not supposed to admit this, but the truth is I don't really like music."

He clearly had no response to that, so she added, "I'm sorry to disappoint you. I'm sure you must think me a Philistine. Doesn't like art! Doesn't like music! What next? But I thought you were someone I could be honest with."

"Aren't you honest with everyone?" he asked, and then he smiled. "My guess is, probably not."

"You might be right." She thought for a moment. "There's often some risk involved when you're completely honest with someone. And not everyone's worth taking that risk for."

"So I should find your confessions encouraging?"

"Yes, but there's a caveat. Reciprocity is involved."

"I was afraid of that," said Noah, and he walked to the kitchen. "What can I get you to drink? Shall I open some wine, or would you like something else?" Cassandra followed him. The kitchen was identical to her own, but there were no boxes on the floor, and the counters bore an array of small appliances and a collection of condiments, as if someone actually cooked here.

"You mean a *drink* drink?"

"If you are referring to a cocktail, then yes."

"What is the house pushing?"

"This house does not push. It merely offers."

"In that case, what does the bartender recommend?"

"How about a Pimm's cup? It's a summer drink, but summer is not that far off, and it's warm this evening."

"I never heard of it. But I trust you not to poison me. Do you have anything to eat, though, in case the drink is a bust?"

"I anticipated that. I have an unassuming brie and a good stilton. Take your pick."

Cassandra opened the refrigerator and took out the two chunks of cheese from the compartment in the door. She took a sniff. "Are you sure this isn't a bad stilton?" she asked.

"The crackers are already out on the cheese plate," said Noah. "You can put out both cheeses if you like."

Cassandra unwrapped the cheeses and placed them at opposing sides of the wooden plate, where crackers had already been fanned out artistically. In a contest for smells, the stilton would win, hands down.

"It's strange to see someone leaving food out on the counter like this. I always have to think about it because Melville will grab anything. One time he got the Thanksgiving turkey."

Noah was adding ginger ale to the glasses. He looked up. "I suppose you found that amusing?"

"Well, even you would have been a little amused. I had barely left the kitchen for a minute, and then I heard the pan crash to the floor and raced in to see Melville wrestling this poor dead bird. But it turned out to be fine. I just cut away the worst parts and washed off the rest and carved the turkey in the kitchen. No one was the wiser."

"Your solution does not inspire me ever to eat a meal at your table. By the way, I'm curious about your choice of canine names. Are you a Herman Melville fan?"

Cassandra laughed. "Quite the opposite. It was a joke, actually. *Moby-Dick*—the world's longest, most boring novel—was required reading in a course in American literature I mistakenly took in college. I was going to call him Moby, but it sounded somewhat melancholy— like mopy?—but Melville had a nice ring to it."

"Boring?"

Cassandra took her drink from his outstretched hand. "I suppose you're now going to tell me it's your favorite book."

"It is a beloved book that I have taught many times, and each time have discovered more to admire."

"Does your cat have an appropriate literary name?"

"My cat has no name at all."

"You know even a cat that is thoroughly disliked still needs to have a name."

"I'll let you name it, then."

"Oh, no. You should ask Cammie to do that."

"Not a bad idea. I will." Noah took the cheese platter and led the way to the balcony. "I thought we might sit outside and enjoy the view and sunset."

Cassandra hesitated and was about to say something, but she followed him, and he held the door open for her. She walked cautiously outside and sat down quickly on one of the two chairs. He set the cheese plate on the table between them.

"If you're cold, I can lend you a sweater."

"That's so gallant of you I'm almost inclined to accept. But actually, I'm fine, thanks."

"What shall we toast?"

"The view. It's certainly different from up here. Down below it's blocked by the trees."

"They have a habit of doing that, don't they?"

"One of their many flaws," said Cassandra. "The other being their tendency to produce leaves that require raking in the fall."

"Which is why you emigrated to Clarion, so you could avoid that pleasure. They do everything for us here, don't they?"

"I wasn't fair to the leaves. Actually I enjoyed raking them—the smell of them, the crackle and crunch. I liked playing in the leaf pile with the girls when they were little—just lying back and looking at the sky. I once made a huge leaf pile on the lawn, and when Ethan, my then-husband, finally got around to raking it up, it left a brown spot that never recovered."

"You'd left him with the raking up?"

"I was the one who created the leaf pile. Did you create leaf piles for your son?"

"I'm afraid I do not remember, but my guess is probably not."

"Your grandkids?"

"Alas, they have been similarly deprived. Speaking of my grand-children, my son called me last night to let me know that Cammie's school bus was involved in a minor accident—no children were on it at the time—and the driver has been suspended. So now they'll be driving Cammie, and they have to figure out how to manage drop-off and pickup."

"Oh, that's too bad."

"There will be a new driver on the route, but Larry's still concerned about safety issues, and Elizabeth is a generic worrier. Larry is taciturn by nature, but when he starts getting anxious about something, it's hard to calm him down."

Cassandra watched the sunset, and the small, meandering river catching its last light. The drink was surprisingly sweet, like something she might have liked even when she was a kid, if she'd been allowed to drink as a child, which she wasn't. Noah had sliced a strip of cucumber, and it stood rather incongruously at the side of the glass. The stilton had more personality than cheeses deserve, but the brie was smooth and seemed companionable for the drink.

"I saw someone taken away in an ambulance last night. I wonder if it might have been David Sussman."

"Why him?"

"He's been sick enough to miss Scrabble. Jennifer said it was the flu, but Barbara raised the specter of pneumonia."

Noah looked dubious.

"Supposedly it fells the elderly—that's us, Noah!—rather quickly. In any case, I thought it was strange the ambulance came to the rear entrance, not the front, but Jennifer said they always do."

"She'd know."

"She thought it was because it was easier to wheel stretchers that way, but I bet it's because it doesn't look good if sick people are carted out through the front entrance."

"Not to mention the corpses."

"Oh, dear. I forgot about the corpses."

"You wouldn't have gotten your apartment if it hadn't been vacated by one."

He stood up suddenly, walked to the side of the balcony, and leaned over. "If you stand here, and feel the breeze on your face, it's possible to forget for a moment that you aren't in a real house." He turned and waved her over.

She got to her feet more slowly and took a few steps towards Noah. The railing was steel and looked strong enough, but below it was a glass panel instead of a solid wall of brick or concrete. When she moved her head, the glare that gave it presence disappeared, and it looked like there was nothing there at all.

"Sandy?"

She staggered backwards towards her chair, sat down, and closed her eyes.

"Are you all right?"

She looked up at him. "I'm not great with heights."

"Want to go back inside?"

She nodded. But the balcony, a tiny platform thrust out into space, seemed so fragile it might snap right off, and she teetered when she began to stand.

"I'll help you. OK?" He'd already put his hands under her elbows to steady her. Her forehead fell forward against his chest. He slipped his arm around her waist and held her other hand.

"Close your eyes," he said.

She closed her eyes and let him walk her back into the apartment.

"OK now?"

She opened her eyes. The walls of the living room, the carpeting on the floor, the massive brown sofa, were reassuring. Noah's arm was still around her. He had never touched her before. They stood that way, and she wasn't sure if he was still holding her because he was concerned she might fall or because his hesitancy meant something else. She couldn't calculate the passage of time. It seemed as if everything had slowed down. Largo. Dance partners, motionless on the dance floor, after a song had ended. Was the reluctance to move apart hers or his?

"I'm OK," she said finally, her voice as bright as she could summon.

He released her and stepped back.

"Was it the Pimm's cup?"

"No. And it wasn't that strident stilton either. The balconies here just don't seem sufficiently—uh, secure. It's that glass, I guess."

"It's a good thing your apartment is on the first floor, then."

"A necessity because of Melville. He isn't partial to perilous balconies, either."

"The balcony has always felt secure to me. But I'm not sure I would want it tested by anything his size."

"I think I better be going back down to check on him," she said. And she started towards the door.

"Would you like me to walk you down?"

She looked back at him and wavered for a moment, then she said, "Thank you, but no. I'll be just fine." And she stepped out the apartment door before he could object.

# V

It had been two days since Cassandra had visited his apartment, and Noah hadn't spoken with her since, and she hadn't made an appearance in the dining room. From his balcony, he'd watch her being dragged along the river path by that beast of hers, so he knew she hadn't abandoned Clarion. He considered the possibility that she was deliberately avoiding him—though he couldn't imagine why—and realized that with someone like Cassandra, anything was possible. He had a cello lesson coming up that afternoon, and he put his energies into practicing and listening to his favorite cellists online—Jacqueline du Pré and Yo-Yo Ma—effortlessly playing the Bach cello suite he was struggling to learn.

Although Noah would have preferred the digital revolution had never happened, he'd taken on the internet with the same determination that he'd applied when learning Mandarin. He was a devotee of Google, which augmented the storehouse of information (both useful and useless) packed away somewhere in his brain. When he was still teaching, it enabled him to avoid the old-fogeyishness cultivated by some of the other senior professors. He had no delusions of being hip, but he did want to appear relevant, so he kept abreast of his students' colloquialisms and cultural (though he could not bring himself to call them "cultural") references. He delighted in using Google for tracking down plagiarized passages in students' essays. Now spared the necessity of checking up on his students and learning their lingo, he used Google to find material on music and YouTube videos of cello performances.

He loved being able to bring the cellists he admired to life, right there in his Clarion apartment, and watch their technique.

That morning he watched an impassioned Jacqueline du Pré playing rapturously and shaking back her wildly unrestrained hair, and while he wanted to reach into the moment and give Jacqueline a hairclip, the decidedly not-paternalist part of him had a rather different fantasy. Surely he wasn't the only man who would have liked to have her grip his body with her knees, hold him against her chest, and bow feverishly across his back.

He did not feel this way about Gertrude Dubrovsky, his cello teacher, former colleague, and good friend. She was a corpulent woman with hair dyed too black for her pale skin and thinning in the front, exposing her vulnerable, pale scalp. She was married to Milton Presser, a composer in the music department whom Noah did not even pretend to like. His compositions were random clumps of discordant, headache-inducing noise, and Noah thought he should have been prohibited from teaching composition at any institution of higher learning but restrained himself from saying so to Gertrude, though he sometimes wondered if she might agree.

Noah had taken up cello again when he retired, after a decades-long hiatus. Now, since he no longer drove, Gertrude kindly came to Clarion for his weekly lesson. When she arrived that afternoon, lugging her cello, she was sweating profusely, even in climate-super-controlled Clarion. She set her cello case down, lifted her blouse away from her fleshy underarms, and shook out the fabric.

"So, how has life been treating you?" she asked. It was her standard greeting.

"I am surviving as well as can be imagined, given the surroundings."

"Whenever my daughter suggests maybe it's time for us to move into a place like this, I tell her I'll put a plastic bag over my face and put a quick end to things first. I keep one handy."

"If you gave up your place and moved to Clarion, would she take on your goats?"

Gertrude snorted.

"May I get you something to drink?"

"Let's attack your Bach and then play some duets first."

"I watched a video this morning of a seven-year-old Yo-Yo Ma playing on what looked like a toy cello. His little hand moved fluidly up and down the neck, as if changing positions were as easy as breathing."

"Don't compare yourself to *any* kid, Noah, you'll get discouraged. Their bodies are like rubber—they just *move*."

"My body moves," said Noah. "But it protests."

He wasn't far into the Bach before Gertrude had him pause.

"Why do you have your bow tightened like that?"

"It's not right?"

"No!" She took it from him, frowned, and loosened it. "The hair should hug the strings." She handed the bow back to him. "Start again from the beginning."

"You are a tough instructor."

"Isn't that why you hire me?"

The issue of payment had been problematic when they'd first started. Gertrude argued that since Noah was an emeritus professor and therefore part of the college, as well as a friend, there was no fee. Noah argued that he should pay her the same as her few private students. They finally settled it that he'd give her a bottle of single malt Scotch whisky at the start of the New Year. He also kept one on hand for her visits.

Noah found his cello lessons engrossing, but it was playing duets with Gertrude that he looked forward to. He actually sounded good when he played with her—or rather, they sounded good when they played together. The walls in Clarion apartments were notoriously thin, but Noah was fortunate that the octogenarian whose living room adjoined his was practically deaf, so he could play at full volume without apologies.

Once Gertrude had packed her cello away, she sank down on the old velvet sofa and kicked off her shoes. Noah brought them both drinks and sat across from her in his leather chair.

"So," Gertrude began, "any nice widows got their talons into you yet?"

"I have done my level best to fend them all off," said Noah. "I did run into someone here I knew in college, though—small worldism. She's livelier than most of the old ladies around here—"

"I don't like that term!" cried Gertrude.

"Female person over the age of sixty-five?"

"Better. I'm waiting for the 'and' clause."

"It's not an 'and' clause, it's a 'but' clause."

"That's disappointing."

"What were you expecting?"

"Something like 'And I don't mind her talons.' What's the 'but'?"

"She doesn't like music."

"A deal breaker, for sure, unless you decide this would be an opportunity to educate her."

"As you so kindly pointed out, I am fortunately no longer in the business of educating anyone about anything. And besides, you can't educate someone to *like* music, can you?"

"I suppose not," said Gertrude. She took a sip of her whisky and smacked her lips ostentatiously. "You are so fortunate you retired. The college is embracing technology at an alarming rate, and they expect the faculty to come on board. They want us to offer online alternatives for courses so they can still get tuition revenue from students who choose to be away for a semester. I'm supposed to be setting up Zoom in my studio to accommodate students who want to continue lessons while they're studying abroad."

"How can you teach cello that way?"

"We'll find out."

"It sounds like the college is trying to stay competitive."

"It won't be a college anymore. It will be a pricey online factory."

"What a pessimist you are!"

"No, a realist. Kids would rather lounge on the beach on Barbados and work—if you call it work—on their laptops than sit at a desk in a classroom. Residential colleges are doomed."

Gertrude took a small sip of her drink and was quiet for a moment. "Enough about the miseries of academia! Let's talk about your summer retreat on remote Cape Cod. When were you planning on doing your annual migration?"

"Depends on when Larry is allowed to drive me down there."

"Allowed?"

"Whenever Elizabeth decides it will inconvenience her the least."

"Here's what I don't understand, Noah," Gertrude said. "Why don't you get your driver's license renewed, get yourself a new car, and drive yourself?"

"It's not that simple."

"Only because you don't want it to be." Gertrude downed the rest of her drink and set the empty glass on the table. "What *is* this about your not driving, Noah? Do you really like being dependent on Larry to get you to the Cape?"

"God, no!"

"Well then?"

"I'm just not ready to drive—"

"Ready? What does that mean?"

"Not able."

"Why not?"

Noah closed his eyes and shook his head so slightly Gertrude probably didn't notice. He didn't want to talk with Gertrude about this. There were things he didn't even want to think about.

Gertrude got to her feet. "Stop making excuses for yourself! You're not in a casket yet, Noah. You'll have plenty of time to not drive when you are."


After she left, as Noah was putting his cello away, Larry called, as if he'd known Noah had talked about him. He was in his car on the way home from his office, an Elizabeth-free zone.

"Just calling to see how you're doing, Dad."

"I'm doing just fine. Why shouldn't I be?"

"Just wanted to make sure everything was good at Clarion Court."

"Nothing is ever good at Clarion Court, Larry, as I have expressed often enough in the past. How are *you* doing?"

"Elizabeth's administrative assistant has decided to go on maternity leave just before their annual meeting, and none of the job applicants Elizabeth's interviewed so far seem right. You can imagine how distressed she is."

"I certainly can."

"Elizabeth is under a lot of stress."

"As I'm sure you are too. Here's a thought. I'd like to go to the cottage early this year, and when you drive me down, why don't you stay a day or two? Relax. Maybe we can get the boat out. I'm eager to leave here soon as you're free to go."

There was an unpleasant pause at Larry's end, and before he said anything, Noah could guess what was coming.

"Sounds like it would be a great thing to do, but here's the thing, Dad. I'm not sure when that's going to happen. Things are kind of tense right now, and I don't think this is a good time to be leaving Elizabeth alone to manage the two kids."

"Her parents are only half a mile away. They're always ready to jump in and help." Too ready, Noah thought but didn't say.

"It's not just that. There's just—"

Noah cut him off. "Whenever you're available, let me know."

There was undisguised relief in Larry's voice. "Oh, of course, Dad. I will."


When Noah was heading to the pool the next day, he ran into Cassandra coming out, a towel wrapped around her head.

"Water-aerobics class?"

"Not before I'm ninety," she said.

"I thought the class was just finishing."

"It is. But they leave two lanes open, so I can swim laps. I do backstroke, and then I can usually get a lane to myself because people don't want me crashing into them."

"Remind me to avoid sharing a lane with you."

"OK."

Noah cleared his throat. Did Larry pick up his annoying habit from him? "Speaking of avoiding, I wondered if you were avoiding me. I didn't see you at dinner last night."

"I decided to eat in my own little dining nook."

"I thought you didn't cook."

"I don't *like* to cook, but I'm not incompetent in the kitchen. It's not that different from running a lab."

"That's right, you worked with bugs!"

"Not bugs—beetles. Tiger beetles. To be precise: a threatened species, the Northeastern beach tiger beetle, *Habroscelimorpha dorsalis dorsalis*."

"Bugs."

"Beetles are Coleoptera. Bugs are a different order, Hemiptera."

"I stand corrected."

Her towel had loosened, and she tried to tuck it back in, then gave up, put the towel over her arm, and shook out her hair. Tiny water droplets flicked out and touched his face, but she didn't seem to notice.

"Since we are old friends, I actually owe you an apology. I wasn't quite forthright."

"No?" He smiled.

"Shall I tell you the truth?"

"You led me to believe you always would."

"The truth is I *was* avoiding you, which is why I didn't make an appearance at dinner, or invite you to have an after-dinner drink with me, since, I believe, it's my turn."

Her turn? He wondered if they'd already established some sort of tradition. "And why was that?"

"Because I was embarrassed about what occurred when we were last together."

"Meaning?"

"The mortifying episode on your balcony."

"I didn't see it as mortifying."

"There aren't many things I'm afraid of. And I'm not the kind of person who likes to appear fragile."

"I didn't think so."

"So I shouldn't have gone out on the balcony in the first place."

"Then why did you?"

"Because you invited me to. And when I thought about our disagreement about art and music and that eighteen-pound novel you're so fond of, I wanted to be agreeable about *something*."

"I appreciate the intention, and I'm sorry about the outcome."

"Friendship reinstated, then?" She held out her hand.

"I never thought it had been on hiatus," he said, although that was not exactly true. He took her hand, and they shook rather ceremoniously, though perhaps longer than necessary. Then she said goodbye and started down the hall. He'd opened the door to the Aquatic Center and gotten the first waft of chlorine-scented air when he heard her call out his name, and he turned around.

"How about tomorrow? After-dinner drink. My place."

"My pleasure."

"And don't worry," she added. "I'll instruct Melville to be on his best behavior."

He watched her walk down the hallway, swinging the towel back and forth beside her.

# VI

It was to be their last dinner together. The special was veal marsala, the veal pounded to such a thinness that it no longer resembled meat, and grilled asparagus, which would have been special except that Clarion must have gotten a deal on asparagus since it had appeared on the menu, in every imaginable configuration, for a week. Jennifer waited until all eight at the table had given their order to the server before she made her announcement. She did not ting her fork against a glass to get everyone's attention—although Cassandra suspected she would have loved to—but instead resorted to leaning out over the table and fluttering her fingers. "Hello, everyone," she said, with the big-eyed glee kids have when relating disasters. "I have some news to share with you." Jennifer always somehow managed to get the news of doings at Clarion ahead of anyone else. (Had she hacked the director's computer?) Jennifer was an agile storyteller, unabashedly hyperbolic by nature, and well schooled in the use of the dramatic pause. When she announced that Clarion Court was now officially part of Oakdale Living and several renovation projects would soon be underway, Cassandra could imagine her promoting a particular trophy house to a potential buyer: "The en suite bathroom off the master bedroom has a marble shower enclosure *and* . . . [pause, pause, pause] a bidet with twelve temperature settings."

And now, Jennifer, exultant with all eyes upon her, arranged her face gravely for the imparting of her final dramatic revelation. Cassandra's eyes were the only pair not behind glasses. She was vain about her eyesight and had succumbed reluctantly to the necessity of glasses for reading and driving at night.

"The first of these is 'The Terrace' dining room. They're reconfiguring the seating arrangements, updating the lighting, and refurbishing the buffet area. It will be closed for two weeks. They'll be sending out a notice tonight."

Cassandra looked around. Would the planters of philodendrons survive the reconfiguration?

"They can't do that!" exclaimed a cadaverous woman whose name was either May or June—Cassandra couldn't remember which. "We do need to eat dinner."

"They'll be serving dinner in 'The Garden.'"

"That's too small!" cried May-June.

"They're extending hours so more people can be accommodated. And you can also choose to have your meal delivered to your door, and eat in your own apartment."

"And the second?" asked Barbara.

Jennifer looked confused.

"Renovation project," said Barbara.

"The pool. They're redoing the tiling, so the pool and hot tub will be closed for a while."

"But what about my water-aerobics class?" May-June asked. "That's one of the amenities I pay for."

"They'll bus people to Brookfield Village so you can use the pool there," said Barbara. "That way they won't be neglecting their contractual duties to you."

Jennifer turned to her, surprised by someone having access to information ahead of her.

"Brookfield Village?" Cassandra asked.

"Brookfield Village is the senior community south of us, owned by the same management corporation," stated Jennifer, reclaiming her position.

"Oh yes, I remember now. I came across it when I was looking into retirement communities, but they don't allow dogs, so I didn't consider it."

"I believe they allow cats," said Barbara.

"Barbara has a cat," said Jennifer. "So she'd know."

"My cat died," said Barbara.

"Oh, I'm sorry. I forgot," said Jennifer.

The arrival of the drinks and appetizers caused a break in the conversation, but as soon as everyone had been served, Jennifer picked right up where things had left off. "When I was researching senior communities, I looked into Brookfield Village. But the apartments there are smaller, and it was farther from my son's house. I'd considered moving in with one of my kids when I retired—maybe add an apartment to their house—but in the end thought it would be best to have my own place. They all wanted me to live with them—"

"All five?" Barbara interjected.

Jennifer heard the question but missed the ironic tone. "At least three, if not four, of the five."

"An abundance of possibilities," said Barbara.

"I'd rather die than have to live with my daughter," said a plump woman whom Cassandra had seen in the dining room before but not actually met. "We'd be at each other's throats in a matter of hours. Her house is a mess, and she lets her kids run wild. I love my grandkids, but live there?"

Her husband—he was her husband, wasn't he?—said quietly, "I think I'd rather enjoy it."

She turned on him quickly. "That's because you're just like her! You don't mind unwashed pots piling up in the kitchen and soggy towels all over the bathroom floor." She looked back at the group assembled at the table. "Craig can function in the midst of chaos. Me? I need an orderly house."

Craig sniffed audibly, and Cassandra couldn't tell if it was deliberate, or if years of living with his wife had made the sniff an unconscious, regular part of his vocabulary. How long would they survive together in their tidy little Clarion apartment without going nuts? She did a quick mental run-through of her own husbands and realized that none of their unions would have had much of a chance if they were at Clarion together for any length of time.

"How is David Sussman doing?" asked Cassandra, before she left the dining room. "Is he still in the hospital?"

It had been he, Cassandra had learned, whom she'd witnessed being carried out to an ambulance past the recycling bins and dumpster that night.

"He is, but they said it was just the flu," said Jennifer.

"That's what they'd say, wouldn't they?" said Barbara.


Cassandra didn't see Noah at dinner, so she called him when she got back to her apartment.

"I decided to grab something quick at the café, a.k.a. 'The Garden,' instead," he said.

"You missed Jennifer's pronouncements about the dire things coming to the Clarion."

"Exactly."

"It looks like 'The Terrace' will be shut down for renovations, so you'll be dining at 'The Garden' for the duration. Unless you want the option of takeout from the dining services in your own apartment."

"An attractive option, though it would preclude the possibility of joining Jennifer's contingent, who, I imagine, will choose the conviviality of 'The Garden.'"

"My daughter called me when I was at dinner, and I need to get back to her before you and I get together. Unfortunately there's no telling how long Laurel will keep me on the phone."

"No problem. I'm practicing that tedious composer, Bach. Just ring me when you're done."

"Where have you been, Mom?" was how Laurel began the conversation.

"Dinner." Cassandra put the phone on speaker, sat on the floor next to Melville, and leaned back against the sofa. It looked like she was in for the long haul with Laurel, so she might as well use her time trying to pull some burrs out of Melville's ears.

"I called you three times. Why was your phone turned off?"

"It wasn't off. But I left it here in the apartment."

"Mo-ther!" Cassandra could just picture the sour expression on Laurel's face as she enunciated the word. "You're supposed to have it with you at all times."

Cassandra wanted to tell Laurel that it was inappropriate for a daughter to be lecturing her mother on what she was "supposed" to be doing, but instead she said, "Don't worry, Laurel, I promise I'll bring my cell phone with me anytime I plan to fall and break my leg when I'm too far to have anyone hear my cries for help."

Laurel did not respond well to humor. "I left three messages for you."

"So you did, and here I am, calling you back. How are you doing, Dear?"

"It's you I'm worried about," said Laurel. "If you don't get back to me when I call you, I imagine that anything could have happened."

"Don't worry, Laurel, I'm just fine. It's unlikely anything can happen to me at a place like Clarion Court, and if it did, I'm sure they will notify you in a timely manner."

"Things happen to people in nursing homes all the time!"

"They die of boredom? But rest assured, Laurel, I'm quite safe here since Clarion Court is not a nursing home."

"Things happen to people in assisted living too."

"Laurel, this is not assisted living, either, this is independent living, which is quite different. And we're all perfectly healthy independent livers." She would have said, "as opposed to other organs," but Laurel would not find that funny, and it would only irritate her further.

"Even so," said Laurel.

"Even so what?"

"Even so, when you decided to give up the house, it would have been better for you to come out here and live with us, and Drew and I still think you should. We have that extra bedroom right off the back hall that we could fix up for you."

"That's so thoughtful of you both," said Cassandra, who was as surprised by this unexpected offer from her daughter, as well as the complicity of her son-in-law, as much as she was horrified at the thought of having to spend more than a night under their roof. "But I assure you, I'm quite happy here in my lovely new apartment."

Cassandra disliked Drew because she found him both narrow minded and pompous. He was perfectly entitled to his opinions, of course, but Cassandra worried that Laurel was simply adopting her husband's views and had stopped thinking for herself. After Cassandra's last visit, the possibility of having a civil conversation with them about anything political had gone out the window.

"You'll just have to find someone to take Melville for you, since we don't really have room for a dog like that," Laurel continued, as if she hadn't heard what Cassandra said. Melville perked up his head at the sound of his name. Cassandra leaned over and kissed him on the nose. Something that would have induced another lecture from Laurel on the dangers of acquiring diseases from a dog.

"If I were considering other places to live—" Cassandra began, but Laurel cut her off.

"You're not thinking about going to live with Maggie, are you!" she cried.

The thought of living near her grandchildren was wonderful to entertain, but Cassandra had no intention of emigrating to New Zealand.

"No, but I'll be visiting them in the fall, when it's spring there."

"What about visiting me?" asked Laurel. "It's spring here now. If you aren't going to live here, you should at least come visit!"

"I'm still settling into Clarion," said Cassandra.

"Then I'll come visit you," said Laurel. "I'd like to check out the place you've moved to. You didn't even consult with me about it—you just moved there—and I'd like to see it for myself."

Cassandra took a long, slow breath, shut her eyes, and said, "That would be very nice, Dear."

"Actually, I can come next weekend," said Laurel. "Drew has something planned with some buddies of his."

"That's such a sweet offer," said Cassandra, "but I'm afraid next weekend won't quite work for me. I have something already planned for then."

"What?" Laurel was persistent, as always. Cassandra had to invent something quickly, or Laurel would keep going at her. As soon as she thought of an idea, she broke into a smile.

"I'm doing something with a friend."

"Mallory?"

"No. It's a friend from here, who has a place on Cape Cod and invited me to visit."

"You said you weren't going anywhere because you were settling in."

"This just came up, and it's a chance to observe the mating dance of American woodcocks. It's the season."

Laurel was quiet for a moment. She had always found her mother's interest in fauna and flora incomprehensible. "Aren't you retired, Mom?"

Cassandra laughed. "Naturalists never really retire, Darling. You should know that. And my friend has a cottage right on the beach that's ideal for birding."

"Oh," said Laurel. "Well, if she invited you to stay with her, that's very nice. I'll come some other time." It took Cassandra a second to realize that Laurel had assumed the friend in question was another woman. No reason not to let her think so. She'd enjoy informing Noah that she'd used him to protect herself from an impending visit from her daughter.

"So, Dear, you haven't told me about how *you're* doing," said Cassandra, knowing that Laurel, above all, always liked to focus on herself.

"Well, things have been difficult, as I've already told you," said Laurel. "Drew's firm has been trimming its staff—not Drew, of course, because he's so essential—and I'm simply swamped with business. All my clients have tax issues. I'm thoroughly exhausted."

"I'm sorry, Laurel," said Cassandra.

"And I'm having trouble sleeping at night. It's all the stress. Drew says everything will calm down at work after a while, and I know that's true, but I still can't help worrying about how I'll get everything done."

"Worrying isn't useful, Darling."

"That's certainly not very helpful, Mom!"

Time to end the conversation! "Sorry, Dear. But I have to go. Melville is clawing at the door and needs to go out." Melville looked up. He was quite used to being an excuse for Cassandra's exit from phone conversations with Laurel.

"I'm still amazed they allowed you to bring that dog with you."

"They love dogs here," said Cassandra. "They brighten the lives of the elderly. Oh—gotta go. Melville requires his walk. Hope things ease up for you soon. Talk to you next week."

The word "walk" had brought Melville to his feet. Cassandra was about to get his leash when she remembered Noah was waiting for her call.

"I'm freed," she said, when she reached Noah. "Would you like to take a walk with me before or after we have a drink?"

"Were you asking me if I wanted to take a walk with you and, I'm guessing, that oversized canine of yours, or were you assuming you could cajole me into accompanying you and were merely asking my preference as to the time."

"The latter, of course."

"In that case, let's get it over with so we can enjoy our wine afterwards."

"Don't grumble. A walk will do you good."

"I'm glad you have my welfare at heart. And grumbling is a time-honored way to communicate emotions."

"I'll meet you outside in ten."


Noah arrived flourishing a piece of paper with the Clarion logo on top. "This was just slipped under my door. Did you see it?"

"I saw it, but I didn't read it yet."

"I'm sure it's all posted on the board downstairs, but they wanted to be sure people saw the information, and they knew not everyone would be checking their email after dinner."

Noah put on his reading glasses, which hung from a cord around his neck, and read: *"The Terrace" dining room will be closed starting tomorrow evening, and "The Garden" will be offering extended dining hours for your convenience. Residents may also choose to have our dedicated dining staff deliver your dinners to your apartment door. Please indicate your dinner preferences on the menu now available online and submit the form or call the main desk by 5:00 p.m. tomorrow so we can accommodate you.*

"Don't you love the language? 'For your convenience,' 'dedicated dining staff,' 'accommodate you.' Someone has had a grand time writing this!"

"Jennifer was exultant to be a few hours ahead of Clarion's public announcement."

"Actually it suits me quite well to have room service for my dinner. I'll be like the Queen of England and eat on a tray balanced on my knees while I watch the telly."

"You have a telly?"

"No. But it sounds better than 'stream NPR on my iPad.'"

"Unfortunately, Jennifer said they'll be closing the pool for renovations too."

"So we'll be lapless?"

"I gather they'll be busing people to this other facility, Brookfield Village, to use the pool there."

"In that case I will take a hiatus from exercise," said Noah. "I will not be bused anywhere."

"I believe it's a van, not a bus—"

"I will not be bused *or* van-ed."

"I, at least, have an exercise plan that is unaffected by renovations," said Cassandra. The exercise plan, suddenly fearing he was going to be cheated out of his walk, started tugging on his leash, and Cassandra said, "We better get moving."

The path along the river widened and narrowed for no apparent reason, so sometimes they walked side by side and sometimes one in front of the other. When Melville looked as if it was likely he was going to be doing something unattractive, Noah dropped farther behind or hurried ahead.

"Would you like to have the experience of walking him yourself?" asked Cassandra, offering Noah the leash.

"I will forego the pleasure for now, thank you, and, I might add, forever."

"Others have had your response initially," said Cassandra, "but in time enjoyed the opportunity."

"Those were others," said Noah. "Not I."

When they returned to Cassandra's apartment and Melville was safely stretched out on the floor by the faux fireplace, Noah sat in the chair where he'd sat before.

"I found some wine," said Cassandra. "I was looking for a field guide on fungi, and there they were. I'd thought the box was books, but I was wrong."

She handed the opener to Noah. "I'll get the glasses." In the kitchen she looked around for something to serve with the wine. The only cheese was a dismal scrap of cheddar, and the only crackers she could find were probably stale.

"Would you like some chocolate?"

"Why not?"

She pulled over a liquor-store box filled with pots she hadn't found a place for yet and used it as a step stool to climb up onto the counter. She'd stored the chocolate on the highest shelf in the cabinet so she wouldn't eat it all up. It was individually wrapped, cheap milk chocolate in a bag, the kind she handed out for trick or treat. Clearly Noah was expecting a different sort of chocolate, but he took a piece anyway.

Cassandra sat down across from Noah. "I needed this," she said. "I had a typically difficult conversation with my daughter Laurel." She unwrapped a piece of chocolate and put it in her mouth. "She's still riled up because I didn't consult with her when I moved in here. She says if I was selling the house, I should have moved in with her and her husband. They live in a politically incorrect outpost in upstate New York. My daughter's husband doesn't embrace my concern about the environment and climate change, and my daughter, who has a strong mind of her own when it comes to many things, has benightedly been echoing him. Things started going downhill when she asked me why, exactly, I thought wetlands needed to be protected."

Cassandra helped herself to another piece of chocolate. "Even having dinner with both of them is unbearable," she said. "I suspect Laurel was relieved when I declined the offer to live with them. And now she can feel superior that she extended an invitation to me, whereas her sister hasn't. Of course, since Maggie lives in New Zealand, it wouldn't be exactly practical."

"At least she invited you. I can't imagine Larry and Elizabeth would ever consider extending an invitation to me. My daughter-in-law has minimal tolerance for retired professors who get incensed by dangling participles. Not, of course, that I would ever accept such an invitation."

"Laurel persistently confuses senior living communities with assisted living and nursing homes."

"A common error," said Noah. "Once they succeed in putting their parents out to pasture, children don't observe the distinction between one sort of pasture and the other."

"I'd hardly call moving in to Clarion being 'put out to pasture.'"

"No?"

"If you feel that way, you have your Cape Cod retreat to escape to."

"I'd be happy to escape from here tomorrow, but now it seems unlikely Larry will be able to drive me there."

"You do know how to drive, don't you?"

"Yes, but I do not possess a car."

"You could always rent one."

"There's another small issue. At the moment I do not have a valid driver's license."

Cassandra raised her eyebrows.

"It's not worth talking about."

"Whenever someone says that, it usually means it's something they'd rather not talk about."

"All right, then," said Noah. "Rather not."

"Why?"

"That is a long story."

"I'm listening."

"A story for another time." Noah concentrated on his glass of wine.

"OK," she said. Noah looked up, as if he was surprised she hadn't persisted, then looked down again. After a while she said, "I used you."

"What?"

"When Laurel suggested she was going to come visit me next weekend, I told her I was going to be away. Because she continued her interrogation, I had to invent an excuse quickly, so I said a friend from here had a house on the Cape and I was going out there for a little vacation and the opportunity to observe the mating dance of American woodcocks. She assumed it was a female friend, and I did not correct her."

"Would she think it untoward for you to be shacking up with a man you were not married to?"

"Unfortunately, yes. There was a time, in fact, she thought I was untoward shacking up with a man—not her father—whom I *was* married to. Laurel has something critical to say about most anything I do, so I play it safe and give her as little information as possible."

"But sometimes you make things up?"

"Only in self-defense."

They both sat quietly for a moment. Then Cassandra said, "Our children fail us in ways we could never have predicted, don't they?" She paused for a moment, then added, "But perhaps we failed them too. Or at least they like to claim we did."

This silenced them again. After a while Noah said, "There's been something I've felt obliged to confess to you, and now seems as good a time as any. I've used you, too."

"How so?"

"After you met my granddaughter, Cammie, when she was here for lunch, I told her I was thinking of getting married again, and I'd chosen you."

"Why would you tell her that?"

"Because I expected she'd let her parents know, and that would rattle them a bit, make them more considerate of me. And Elizabeth would be eager for Larry to drive me to the Cape."

"You used Cammie, too."

"That's true, but I didn't think it would harm her."

"What was Cammie's response?"

"She thought I'd made a good choice. The dog and tarantulas helped."

"They usually do."

They sat rather companionably after that, drinking their wine and slowly unwrapping and eating chocolate, crumpling the paper and tinfoil into little balls that they piled together. Cassandra had thought their relationship was one that was primarily verbal, and she was surprised to discover they were comfortable together this way, as well.

As Noah was leaving, a while later, he hesitated at the door.

"It's not such a bad idea, you know."

"What?"

"Your little plan."

"What are you talking about?"

"I mean the plan you described to your daughter. In fact, it makes perfect sense. I have a place to retreat to, but no way to get there. You have a vehicle and would enjoy a little vacation on Cape Cod so you can do your birdwatching. It dovetails perfectly."

Cassandra laughed.

"Think about it," said Noah.

"Sure," said Cassandra, and she laughed again.

# VII

Dinner the next day appeared on a tray left by his door at 6:00 p.m., the appointed time. Noah had spoken to the head of dining services to request they bring up his stored case of wine as well, but it hadn't materialized. He carried in the tray and set it on his portable laptop table. The plates were covered in tinfoil, which had done an inadequate job of keeping things warm, so Noah reheated his pork chop and lima beans in the microwave before he sat down for dinner. He'd checked "balsamic" for his salad dressing choice, but the little pitcher next to the clump of mesclun was filled with something gooey that bore an unfortunate resemblance to phlegm. He got up and went back to the kitchen to make his own vinaigrette, and by the time he sat down again, his pork chop was no longer warm. Dessert was a piece of chocolate cake that had slid during transport and deposited its icing on the rim of the plate. When he'd finished eating the cake with a fork, Noah lifted the plate to his mouth and licked up the icing. There were advantages to eating in the privacy of your apartment.

Another bulletin had been issued that day by the Clarion director, saying that the water-aerobics class at Brookfield Village was being offered at 11:00 a.m. and there would be shuttle service twice daily so Clarion residents could make use of the pool at Brookfield. It was a cool gray day, and Noah might not have been inclined to venture anywhere beyond his apartment, but the idea of being herded into a Clarion van to go anywhere made him bristle. Even Bach failed to soothe him, and he decided to resign himself to reading instead. Nothing erudite; just a nice, clever British murder mystery featuring dour upper-class characters whom you didn't mind seeing knocked off.

Noah had just deposited his dinner tray and dirty dishes outside his door and settled in his chair when Larry called.

"Just checking to see how you're doing, Dad."

"How do you think I'm doing?" said Noah. "I'm stuck here in this apartment instead of being out on the beach at the Cape."

"At least you're in a comfortable, safe place."

"Comfort and safety are highly overrated."

"It's a top-rated facility, with a rich offering of activities," said Larry, a quote from the brochure he'd used before when he'd been persuading Noah to move there.

"Tinkering with sailboats does not seem to be among them."

"Yeah, well, as you've always pointed out, life isn't always perfect," said Larry, paraphrasing Noah inexactly, though Noah refrained from saying so and instead asked, "How are you and the family doing?"

"This is a particularly difficult time for Elizabeth at work, and Richard has been acting up at home, so we're all under a lot of stress."

"And how is Cammie?"

"She's finding Richard trying," admitted Larry.

"Send her to stay here with me," said Noah.

Larry sighed, and Noah quickly said, "I'd enjoy a visit from her at least."

"We'll try to arrange something," said Larry, "but we've been incredibly busy, as you can imagine."

Busy. It was Larry's family's standard mode of life.

"Yes, of course I can imagine. My memory may be slightly imperfect, but my power of imagination is still operating at optimal level."


The next night, instead of dishes on a tray, Noah's dinner arrived in plastic take-out containers stuffed into a paper bag, with his name and apartment number written in red marker on the front. Noah unpacked it in the kitchen and tossed out the plastic cutlery. Dessert was something gelatinous—pudding?—that quivered when he set it on the counter.

He called Cassandra. "Was your dinner delivered yet?"

"Let me check," she said, and he heard her walking across the room and opening her apartment door. "If this paper bag is holding mushroom ravioli, then yes, it was."

"How do you feel about bringing your dinner up here?"

"I'd love to!"

"Sans dog, please."

"If you insist. I'll give Melville his dinner before I leave, in consolation."

Before she arrived, Noah pulled the dining table farther away from the wall and found some woven blue place mats and matching napkins in a drawer. He set the table with stainless steel cutlery (he'd never unpacked the silver) and china plates that had been purchased on a trip to England. Another life. His wine had still not been delivered to his apartment, but he managed to find a bottle he'd stashed.

"Almost as elegant as 'The Terrace' dining room," said Cassandra. She paused before spooning her ravioli onto the plate. "Lovely china. I hate to cover this nice sailboat with tomato sauce."

"It was meant to endure such things. And it's actually a clipper ship."

"Which is more tolerant of tomato sauce than other sailing vessels?"

"No doubt."

"At least this looks more appetizing on the plate than it did in that plastic container."

"It certainly couldn't look less appetizing."

"Ready to submit to dining at 'The Garden'?" asked Cassandra. But one look at Noah's face and she added, "I didn't think so."

When they were done with the main course, Noah pointed to the gelatinous concoction on the kitchen counter. "I am foregoing the dessert."

Cassandra took a look at hers. "Wise decision."

"Let's have coffee in the living room."

They brought their dishes into the kitchen, and Noah made the coffee. He had once been a perfectionist about coffee, but now he bought it ground rather than grinding his own beans, though he still used his old Chemex coffee maker.

"No matter how bad the food was when we were at 'The Terrace,'" he said, "at least you didn't have to clean up afterwards."

"I didn't think the food was bad at all, though I know it was fashionable to complain about it."

"Someday, maybe, I'll cook a real meal for you, just so you can have a comparison."

"I'd like that. I have a little proposition for you—" Cassandra began, but she suddenly jumped back and looked down in front of her.

"What is that?"

"That is the elusive and nameless cat who lives here and expects its dinner."

It was an obese orange cat with orange eyes, and it was rubbing against Cassandra's leg.

"Feed it, please!"

The cat glared at Noah, who filled its bowl with redolent cat food and set it on the floor. The cat gobbled it down with surprising speed, then, perversely, spent a lot of time licking the empty bowl.

When Noah and Cassandra had settled in the living room with their coffee and a plate of mint-chocolate Girl Scout cookies, the cat, still smelling like its dinner, decided to make itself comfortable on Cassandra's lap. She lifted the cat up under the armpits and deposited it on the floor. "This is one heavy cat," she said. It rubbed itself against Cassandra's legs, gave her a baleful look, then disappeared. "Cats always seem to like me. It's probably because I don't like *them*."

"I don't like them either," said Noah. "But they've never liked me. At least this one certainly doesn't."

"Has Cammie named it yet?"

"No. I'm afraid I haven't had the opportunity to consult her yet."

"Perhaps a name would help establish some rapport between you."

"I'm not interested in rapport with a cat."

"Poor cat," said Cassandra, and she bit into another cookie.

"Let me hear this proposition of yours."

Cassandra finished her mouthful of cookie before she spoke. "Remember what you were joking about when you left the other night? The dovetailing of our interests?"

"I wasn't joking."

"No?"

"No."

Cassandra looked at him skeptically but continued. "I was thinking about the American woodcock."

"What?"

"The courtship dance of the male American woodcock."

"Why would you think about that?"

"They're out there on the Cape, in early spring, performing their incredible mating dance."

Noah shrugged.

"Well, they are. So I thought maybe if I decided to drive out there to observe them, and if you wanted a ride out to the Cape, our plans could, in fact, dovetail."

Noah studied her for a moment.

"OK, sorry. Silly idea."

"No. Not silly at all," said Noah. "What I had in mind when I asked you was that you come for a visit to the Cape while Clarion renovations are underway. It looks like it will be another two weeks—or more—before Clarion's version of gracious dining is open again and the pool is restored. I would be happy to have you as a guest."

"So you weren't kidding."

"I wasn't. And, in general, I don't."

"If I did, in fact, end up going to the Cape with you, it would absolve me of lying to my daughter when she threatened to come for a visit. Though I'll still feel a bit guilty because technically it's imperfect absolution, since the excuse was a total fabrication at the time."

"I don't see why there should be any guilt involved if, as you said earlier, you acted in self-defense."

"Oh, Noah, when it's a matter of dealing with our children, there's always some guilt involved, isn't there?"

"Not necessarily."

Cassandra got up, prowled around the living room, then sat down again.

"What are the sleeping arrangements in your house?"

"First of all, it is not a house."

"Right—a cottage."

"*Rough* cottage."

"But with electricity."

"Yes, electricity. Unless the power goes off. Which it does out there, with alarming frequency."

"And no heating."

"There's a woodstove."

"Fan-cy!" Cassandra waited a moment, then asked, "And the sleeping arrangements?"

"Two bedrooms. I thought I'd take the little one, which was Larry's."

"You expected that I'd come?"

"Sandy, I don't know you very well, but I do know that with you, it would be useless to *expect* anything."

"You've just touched on a major problem, haven't you—the fact that you don't know me very well. And I don't know you very well. And here we are discussing staying together in a rough cottage with fickle electricity."

This was true. Noah wondered if the whole idea might be absolutely crazy. "Are you suggesting we stick around here longer and get to know each other better, first?"

"What? Stick around here? And miss the woodcocks?"

"Well, then, what do you suggest?"

"Oh, that's easy. Get to know each other better. A sort of crash course in developing an honest, working, platonic—I am assuming it's platonic—friendship."

"Oh, Lord!" said Noah. "Orientation week for college freshmen."

"But we can't drink coffee; we need something more compelling."

Noah stood up. "Like what? Sherry?"

"Yes, that would be perfect. And do you have more cookies?"

"I'm afraid that's it. I bought only four boxes when Cammie was selling them for her Girl Scout troop. Next time remind me to order a dozen."

"If this friendship proves to have any longevity, that would be a shrewd move."

Noah poured two glasses of sherry and carried them over to the coffee table. "So what am I getting myself in for?"

"I thought we'd ask each other questions, whatever we need—or want—to know. You should go first." Cassandra held out her arms as if she were embracing the world. "So here I am. Ask away!"

"It's your game, Sandy. I think you're the one who should begin the asking."

"It's not a game, Noah."

"Then what is it?"

"It's a tool. A shortcut to what would ordinarily be a long getting-to-know-each-other process. But to make you happy, I'll go first. OK?"

"Do not have the illusion that any of this will make me happy."

"Ready?"

"As ready as I'll ever be."

"Why don't you drive?"

Noah felt a lurch. He wasn't ready for *this*, but to say so might only provoke Sandy, so he said, lightly, "You don't fool around, do you?"

Cassandra shook her head. "There's not a lot of time, so we have to be efficient. Get right to biggies."

Noah didn't say anything.

"You insisted that I go first," said Cassandra, "so I did. You're not allowed to just sit there with your lips pressed together."

"Of course I am! I'm not really enjoying myself."

"This isn't about enjoying ourselves. It's about clearing the decks. Getting some of the important stuff out of the way."

"My not driving isn't particularly important."

"No?"

When Noah didn't respond, Cassandra waited for a moment, then said, "OK. Then why don't you ask me a question? Ask anything you want. See how compliant I am."

"I don't have any questions for you."

"Come on, Noah, there must be something about me you're curious about!"

"All right, then. Are you a widow or a divorcée?"

"What! You don't know?"

"How would I know? You've mentioned a husband in your past, but I didn't know if he was dead or still alive."

"I'm sure Jennifer or any of her cronies would gladly have given you the lowdown, which she ferreted out from me within an hour of our meeting each other."

"I do not engage in gossip. With Jennifer. Or anyone else."

"It's not gossip, Noah. It's facts!"

"You're dodging the question, aren't you?"

"Not at all. The answer is I'm both. I've been divorced *and* widowed. I've been married three times."

"Three?!"

"It does sound like a lot, but we're talking about many years here. I married my first husband when we were both fresh out of college and too young to know better. When we got divorced, I married someone who was twelve years younger. The sex was great, but the marriage wasn't, so we got divorced. Neither my first nor my second husband is still alive. My most recent marriage was to a former colleague of mine, who was twelve years older than me—and he died, so that makes me officially a widow."

"A dozen years too young, then overcompensating with a dozen years too old."

"Something like that."

"You are certainly hard on husbands, aren't you?"

"What about you? Jennifer said you were a widower, but she didn't mention how many wives you've had."

"Just the one."

That put the conversation on pause. They both drank their sherry and waited for the other to speak again.

"Did you have another question for me?" Cassandra asked.

"I'm done with questions."

"But that's hardly fair, since you haven't answered my first one."

"All right, I'll answer your question, and then that's it. The reason I don't drive is that my license expired, and I didn't get it renewed." He held up his hand before Cassandra could say anything. "And the reason I didn't get it renewed was that I was involved in an accident that was entirely my fault and I didn't feel comfortable driving anymore."

"What happened?"

"I believe I've already fulfilled my obligation to answer questions. And here you are, asking another one."

Cassandra held up her hands. "Sorry."

"But you're not really sorry, are you?"

Cassandra laughed. "Of course not. When you hear that a friend was in a car accident, it's perfectly natural to ask more about it, since you want to find out what happened to said friend and said friend's car and whoever else was involved."

"The cars were totaled. The people were not. Are we done?"

"For now."

"I was afraid of that."

"My car would be totaled," said Cassandra, "if it had been only a fender bender. Its book value is not much more than the price of a toaster."

"How old is it?"

"Oh, a decade or so."

"Maybe I should reconsider driving anywhere with you."

"It's all right, it's a Volvo, they last forever. Like us old folk. And if the engine gives up before we get there, we'll have Melville push."

"Wait a moment," cried Noah. "You aren't thinking of bringing that beast with you?"

"Of course I am," said Cassandra. "He loves the Cape."

"That may be true, but I don't love the idea of him invading my cottage."

"He'll grow on you." She was quiet for a minute. "Are we seriously contemplating this adventure?"

"I certainly hope so," said Noah. "Otherwise you've wormed information from me under false pretenses."

"I think we need to sleep on it and reconvene tomorrow. And no hard feelings, right? If either of us comes to our senses overnight."

"No hard feelings," said Noah, but in spite of the prospect of Melville joining them, he was already anticipating the pleasure of removing the plywood panels covering the front windows of the cottage and lugging the Adirondack chairs out onto the deck so he and Cassandra could watch the glow of the sunset on the bay.

# VIII

Fog was hovering over the landscape when Cassandra took Melville for his walk the next morning. She'd always loved the intimacy of fog. The way it turned the outdoors into a space that felt interior. And she loved the way it muted the infinite sky, since she found the concept of infinity disquieting.

The fog obscured the river's distant meanderings, and when Cassandra had walked for a while and looked back, it obscured the sprawling edifice that was Clarion Court, where all those residents were safely tucked away in their "spacious" (a.k.a. small) apartments. Except for the residents who had dogs that required walking. Most of the dogs were diminutive, and she was one of the only residents who walked her dog daily beyond the immediate grounds.

Melville had an excellent sense of smell, and when it was foggy, his nose went into overdrive, making up for the limitation of sight. Judging from his quivering excitement at discoveries that morning, you'd think wolves and mountain lions had been leaving their scent all along the trail. Cassandra's arm was sore from his pulling. After a while the fog started clearing, and she was able to observe a great blue heron moving slowly through the marsh, lifting its legs as delicately as a dancer, then posing a moment, perfectly camouflaged among the reeds, before it lifted up and flew off.

She'd slept on the proposition she and Noah had discussed the night before, as she had suggested they do, but when she had awakened, instead of seriously weighing the benefits and potential difficulties, she'd felt exhilarated at the prospect of an adventure. She always embraced an exciting, new plan and figured she'd work out the wrinkles as it unfolded. Now, instead of considering the feasibility of going to Cape Cod, she just imagined herself gleefully running with Melville down a beach. And having turned her lie to Laurel on its head, she wouldn't have to consider the dreadful prospect of hiding out at Clarion during the time her daughter had wanted to visit. As she walked along the river, her back to Clarion, her mind swirled as she thought about what needed to be done so she could make the trip. She listed things to bring: dog food, marrow bones, stick insects, tarantulas, crickets, binoculars, net, jars, hiking boots, raincoat, bathing suit. Bathing suit? It was definitely too cold for swimming in the ocean now, but you never knew.

She'd inform Laurel and Maggie about her plans, and she'd call Mallory, who, no doubt, would try to reason with her, and, as always, when she'd acknowledged that Cassandra was unpersuadable, she'd sigh and enumerate things to be careful about.

Cassandra's bagged breakfast awaited her when she got back to her apartment. The waffles had survived transit poorly, so she gave most of them to Melville, who swallowed them whole without expressing gratitude, and she started writing down items on two lists: TO DO and TO TAKE. She cleared a staging area near the french doors where she could pile things.

She called Noah and told him she'd be up to talk with him shortly, and before he had a chance to initiate a conversation, she said "See you!" and hung up. Then she called Mallory to tell her where she was going.

Mallory's immediate response was entirely predictable: "Sandy, you can't do something like that!"

"Of course I can," Cassandra said. "This will be a little vacation while Clarion is being spruced up. I love the Cape, and it would be great to be there now, off season. Give me one good reason why I should be dissuaded."

"I don't know where to begin," said Mallory.

"If I get a little distance from Clarion, it will help me feel better about my decision to move there."

"What if it makes you feel worse?"

"Well, I should find that out, shouldn't I? So that's another argument in favor of my going."

"But you don't know what it will be like when you get there. I mean, you've never even seen his house and—"

"It's not a house; it's a rough cottage."

"Oh, Sandy!"

"Mallory, you forget I'm used to roughing it. When I did fieldwork, sometimes I was lucky to have a tent to sleep in. This place has a roof and windows and an indoor toilet. No heat, but there's a woodstove."

"And you'll be cooped up with this man whom you barely know. I mean, you knew him when you were twenty, but—"

"I know him well enough. And it will be fun, Mallory. He's as opinionated and stubborn as I am. We'll have a grand time arguing with each other. We won't be bored!"

"Sandy, that's exactly what you said about Dennis when you married him."

"The main problem with Dennis was that I married him. And I have absolutely no intention of marrying Noah."

"Uh-oh," said Mallory. "Whenever you say that, it makes me nervous. You have a terrible track record for marrying people you had no intention of marrying."

"I'm older and wiser now. And I deserve an adventure, don't I? It's been four years since Rob died."

"All right," said Mallory. She waited a moment before continuing. "This does sound like an adventure—and I'm actually a little jealous of you. But please, be careful!"

"I always am."

"I wish that were true!"

"And, Mal, remember that I'm going to have Melville with me, and he'll chaperone and protect me from all dangers."

"It's a good thing that Noah likes dogs."

"He doesn't," said Cassandra. "But maybe after they've lived together in close quarters for a while, he will."

Mallory, who had perfected "the sigh" as a response to most of Cassandra's doings over their many years of friendship, sighed dramatically, and she laughed, the way a fond parent would at an offspring's endearing transgressions.

"And Mallory, if it doesn't work out, I'll just come back here and make do."

"If you want a place to get away from Clarion for a while so you can get some perspective on it, come stay with me!"

"You're forgetting Melville."

"We'll work something out."

"That's sweet of you!" said Cassandra. "You're the sister I never had. But I think this trip is just what I need now."

"Sandy, you *have* a sister."

"The less said about her, the better."

"Even after all these years, you still feel that way?"

"It's not that I haven't tried, but nothing's changed, Mal. Judy is still praying for my soul. I'm just lucky I have *you*."

They were both quiet for a moment. Then Mallory said, "Let me know how things are going. I want to hear *everything*."

In college they would sit cross legged on their beds when they got back from a date and recount all the details to each other. They had both been less sexually active than many of their classmates, so, in retrospect, it was all quite innocent, but at the time they had felt adventurous.

"This is not what it's about!" said Cassandra.

Mallory didn't say anything.

"You're skeptical. I can hear it in your silence."

"Of course I'm skeptical. I know you! And when you were here, you admitted that you'd found Noah attractive."

"That's right, I did—when he was twenty. He's an old man now."

"Rob was an old man, and you fell in love with him and married him."

"I loved Rob, but I didn't fall in love with him. I *needed* Rob. I needed someone who was steady and sensible and caring and—"

"And wildly in love with you."

"That always helps."

When she hung up with Mallory, Cassandra realized she'd been on the phone for quite a while, so she called Noah. "I'm on my way now."

She grabbed a notepad and pen and took the stairs up to the third floor at a fast pace. She was panting when she got to Noah's door. He looked at her questioningly.

"The elevator is pokey, so I used the stairs."

"Your alternative to swimming laps?"

"With the advantage of no wet hair." Cassandra held up a strand and smiled. "Now, let's get to work!"

"Work?"

She took a seat in the living room and at the top of the pad wrote To Do. She turned it so he could read it.

"Does this mean you've decided to go?"

"Of course. It wasn't actually a thought-out decision—more something I arrived at unconsciously. I was down near the river with Melville, and there was a great blue heron in the marsh, walking like this"—Cassandra made a beak with her hands and stepped slowly across the room, one leg lifted high, then the other—"and then it took off—you know the way their wings just spread." She flung her arms wide. "And that clinched things. It seemed like an omen."

"You believe in omens?"

"Of course not. But it makes a nice story, doesn't it?"

"And do you usually go around imitating herons?"

"Only when I'm doing a nature program with kids. I told you, didn't I, that since I retired from the university, I started teaching courses at the wildlife center?"

"Yes, you did. Your excuse for the cage of bugs that decorates your living room."

"Stick insects," said Cassandra. She picked up the pad and pen. "Now, down to business. What are the things that we need to do before we leave?"

"When do you imagine we're leaving?"

"How about tomorrow?"

"Tomorrow!"

"I thought you were eager to get there. And there's no reason to stay around here any longer, is there? The food is not going to improve, and the pool is not going to open for a while. I just have to meet with the Clarion residential director, Stephanie Cruikshank, before I go."

"To lodge a complaint about the pool?"

"Actually, no. She's the one who got in touch with me. Probably likes to check out all the new residents face to face. When I came for my tour, I was shown around by her subordinate, the program coordinator, and I haven't met her yet."

"More likely she wants to encourage you to do a better job cleaning up after your dog. She never invited me to meet with her when I arrived, but that's quite all right. My experience with administrators of any sort is they are conversationally predictable. Unless, of course, our Ms. Cruikshank is related to the celebrated George and inherited some of his wit."

"Who?"

"George Cruikshank, the nineteenth-century British illustrator famous for his caricatures."

"I think it would be more appropriate if you were the one to ask her about that. By the way, how long is the drive? Two hours?"

"Closer to two and a half."

"I drive fast. Let's aim for two."

"What am I getting myself into?" asked Noah.

"It will be fun. We'll take the bag lunch and eat in the car on the way there. Once we hit the highway, we'll tune into that oldies station, roll down the windows, and let our hair flow in the wind!"

"My hair does not flow."

"A metaphor, Noah. Surely you recognize a metaphor."

"Are you always this energetic?"

"Actually, no. It's just that I'm ready for a vacation. I've been cooped up in Clarion Court, working to get my stuff unpacked and my apartment in shape—"

"You haven't been cooped up—you've been out there tramping around in the conservation-land wilderness with that dog of yours."

"Yes, but psychologically I've felt cooped up. It's all those books in boxes, waiting for me to set them free, passing judgment on me because I've been here all this time and still haven't unpacked."

"A valid point."

Cassandra looked around the living-dining area as if taking stock of things. "We should think about what we're bringing so I can visualize packing the car. Melville takes over the back seat, but there's the back end."

"I'll put the cat there."

"Oh, I forgot about the cat!"

"I don't have the luxury of forgetting about the cat. Once my daughter-in-law bestowed it on me in the mistaken notion it would improve my attitude towards life at Clarion Court, I was denied that privilege."

"I don't know what we'll do. I can't imagine driving even ten minutes with Melville and any cat in close proximity. Ordinarily Melville is pretty laid back, but he finds cats alarming."

As if on cue, the cat made an appearance. It pranced across the living room to the kitchen. It must have leaped up on the kitchen counter because it rattled some pans there, and when Noah got up to investigate, it tore out of the kitchen and disappeared back into the bedroom.

"Even I find this cat alarming," said Cassandra.

"It will be in a cat carrier."

"I'm not sure that will help. Melville will smell the cat, and he'll realize it's there. I can't possibly drive anywhere with a Melville-cat encounter going on in the back seat. It would be a safety hazard."

"We can put the cat in the back end."

"Which means Melville will climb over the seat to get into the back—claw his way through all the stuff we've packed back there—and he'll take on the cat *while* it's in its carrier. Cat carriers were not designed to encounter Newfies!"

"What worries me now isn't just the car trip to the Cape. It's how your beast and mine can possibly coexist for any time at all in my small cottage. In fact, last summer the cat even had difficulty adjusting to being there on its own. It's a cat more suited to comfort-controlled Clarion than a drafty seaside cottage."

"So what are you proposing?"

"That we take only one of them."

"I realize that it may seem only fair to give priority to your cat since we're going to your cottage. But I'd like to point out that I'm foolishly devoted to Melville, whereas you don't even *like* your cat."

"I may not like my cat, but even I am not so heartless that I'd leave it behind in the apartment."

"Noah! Did you really think I was suggesting you abandon it? I was imagining you'd look into alternate arrangements. Find someone to take care of it for you."

"That would be a rather long-term cat sitter."

"How about finding someone to give it to? It's not fair to the cat—or any pet, for that matter—to be stuck with an owner who doesn't really want them."

"Who'd want this cat?"

"People living alone need companionship, and not everyone who'd like a cat already has one."

"I can't think of anyone."

Cassandra studied him. "Would you like me to handle this, then?"

"That would be the general idea. After all, it's an equitable arrangement, since no one is suggesting that you relinquish your dog."

"All right, I'll take it on. This cat will be a hard sell, but I'll do my best. I have someone in mind who might possibly take it on, and I'll give her a call. If it works out, you can deliver the cat to her. Get out the cat carrier and pack up its food and gear."

"So we're really going?"

"Why not?"

They looked at each other for a moment, then Cassandra said, "I better be off now. There's lots to do."

New Zealand was sixteen hours ahead of Massachusetts. Maggie was usually up early with the kids, so Cassandra called her at four that afternoon so she'd catch her at breakfast. She decided not to bring up the trip to the Cape till the end of the conversation.

"I'm glad you called, Mom," said Maggie. "I've been wondering how you're doing. I've been worrying about you."

"I'm doing just fine, Maggie. I don't know why you would be worrying about me."

"I was afraid you were feeling sorry that you sold the house and moved into this retirement place."

"Oh, no, not at all! I'm unpacked—well, almost unpacked—and settling in nicely."

Maggie didn't say anything, and after a minute Cassandra asked, "What is it, Maggie?"

"You just don't sound very convincing."

"What do you mean?"

"I mean you have that cheerful little voice you get when you want everyone to think you are happier than you really are."

"Oh. Well the truth is, Maggie, there's a lot to like about this place—so I should be perfectly happy about the move."

"*Should* be," said Maggie.

"Well, no place is perfect. And it's a huge relief not having that big house to take care of."

"But?"

"I didn't say 'but.'"

"You didn't have to."

Cassandra hesitated for a moment. She always tried to sound confident while talking with each of her daughters. With Laurel it was because Laurel didn't understand ambivalence and was always quick to disapprove. Maggie understood ambivalence too well and was always sympathetic, but Maggie had two children who had conspired to deny her sleep and sanity, so Cassandra was reluctant to burden her. Still, Maggie's insights had a way of hitting home.

"All right, Dear. I'm just not sure this is the right place for me."

"You don't have to stay there, Mom!"

"That's what Mallory told me. She said, 'You're not stuck at Clarion forever!'"

"So your best friend and your favorite child have given you permission to admit that you may have been wrong about moving there."

"First of all, I don't play favorites with my offspring. And second of all, I've always been very good about admitting it when I'm wrong."

Maggie laughed. "Sure, Mom. You may be good about *admitting* it when you're wrong, but you're not very good about recognizing it in the first place."

"No one's good at that!" said Cassandra. She paused. This seemed like a moment to change the subject and bring up the trip with Noah. "You'll be pleased to hear that I'm going on a little vacation."

"Where are you going?"

"Out to Cape Cod with a friend. It's a great time of year for birding."

"Where are you going to stay?"

"He has a cottage."

"He? Who is he?"

"His name's Noah Shilling. He's someone I knew in college, and it turns out he's a resident here, too."

"And you'll be staying with him in a cottage, just the two of you?" Maggie was sounding more like Laurel now—that is, what Laurel would have sounded like had she known about Noah.

"It's nothing like that, Dear. We're just friends. Old friends. Someone to talk to."

"I don't like it," said Maggie.

Cassandra wanted to say that she didn't care if Maggie liked it or not, but she was always careful when she talked to Maggie. If they squabbled, it was not easy to repair things with Maggie so far away. If Cassandra got going, she might point out that Maggie always expressed concern about her, but she was not concerned enough to live closer than nine thousand miles away, and she hadn't even been back to the US to visit once since Rob had died. She hadn't really earned the right to criticize what Cassandra was doing.

"Don't worry, Darling," is what Cassandra said instead. "Noah is perfectly safe. He's an old man, and I'm an old lady. And it's really kind of him to offer me a room in his house on the Cape."

"I thought you said it was a cottage."

"Cottage, house. Whatever. I'm just happy to be able to get away for a bit right now. It's been depressing confronting all my boxes. On the Cape I'll be able to take Melville on long walks on the beach, and I'll go birding!"

"I don't know . . . ," began Maggie. "Oh, Mom! I wish you'd moved here with me." And Maggie sounded so sad, Cassandra forgave her for what earlier had seemed like false concern.

"Remember when you were a kid and I took you and Laurel camping at the Audubon Sanctuary? And we walked to the bay in the early morning, and you sat on the boardwalk and watched the fiddler crabs?"

"Yeah."

"And we spotted those three oystercatchers poking along the sand, and you said it was like our family because we liked oysters too."

"Yeah."

"Be happy for me, Sweetie, that I have this vacation to look forward to. OK?"

"OK," said Maggie. But she didn't *sound* happy.

# IX

Noah started by boxing up the books. His cottage was filled with books, but there were always more to bring—books he wanted to read and books he felt he should read even though he didn't really want to. He packed his cello in its case and packed a box with music books and a pile of CDs, including a generous assortment of Bach. He had clothes at the cottage, but he took a suitcase of additional clothing and the waterproof watch with the tide chart his wife, Helene, had gotten him when he'd retired. On second thought, he decided not to bring the watch because it invariably dredged up memories. He leaned his new kayak paddle against the wall and laid the key to the cottage on the table next to his cell phone. There was an extra key hidden in one of those fake rocks, but he wasn't exactly sure where he'd put the rock. He packed up food from the cupboard and dragged out the cooler from the back of his storage closet. He put the cooling pack in the freezer so he would be ready in the morning. He'd load the cooler right before they left.

Cassandra came by before dinner. "You've lucked out," she announced. "I have persuaded Barbara to take your cat. Fortunately hers died recently, so she is a cat person currently lacking a cat. She was reluctant at first because she might go visit her sister, but when she heard your cat's plight—"

"Plight?"

"Yes, plight."

"Cassandra, what story did you make up about my cat?"

"I explained that you were going to be with family, and at least half of them had an allergy to cats and you were afraid they might not let the cat in the house. And I couldn't take it because of Melville."

"Oh my God, will you stoop to anything?"

"OK, Noah, so what was your plan for the cat? Huh?" Cassandra looked up at the ceiling. "Forgive me, Lord, because I've lied a little so that Noah can be restored to his beloved cottage on Cape Cod?"

"What have I gotten myself into?"

"Stop moaning! Right now, what you've gotten yourself into, is getting the cat into the cat carrier and hauling it to Clarion 239 East. Along with the bag of cat food and kitty litter. I'll bring the cat's gear."

"How do you expect me to face Barbara after this ridiculous story you concocted about my family?"

"If you don't want to see her, leave the cat and run off. I'll say you had a pressing appointment. She won't ask more, because people our age understand bathroom emergencies."

Noah groaned.

"I have a feeling that putting the cat into the carrier may be a two-person job. Set up the carrier on the kitchen floor, and I'll get the cat."

Noah unzipped the door of the cat carrier and placed the carrier down by the refrigerator. Cassandra got down the canister of cat chow. "Do you have anything more tempting than this?"

"Like what?"

"Tuna fish?" Cassandra started looking through the kitchen cabinet and pulled out a can.

"Wait, that's gourmet tuna—not intended for cats!"

"I'm sure the cat won't object," said Cassandra. She removed the lid and set the can deep into the cat carrier, smearing some tuna along the front.

"Stay around the corner out of sight until the cat's going into the carrier," she instructed Noah. "Then block its escape."

The cat was lurking in the bedroom and trotted over when Cassandra dropped some cat chow on the floor. It gobbled some morsels and curled around Cassandra's shin. She didn't try to catch it but walked towards the kitchen, ignoring the cat, and sprinkling a trail of cat chow behind her. The cat got a whiff of the tuna and bounded ahead but was smart enough to be suspicious of the cat carrier. The pricey tuna, though, proved irresistible, and the cat had a paw inside the carrier when it spotted Noah approaching and bolted. The cat bounded past Cassandra, who cried, "Catch it!" Noah lunged at the cat and managed to grab it from behind. The cat clawed wildly, Noah yelped and dropped it, and the cat leaped onto the kitchen counter, knocking the sugar bowl to the floor. It tore across the stove top, scrambled over the dish-drying rack, clattering dishes and scattering spoons in its wake, sprang on top of the refrigerator, and cowered in the space in the back under the cupboard. It was miraculous that such a large cat could fit in such a small space.

"We'll never get it now."

Cassandra snatched some oven mitts hanging by the stove, shoved her hands into them, and pulled over a step stool so she could climb up on the counter.

"Get the carrier, and turn it upright," she commanded Noah. "Soon as I drop the cat in, close the door and hold it shut."

She reached back into the space between refrigerator and cupboard and dragged out the cat. She held it under the armpits, away from her body, and dangled it over the open carrier that Noah had positioned by the counter. The cat splayed its four legs wider than the carrier opening. Cassandra grabbed it by the scruff of its neck with one hand and grabbed its two back legs with her other hand, and before the cat knew what was happening, she pushed it into the carrier. She hopped off the counter and zipped the door closed. She put the carrier right side up and squatted down beside the screened door.

"See, Baby, you're OK. That wasn't so bad, now, was it?" The cat yowled in protest. "Believe me, you'll thank me in the end. Barbara loves cats, and she'll take wonderful care of you."

98

Cassandra stood up. "You're bleeding!" she said, looking at Noah's hand.

"I told you the cat didn't like me."

"Should I get you a Band-Aid?"

"I'll manage."

"I'll wait while you get yourself one. If Barbara sees that claw mark, the deal might be off."

"I don't intend to be seen by Barbara," Noah said, but he did put something on his hand before they left. He carried the cat and its supplies down to the second floor, set them down by Barbara's door, and disappeared before Cassandra rang the bell.

Cassandra was smiling when she returned to his apartment a half hour later. "Believe it or not, you have now earned brownie points in heaven. The cat liked Barbara even better than it liked me—which is odd, since Barbara *likes* cats. She was actually grateful to you for providing her with a pet. If she were a huggy sort of person—which she is not—she'd have asked me to hug you on her behalf."

"I consider myself fortunate."

Cassandra's eye was distracted by the cooler on the kitchen floor. "Is that what I think it is?"

"If you think it is a cooler, then you are correct."

"And you expect us to take it?"

"We're not going to leave anything in our refrigerators, are we?"

"There's very little in my refrigerator, and what there is, is not worthy of transport."

"Then I'll make use of your allotted space."

"That cooler will take up half the car!"

"Good. Then we'll have the other half for us."

He had watched her as her eyes moved, dangerously, across to the hall. She pointed at his kayak paddle.

"And what about that?"

"It's a special lightweight paddle with a carbon shaft and—"

"And you're planning on bringing it?"

"Of course. It was a present I gave myself. I've been waiting since Christmas to try it out."

"What's in those boxes?"

"Books."

"Two boxes of books?"

"That's my primary indoor activity. Reading. Sometimes my outdoor activity, too. I have a particular hammock dedicated to the purpose."

"Anything else?"

"Just some clothes in a small suitcase. And the wine. I finally got someone in dining services to deliver it to me."

Cassandra pointed accusingly to the cello. "You're not bringing that, are you?"

"I am."

"Do you have any idea about the storage capacity of a Volvo wagon?"

"I do."

"And do you realize how much space your cello will require?"

"If we want to talk about something requiring a considerable amount of space, I suggest we talk about your dog."

Cassandra ignored his remark and swept her arm across the guilty items she spotted in the living room, hall, and kitchen. "But you're bringing all these other things too!"

"My cello is the companion of my solitary years. I don't travel without it. And I'd like to remind you, because of you, I just parted with my cat."

Cassandra glared at him—it was impossible to tell if it was mock fury or real fury. "I have just completed a difficult job on your behalf," she said, "a job that, as you point out, required me to compromise my moral commitment to the truth in order to accomplish the end you required. I suggest that when it comes to the subject of your cat, you express nothing but eternal gratitude to me for not only freeing you from an unwanted burden but also assuaging your guilt by providing your pet with a home infinitely superior to the one you so begrudgingly offered."

"Are you done yet?"

"That will depend on whether you're sufficiently contrite."

"You really are impossible, you know it?"

"And you believe that *you* are *possible*?"

Noah had to laugh. "Of course I am!" He waited a moment before he said, "Truce?"

"OK, truce. Now let's get this stuff down to my place. We'll take a break for dinner and then load the car."

It took several trips to relocate Noah's stuff to Cassandra's apartment. They piled it all next to Cassandra's stuff in the staging area by the french doors. Cassandra collapsed on the sofa and surveyed the mound.

"I am a genius at packing," she informed Noah. "However, I am not a magician who can abracadabra things to make them tiny." She opened one of Noah's boxes of books, shook her head, and then started emptying the box.

"What are you doing?"

"We've got to pack more efficiently. There's wasted space in here." She repacked the box, stacking cans from Noah's grocery bag across the bottom and filling in a side with boxes of noodles. Melville, who seemed to be able to detect the presence of food even when it was sealed in cans, came over to investigate. When he had drooled sufficiently on the contents of the box, he went back and curled up on the rug.

Cassandra added a stack of her own books to Noah's book box. "We'll consolidate things."

"Is this healthy?"

"It's merely a temporary co-mingling. When we arrive at your cottage, you'll liberate your books and place them on your shelves—you do have bookshelves, don't you?" She looked up at Noah.

"Of course I have bookshelves!"

"And I'll use the box to store my books in the bedroom you have assigned to me." She paused, then added, "It's just for a week or so, right? Till Clarion is restored to its full glory."

"Right," said Noah. Though he realized he didn't like imagining the end of her visit, having that hovering there before they'd even started. "You are certainly bringing a lot of stuff for a short stay." He pointed to the field guides she had piled on top of his sheet music. "And why are you bringing these, anyway? These days you can look up anything on your iPhone; you don't need to lug books."

Cassandra's eyes widened. "I can't believe you're saying that, Noah. I took you for a man who respected—no, that's too mild, who *cherished* the printed word. Printed on paper, that is."

Noah didn't answer. Instead he pointed at Cassandra's insect net. "Is that a necessary addition?"

"Do you have one at your cottage for me to use?"

"I have a fishnet."

"I have no interest in catching fish."

"You do eat them, don't you?"

"Yes."

"We will feast on the bounty of the sea and what we forage."

"What do you forage?"

"Quahogs, steamers, oysters."

"Oh, goody," said Cassandra. "I love to forage, but I shy away from exotic fungi. A colleague of mine who was a specialist in the field nearly poisoned himself and some of his friends. He'd led them on a foraging trip, and then they all went to his home and cooked and dined on what they'd gathered. Apparently he'd misidentified some rare fungi."

"A cautionary tale. Let's stick to the bounty of the sea. Except for cranberries. But they won't be ready for picking until the fall."

"I'll come back and visit you then, if you're still on the Cape. OK?"

"I intend to stay until the first snow drives me away. As long as I'm still alive and have my faculties intact."

Cassandra sat down on the box of books she had taped shut. "Why are you saying something like that? It's depressing."

"I'm not an optimist like you, Sandy."

"I'm not really an optimist, it's a veneer. Underneath I'm as pessimistic as you."

"I hope that isn't true," said Noah.

"I've come to terms with the fact that I'm mortal. That's pessimistic, isn't it? And I've made a will. But you said something earlier about maybe leaving your paintings to a museum rather than your son, which sounded as if the designation of your inheritance was still in flux."

"And—?"

"And if that's the case, I'd say it was optimistic. You believe it's a way you can keep yourself alive."

"What?"

"People put off making wills because they're afraid that the existence of a will might hasten the occasion when it would be put to use."

"I'm not afraid to make a will—it's just that there are some things I haven't made my mind up about yet."

"People also put off making wills as a way to leverage power over potential heirs. Though my guess is such power is purely illusory. Which is why I just went ahead and informed my two children that I'd divided the spoils of my demise evenly between them, regardless of who deserved it more." Cassandra smiled, then she added, "Oh, and I included a generous proviso for Melville, should I predecease him."

"I'm not surprised," said Noah.


Noah went up and collected the paper bag with his dinner and rejoined Cassandra in her apartment. He had a bottle of wine in his hand.

"I thought we should toast our last Clarion dinner."

"Lovely idea, but we still have to pack the car. So let's not finish the bottle till later."

Noah had opted for the meat loaf, and Cassandra had opted for the lasagna. Neither choice was the right one. The vegetable was asparagus, yet again, this time in a cream sauce that was an unnatural shade of yellow. At least the dessert was an oversized cookie, though unfortunately oatmeal raisin.

Cassandra took Melville with her when she fetched her car from the lot and drove it up to the back of the building, as close to her apartment as possible.

"Melville always loves excursions, so he'll sit happily in the back seat while we load the car. And if anyone starts to question why I've parked there, I'll just say I'm taking Melville to the vet."

"At night?"

"An emergency visit. He ate a chocolate cake. Chocolate, as you know, can be lethal to dogs."

"I didn't know," said Noah. "But I'll keep it in mind."

Cassandra punched his shoulder.

Noah had to admit that Cassandra excelled at car packing. Not a genius, as she claimed, but better than anyone he knew. She approached the problem as if it were a giant three-dimensional puzzle, moving things around till they were a snug fit, squatting to tuck things into low corners, and stepping back now and then to reassess and make adjustments. Noah hefted the boxes, which she felt was an appropriate division of labor. When it was done, there wasn't a cubic inch left. An empty box held the place for the stick insects, crickets, and tarantulas, who'd be added in the morning. She stood back and admired her work.

"You forgot something," said Noah.

"I got everything from the pile."

"But you didn't leave room for the cooler. It's still up in my apartment."

"Fuck! Double fuck!"

Noah grinned. "I wondered what it would take to get you to say something like that!"

Cassandra closed her eyes, took a deep breath, exhaled slowly, and opened her eyes. "OK, no problem. There will be plenty of room for the cooler on your lap."

# X

Cassandra was already in bed when Laurel called that night. When Laurel called this late, it was usually because she had a crisis—real or invented—and her capacity for rational discourse was diminished. Cassandra pulled herself up, turned on the light, and invoked her most maternal, calming persona. "Is everything all right, Darling?" she asked.

"Deborah's mother died."

"Deborah?"

"Deborah Malik."

Cassandra wasn't sure who that was, but fortunately Laurel continued, "Eve called me tonight to tell me." Eve was Laurel's college roommate, and Cassandra was able to recall a Deborah who'd lived in their suite.

"She was in a nursing home and had a stroke and died in the hospital. Deborah didn't get there in time to say goodbye to her."

"I'm sorry to hear this," said Cassandra.

"She died all alone!" cried Laurel.

"That's so sad."

"I'm not going to let that happen to you!"

"I'm certainly not going to let that happen to me, either, so there's nothing for you to worry about."

"I've been so upset thinking of you in that nursing home, so far away!"

"I keep telling you, Laurel, this is a senior living community, it's not a nursing home. They're entirely different—"

But Laurel wasn't listening. "I wish you'd reconsider moving in with us! I was going to take the day off from work and come see you right away, but Drew said I should wait till this weekend."

"I'm glad to hear that, because I'm—"

"But now I'm not so sure I should wait. Deborah's mother wasn't even sick—I mean, she was old—but there wasn't anything else wrong with her. Deborah got on a plane as soon as the nursing home called, but it was already too late!"

Cassandra wanted to tell Laurel not to be hysterical but knew that would be futile. She took a breath and spoke in the most soothing voice she could summon. "I want to reassure you, Sweetheart, that I have no intention of having a stroke or anything remotely like it. Please keep in mind that just because people are old, it doesn't mean there's anything *wrong* with them. And although it's sweet of you to think of coming to see me, this isn't a good time, because I'm leaving tomorrow morning."

It was deeply satisfying to be able to offer this bit of news to Laurel, and although Cassandra believed Laurel's concern was genuine, she guessed that Laurel was relieved to be spared the trip. And she was certain that both Laurel and her unfortunate choice of spouse were as pleased with themselves for their offer of hospitality as they were glad that she hadn't taken them up on it.


Melville woke Cassandra early the next morning. "Paws off!" she cried, as she always did, and he obediently removed his offending front paws from the side of her bed and replaced them with his giant head and his slobbering tongue. The bedroom looked tranquil and lovely in the morning light, the walls milky white—still bare, because she hadn't gotten around to hanging any pictures yet—the carpeting a shade of gray that made her think of mist in the mountains. She threw on the clothes she'd worn the day before and left draped over the armchair by the window and went to fetch Melville's leash. Her living room looked gracious, in spite of the boxes. The french doors opened up to a green world. It was as if the photographs on the Clarion Court website, which showed a "typical" two-bedroom apartment, had been laid out for her with cunning reality. It had been the photos of a prospective apartment just like this—in addition to the pet-friendly environment—that had lured her to Clarion Court.

"Come on, Baby," she said, and she grabbed a sweater and took Melville on their usual walk. The river seemed to curl endlessly in the distance, with the encouragement of the sunrise. A cardinal, glowing red in a shaft of sunlight, began singing with glorious certainty to an invisible potential mate—or perhaps for himself, in response to the sunshine and the morning and the sweetly meandering river. How was it possible that such intense sound could be produced by a body that small?

No one else was out walking on the path, and there were no other people in sight. It was hard to believe that this conservation area was just a small preserved pocket of nature and that civilization—if you could call it that—was there, pressing on all sides, ready to encroach. When Cassandra turned to start walking back to her apartment, instead of Clarion Court seeming like an institution housing a multitude of aging residents, it looked more like a huge, stately mansion on a vast estate. Melville tugged at the leash, but she stood for a moment, watching for people to start appearing—but no one did.

When she'd told Mallory that she was going to the Cape with Noah, Mallory's first words had been, "Sandy, you can't do something like that!" Now Mallory's voice came, unbidden, into her head. She tried to push it out of her consciousness, but it snuck around the recesses of her brain. All of the concerns Mallory had expressed—which she had so determinedly ignored or pushed away—now swarmed. "You don't know what it will be like when you get there," Mallory had said. No, she didn't. She'd never seen Noah's cottage. And she'd be, as Mallory put it, "cooped up with this man whom you barely know." And what if she got there and realized it was a mistake? She'd have to come up with a politic exit strategy. And why was she going off with Noah? Because instead of dining in "The Terrace" dining room, she had to settle for dinner in a plastic container on a tray left outside her door? Because she'd have to do without swimming laps for a week or two? Because she imagined getting some distance from Clarion Court would enable her to decide whether she wanted to continue living here? But that didn't make much sense, did it? She hadn't even finished unpacking; she'd hardly had a chance to see what living at Clarion Court was really like. And where was she going? Someplace entirely unknown. Perhaps she'd gone crazy. She hadn't dared tell Laurel about Noah, and Maggie, her adventurous daughter, had been alarmed. Her voice, spoken nine thousand miles, sixteen hours away, had been absolutely clear: "I don't like it."

Maggie's voice and Mallory's voice; sane voices. And in spite of all their reasonable doubt, she'd been her bright, effervescent self—giddy with the scent of the adventure. Flighty, childlike, irresponsible. The sight of her packed car, which she had parked in a spot that said "SERVICE VEHICLES ONLY," was a dramatic reminder of her foolishness. Worse: her recklessness. She'd had fun working to fit everything in—well, almost everything; there was still that cooler—but she'd let the excitement about the trip sweep her along. She hadn't really faced the basic essential questions: What was she really doing? And why? She'd married Denny in the same fever of adventure, and how had that ended up? For God's sake, she was seventy-two years old. Had she learned absolutely nothing? Nothing!

As for Noah—he was just some guy she'd come to like because he was amusing, and because he seemed to enjoy her company. He'd find another ride to get him to his Cape Cod cottage. She'd just started settling in to Clarion, and she really wasn't ready—was she?—to be going away, anywhere, this soon. Yes, there were some temporary inconveniences, but that was what life was. (And possibly death too—though no one had been able to report about it.) She'd been tempted by the lure of Cape Cod, by the dance of the woodcocks, by the call of the open road, like hapless Toad in *The Wind in the Willows*. Tempted by the prospect of escaping from the drudgery of unpacking and facing all those boring decisions about where things should go or how to fit in the things that didn't seem to want to fit in anywhere. Maybe sometime later she'd make a trip to the Cape, but this was not the right time. As soon as she got back to her apartment, she'd call Noah and tell him she'd come to her senses, reconsidered their plan, and decided she wouldn't be going.

As she got closer to the building, Melville recognized her car and started pulling her closer to it. He loved car rides.

"Sorry, Baby," she said. "Maybe another time." The sight of Noah's kayak paddle through the back window, optimistically awaiting its maiden voyage in the sea, gave her a sudden pang. If only her decision affected her alone. That was the problem with doing anything with someone else. Nothing was emotionally streamlined anymore. Every step caused little eddies of turmoil, little wisps of guilt.

"Come on, Melville," she said. But Melville, all 150 pounds of him, was hard to dissuade once he got determined about something. Was it possible he spotted the bag of dog food that she had wedged in along the back window? There was no way Cassandra could out-pull Melville, but fortunately he was persuadable when it came to dog treats.

"Treat, Melville, treat! Let's go get your treat!" cried Cassandra, and Melville quickly weighed the choices and decided that a promised treat was a better option than vague possibilities associated with a bag of dog food stowed behind glass. He trotted alongside Cassandra back to their apartment, where he was suitably rewarded, and Cassandra realized that although she had packed the dog food for the Cape, she had neglected to pack the bag of dog treats, which would have been a disaster—if she had gone.

"OK, Baby," she said to Melville as he gobbled the second treat she gave him, "time to call Noah now and let him know things have changed." But when she finally found her cell phone (it had hidden itself on the kitchen counter next to the toaster oven), she decided to wait until after she'd eaten breakfast. After all, she had no idea what time Noah got up in the morning, and she didn't want to wake him. She had no idea if he was an early riser or not, just one of the many things she didn't know about him—this man with whom she had been planning on going off with to spend who-knew-how-long in a small cottage.

She'd ordered a breakfast less likely to disappoint than the waffles of the day before. But the eggs, which were supposed to be soft boiled, were closer to hard, and the croissant looked as if someone had rested an elbow in the center of it. There was orange marmalade rather than strawberry jam, and the butter had failed to make an appearance at all. Dinner was included in her monthly fees, but she was charged separately for breakfasts and lunches at Clarion Court. She had liked the breakfast buffet in "The Terrace" dining room. But there was no reason to pay for breakfast now; she had a kitchen and could certainly make it herself. Even she, the anti-chef, could produce something better than these brown-bag eggs.

She made herself coffee and lingered over it and picked at the extremities of the croissant. Melville had settled down in his favorite spot by the pseudofireplace, but he glanced up at her now and then. His expression was naturally reproachful, but she had a feeling he was aware that she was putting off calling Noah as long as she could.

When her cell phone rang, she was so sure it was Noah she almost didn't answer it because she hadn't yet prepared how to say what she was going to say. But it wasn't Noah. It was Barbara.

"I haven't been able to reach Noah, and I was hoping you'd see him before he left to tell him about his cat."

"What happened?" asked Cassandra.

"Happened? Nothing happened. I just wanted him to know how well his cat is doing."

"Oh," said Cassandra. "Oh!" She could not disguise her relief.

"As you know, cats hate change"—Cassandra didn't know, but didn't say so—"but this cat has adjusted beautifully to being with me. And she's such a sweet and friendly cat!" Barbara almost cooed, which seemed entirely out of character. Cassandra was tempted to ask if this could possibly be the same cat she had dropped off the day before, but that seemed imprudent, so what she said instead was, "I'm so glad this worked out!"

"I'm sure it was hard for Noah to give her up," Barbara continued, "but he can rest assured his cat will be well taken care of and greatly appreciated."

"There wasn't any doubt about that," said Cassandra. As for Barbara's idea that it had been hard for Noah to part with the cat, why spoil the myth? "I'll be in touch with him shortly, and I'm sure he will be happy for the update. And thank you, Barbara. Since I couldn't help Noah out, I'm tremendously grateful to you for coming to the rescue. And by the way, this cat is not sweet and friendly to everyone—you clearly have brought out the best in her."

"It's not me," said Barbara. "She's a truly sweet animal, and my sister said it would be fine if I brought the cat when I go visit her. She's in rural Vermont. I mean *really* rural. It will be a short visit. By the way, did you know David Sussman died?"

"Oh, I'm so sorry!"

"The director here prefers to control information about all the Clarion residents, but Jennifer is adept at finding things out. I don't trust the director at all, and I don't think you should either."

"Actually, I'm having a meeting with her this afternoon."

"Oh?"

"She sent me an email asking if I would drop by."

"No doubt someone complained because you were singing in the shower."

"I sing only on dry land."

Barbara laughed.

When she was done talking with Barbara, Cassandra had no excuse to put off calling Noah any longer. She decided it would be preferable to tell him in person, rather than on the phone. The problem was that she had never been any good at disappointing people, which accounted for some of the worst mistakes she'd made in her life—including at least two of her marriages. She briefly considered the idea of chauffeuring Noah to the Cape and coming right back, but she doubted he'd accept the offer, and even if he did, it would be emotionally too complicated.

"I'll just fortify myself with a second cup of coffee first," Cassandra informed Melville. "OK?" Instead of a satisfactory nod of his huge head,

Melville ignored Cassandra's question and concentrated on chewing at a burr that had gotten caught in the fur on his paw.

Cassandra poured the coffee in the mug given to her by some of her grad students when she retired, which had illustrations of forty-eight (she'd counted them) varieties of beetles. It always cheered her. She settled herself on the living room sofa with the coffee and the squashed center portion of the croissant left over from her breakfast and decided she'd give Mallory a call before she called Noah and let her know what was happening.

"You got there already!" were Mallory's first words as soon as she heard Cassandra's voice.

"Actually, no, I'm still here."

"Shouldn't you be packing the car now instead of calling me?"

"We packed it last night—except for the critters—but the reason I'm calling is—"

"That was brilliant of you, but—"

"Mallory, listen. It turns out I'm not leaving."

"What happened?"

"I changed my mind. I decided not to go."

"Why would you do that?"

"That's exactly what you said when I told you I was going."

"Maybe so, but you ended up convincing me it was a good idea."

"So now I have to convince you that it isn't? You're the one who listed all the reasons I shouldn't go. And now I'm actually doing what you wanted."

"Are you blaming me?" Mallory didn't sound exactly angry, but her voice had an unusual sharpness to it.

"I'm not blaming you, Mal, I'm just saying that I thought about everything you said and realized you were right—"

"But I said I envied you, going off on an adventure like this."

"Well, maybe you said that in the end, but that was after you'd given me a whole litany of reasons why I was nuts to consider what I was doing."

"I never said you were nuts."

"But you implied that. And now you're sounding disappointed because I'm not going."

"Well—"

"Well, are you disappointed?"

"Yeah. I guess so. I'm stuck here in this big, dull house, and you were heading off on a romantic escapade, and yeah, I was kind of excited. I was going to vicariously experience the great adventure."

"Jesus, Mal!"

"I thought you were eager for a little vacation."

"Maybe sometime—but not now, Mallory. I haven't unpacked all my boxes yet. I don't deserve a vacation."

"I seem to remember you once saying that what people deserve and what people get are entirely unrelated."

"It's not fair to use my own words against me."

Mallory sighed one of her substantial, complex sighs. Then she brightened. "If you're not going to the Cape, Sandy, then why don't you come stay with us for a while?"

"Thank you, Dear. But the reason I'm not going to the Cape is I realized, in spite of everything, this is my home now, so I should be here. I've only just moved in!"

"I thought you weren't sure that you *wanted* it to be your home."

After a space of silence Mallory asked more gently, "Sandy?"

"All right. I'd thought getting away for a while would clarify things for me. But maybe the real reason was it offered an escape. I didn't want to face the possibility that moving to Clarion had been a colossal mistake and I'd have to figure out what to do with myself instead. Maybe it was a way to imagine I could go back in time and reclaim my old life, which I'd abandoned in a fever of misjudgment!"

"Oh, Sweetheart!"

"So, in the end, I decided I couldn't go away. I needed to stay at Clarion, give it a chance, try to make it work."

"Poor Noah. This must have been a big letdown for him."

Cassandra didn't say anything. She looked around the room, trying to come up with a proper reply. Melville had gone to sleep, muzzle on paws.

"You did tell him, didn't you?" Mallory asked.

"Not yet, but—"

"You mean that poor man is happily waiting in his apartment this very minute, expecting you'll soon be driving off with him to the Cape!"

"I'm planning to tell him soon as we're done talking. And I wouldn't call him a 'poor man.'"

"Oh God, Sandy! I can't believe this. He's counting on you, isn't he? You told me he doesn't have a car and doesn't drive and—"

"Mallory, I concocted this whole plan of going to the Cape without really thinking about it. Typical me, right? I just wanted to get away, and it seemed like an ideal escape. But this morning I confronted reality and decided to act responsibly. And I had hoped you'd be pleased."

Mallory didn't concur, but Cassandra persisted. "Aren't you?"

"I'm not your parent," said Mallory quietly. "You shouldn't be doing anything in order to please me."

"I don't have parents anymore," said Cassandra. "So I rely on you."

"I'm hanging up now," said Mallory. "And you're calling Noah." And she did hang up.

Cassandra had barely finished telling Noah she needed to talk with him in person when he cut her off.

"Rather than you coming up here and bringing whatever you want to load in the cooler, wait till later, and I'll just bring the cooler down to you. And I have a plan for fitting it in the car that doesn't involve my lap, or yours."

"I've got that meeting with the director I told you about, and when I get back, I'd like to sit down with you and explain that—" Cassandra began, but Noah interrupted. "Don't castigate yourself about the cooler.

Even genius packers have lapses now and then. See you later." Then he hung up on her. The second person in ten minutes to do so.

The office of the residential director of Clarion Court was separated from the receptionist's desk in the front hall by half walls, with glass waist to ceiling. An obvious attempt, Cassandra thought, to give the appearance of accessibility. She'd once seen the director smile and wave as some residents passed by. But Stephanie Cruikshank was rarely in her office, and when there, she was usually engrossed in something on her computer screen. The director was two or three decades younger than the youngest resident, and so it was an interesting role reversal: a community of the relatively powerless seniors with someone as young as their offspring (those who were fortunate enough to have offspring) wielding power at the helm, though Cassandra wasn't sure if the director actually had any power or if she was just a PR face. And it was unknown whether in the new corporate configuration marrying Clarion and Oakdale Living, she would be further empowered or demoted.

The Clarion staff—fitness instructors, activity instructors, waiters, cleaning staff—sported first names only on their name tags. The director's status was apparent by the fact her tag bore first and last name. Since this posed a conundrum for how she should be addressed, Cassandra waited until the director addressed her first.

"May I call you Cassandra?" she asked, saying her name in what Cassandra thought of as the "snooty way," the second "a" pronounced like an "o" as in "on." When people mispronounced her name, Cassandra felt it gave her a certain edge over them, so rather than correct her, she just smiled and said, "Of course, Stephanie."

Stephanie had a pinched face and impeccably straight blond hair that grazed her shoulders. Her perpetual smile displayed disproportionately large teeth and salmon-pink gums, like an equine with its lips curled up.

"Do have a seat," said Stephanie, and she pointed to one of the two high-backed chairs flanking the desk. Cassandra sat. The chair was upholstered in cozy-looking chintz, but was surprisingly uncomfortable.

"I wanted to make sure you've been settling in here well," Stephanie began. "Do you have any questions or concerns that I could help you with?"

Cassandra considered saying something about the inconvenience of the closure of the dining hall and the swimming pool but decided to keep these on hold. "Everything's fine, thank you," she said in what Maggie would have called her "chirpy voice." As Noah had suggested, she guessed that the request of an interview had been initiated not out of a desire to ensure that Cassandra was a happy camper but to discuss an issue management had about her residency. And she was not proved wrong.

"I thought it would be useful," Stephanie said, "to have a little chat with you to clarify some of our residential regulations and expectations."

In Cassandra's experience, "little chats" were rarely "little." Nor were they "chats." She smiled a bright smile, her lips firmly together so her teeth showed not at all.

"As you know, Clarion is a pet-friendly community," Stephanie began.

"It's one of the main reasons I selected it," said Cassandra.

"When the management made the decision to allow residents to have dogs, what they had in mind were small dogs, or at most medium-size dogs. They didn't expect anyone to move in with a dog as big as yours."

"Your regulations simply referred to 'dogs,' without specifying their size."

"Yes, we're well aware of that now," said Stephanie. "Since you may not have a copy of the contract you signed handy, I thought it would be useful for us to look at it together." She tapped briskly at her keyboard, then turned her monitor slightly so Cassandra could view it. Obviously she'd had this document all ready before Cassandra had arrived for the interview. She scrolled down to the section labeled "OTHER CONDITIONS" and pointed to the screen where it said "PETS."

"As you can see here, it says 'One dog, one domestic cat, a caged bird or fish may be kept in the Living Accommodation only with the approval of the Executive Director, whose approval may be revoked at any time.'" Her smile showed even more gums, if that were possible. "As you can imagine, your big dog has alarmed some of the other residents."

"He may be big," began Cassandra, "but there's no reason for alarm. He's a Newfoundland, a breed renowned for their gentle nature, for their calm disposition and loyalty. Newfies are bred as lifesaving dogs and excel at water rescue. Their two less-desirable characteristics— drooling and shedding—may be unpleasant for their owner but aren't a problem for anyone else. I'm happy to provide you with more information about the breed—"

"Your next-door neighbor says she can hear him bark."

"He barks very rarely, considering he's a dog, and that's what dogs do," said Cassandra. She'd never actually spoken with her next-door neighbor, and she was tempted to comment on the fact that she could hear her neighbor snoring but hadn't complained about it, but said instead, "The apartments here are not exactly soundproof, so I have to endure the sound of her television, which is on most of the day."

Stephanie sat back in her chair. "There is another small matter," she said, and she resumed her overgenerous smile. "It has come to our attention that you are keeping insects in your apartment."

"That's true," said Cassandra. "I do 'keep' insects. I'm an entomologist; they're my profession."

"This is a residential community. If you require them for a business, then they should be housed at your business location."

"I'm retired from being a college professor, but I use the insects when I do nature programs for kids. I volunteer in schools. Why don't we just consider them my pets."

Stephanie turned back to her monitor, tapped at the screen, and read aloud: "Pets. One dog, one domestic cat, a caged bird or fish may be kept in the Living Accommodation.'" She looked at Cassandra. "As you can see, that does not include insects."

"Perhaps when the contract was drafted, it didn't occur to anyone that future residents might have pet insects or arachnids, but they're as much pets as birds or fish. Petunia, for instance is a pinktoe tarantula, *Avicularia avicularia*, which is an arboreal species. She's practically a bird. And my insects are all perfectly friendly. Kids love the stick insects!"

"Stick insects?"

"They're in a perfectly safe cage."

"A member of the cleaning staff saw an enormous spider loose, in your apartment. She was terrified."

"Loose?"

"I believe it was on the bureau in your bedroom."

Cassandra laughed. "That was just an exuvium."

"We can't have any bugs at Clarion," said Stephanie, giving unnecessary emphasis to the "b."

It was obviously not a good moment to give Stephanie a lecture on the meaning of "exuvium," the molting habits of tarantulas, the distinction between insects and arachnids, or the characteristics of "true bugs." So Cassandra said, "That wasn't a live tarantula. It was just the—" She sought a word that would sound harmless. "It was just the shell of Marigold, after she'd molted. I'd be happy to give a talk in your lecture series so residents and staff can become acquainted with my pets. The stick insects are fun to watch, and everyone can hold Marigold, who's a Chilean rose tarantula. I can show them Petunia, but it's better not to take her out of her cage."

Stephanie had managed to maintain her smile, but said only, "We had to rearrange the cleaners' schedule because several of the staff have refused to go into your apartment."

"I'm sorry," said Cassandra—always best to say you're sorry, even when you weren't—"but there's a simple solution. I'll just clean the apartment myself, and no one needs to come into it."

Stephanie turned to her computer again, scrolled to another section of the contract, and tapped on the screen while she read aloud. "Housekeeping of the Living Accommodation will occur on a scheduled basis every week."

"Yes, I know that cleaning's included in my monthly fees, but surely it's not required."

"Actually, it is."

"Then I'll keep the insects in a place in my apartment where the cleaning staff can't see them."

"The point is they are not allowed."

"They won't even know they're there!"

Once again Stephanie turned back to her monitor and scrolled down to the section of the document titled: "RIGHT OF PRIVACY." She read aloud: "Residents recognize and accept the right of Clarion Court to enter the Living Accommodation in order to carry out the purpose of this Agreement. Clarion Court shall have the right to enter the Living Accommodation for the purposes of"—Stephanie pointed to #9, and continued reading—"inspecting the Living Accommodation upon reasonable belief that there is a violation of the Rules and Regulations."

"What? Inspect my apartment!"

"I assume you read this document before you signed it."

"It was thirty-four pages long. I'm afraid I just skimmed it."

"We prefer residents actually read the contract so they can comply with it. We'll make an exception for your dog, for now, and see how things go," said Stephanie. "But the insects need to be removed from the premises."

"Removed? What do you mean?"

"Relocated elsewhere."

"But I don't have an 'elsewhere' to relocate them to."

Stephanie cocked her head—perhaps in an attempt to appear sympathetic—and shrugged.

"How about we give you a week to resettle them. All right?"

Cassandra wasn't sure what to say to this. She gripped the chair's wooden armrests. She was thrust back into a memory from when she was a kid, in second grade. She'd been sent to have a "little chat" with Mr. Brumbaugh, the principal, because she'd drawn in a book from the school library. It was a story about animals at the seashore, and the crab in the illustration had only six legs. She had drawn in the others with a pen and colored them in carefully to match the pinkish color of the crab on the page.

"You know you're not supposed to mark anything in library books," Mr. Brumbaugh had said, cocking his head exactly as Stephanie had. "Don't you?"

She'd nodded.

"But you seem to have drawn in this one, didn't you?" He raised his eyebrows interrogatively, and the brown mole perched above his left one rode up with his brow.

"Yes, but that's because the crab needed more legs. Crabs have eight legs. This crab had only six."

He swiveled the book around to take another look and tapped at the illustration. "I see eight legs," he said.

"Those two are claws."

He shut the book and thumped it for good measure. "Your parents will be contacted, and you will be required to purchase a new copy of this book for the library. If you mark any other books in the future, your library privileges will be permanently revoked. Do you understand?"

She had nodded but hadn't looked at him. Then she ran from the office, trying, but not managing, to keep herself from crying until she was in the hall outside the principal's office.

Her mother was furious with her, but when her father heard the story at dinner, he smiled. He said he'd give the school the money for the book, but he'd have a word with the principal about books in the school library that gave children misinformation about the natural world.

"No wonder she gets into trouble at school," her mother had shouted. "You encourage her!" And she'd left the table, throwing her linen napkin on her chair, and not noticing when it slipped to the floor.

When Cassandra returned to her apartment, she sat down next to Melville on the floor and laid her face against his thick, furry neck. She felt the rise and fall of his breathing and listened to his tongue moving around his jowls. Was her procrastination about informing Noah that she wasn't going to the Cape a symptom of her cowardice, or was it a sign of her ambivalence? Was she afraid of hurting him, or was it that she was afraid of hurting herself, pointlessly depriving herself of something she wanted to do?

Someone was coughing in the apartment next door. It was, no doubt, the old woman who had complained about Melville. An old woman—not old like Cassandra, but *really* old—and her cough came in a pattern of threes, subsided for a moment, then began again. Silent, barkless, blameless Melville looked up each time.

Is this what her life would always be like here? Listening to the sounds of her next-door neighbor: her snoring, her coughs and sneezes and farts, the flushings of her toilet, the humming of her refrigerator, the whirring of her bathroom exhaust fan, the babble of her TV. And would she always have to be vigilant about Melville, since his tenure here depended on his maintaining model behavior and the whim of administrator par excellence, Stephanie Cruikshank?

When Noah arrived an hour later, Cassandra held the door open for him. He hurried past her and set the cooler down on the kitchen floor.

"Why don't you add the things from your refrigerator, and if it's all right with you, I'd like to make myself a cup of coffee. I seem to have run out."

She stood in front of him. "I'd like to talk to you first."

He looked at her questioningly. "All right."

"I need you to know that I had a kind of change of heart this morning about going to the Cape—"

"What?"

"Let me finish! I was out walking Melville, and all the doubts that I had done a super job of tamping down started bubbling up, and by the time I was heading back to my apartment, I'd convinced myself that I shouldn't be going anywhere now, since I just moved in here and haven't even finished unpacking. But you don't have to worry about it. Because I've realized that I don't want to stick around here now, I want to go ahead with our trip."

"If you have major doubts, Sandy—"

"Of course I have doubts. Don't you have doubts? But my meeting with Stephanie Cruikshank convinced me I need to get some distance from this place and think about what I've gotten myself into. I'm not sure now that moving here was such a good idea. Clarion is fine for some people, but I don't think I'm suited to it. I'd been thinking of the conveniences, but I hadn't taken into account what it would feel like to be subjected to all the rules and regulations. I just hadn't considered the depressing paternalistic aspect of it all."

"And?"

"And they have a vendetta against my insects. I was informed I need to repatriate them within a week. I've got to figure out what I want to do with them. Or not."

"What about your dog?"

"Melville has been granted a temporary dispensation. I will be at the mercy of my litigious next-door neighbor and our humorless Executive Dictator. It's certainly not fun."

"I'm not sure my little cottage will be fun."

"But we'll make it fun—you, me, and Melville."

"How do I know you won't change your mind again soon as we're on the road?"

"You won't. But judging from my past experience, it's highly unlikely. Once I get going someplace, once I'm speeding along the highway—"

"Speeding! I hope not!" Noah interrupted, but she went on.

"I'm always happy. But I often experience a bit of a wobble before I take off—a short period of time when all my doubts gang up against me."

Noah leaned back against the kitchen counter. "Nothing is easy with you, is it?"

"Probably not. But nothing's easy with you, either, is it?"

"No."

She reached out and took both of his hands and gave them a squeeze.

"We'll do OK," she said. "I promise."


The cooler wasn't quite as big as Cassandra had remembered it. She guessed it wouldn't fit on the floor behind the front seats, but maybe some things in the back could fit on the floor, so they could trade spaces.

"What are those?" Noah asked, pointing to a bag of frozen marrow bones Cassandra was putting into the cooler.

"Irresistible dog treats for when you need to persuade Melville to do something he doesn't want to do or stop doing something you don't want him to do. Oh, I have some good news from Barbara to pass on to you."

"She's taking Melville, too?"

"I'm sure she'd love to," said Cassandra, "but she's already undertaken the adoption of your cat, and if you recall, the two animals are not an advisable pairing. No, she called to report that your cat has adjusted well, and she'll even be bringing it with her when she visits her sister in a rural outpost in Vermont. She has the misguided notion that your cat is 'sweet and friendly'—and I'm quoting her directly."

"Barbara said that? About my cat? And I took her for one of the more perceptive residents in this place."

"Obviously she and your cat hit it off, and Barbara's modest enough to minimize the influence she has over it. By the way, Barbara mentioned David Sussman died. Did you know about it?"

"I? Know anything about the goings-on at this place? Either you flatter me or you jest."

"It kind of jolted me."

"I am sorry to hear about David, but you get used to death in a place like Clarion. It's the predominant exit scenario."

"Not yours."

"No. At least not at the moment."

"At least Barbara said 'died' rather than 'passed away.' I hate that euphemism."

"It's in vogue now. Part of the current trend to avoid anything that anyone might find offensive."

"It doesn't make the person any less dead. And it's inaccurate. When someone dies, their life is over. They haven't passed anywhere."

"I believe the expression was first used in the Middle Ages to refer to the passing of the soul to the afterlife—heaven or hell."

"I hadn't realized you were such a storehouse of occasionally-useful information."

"I do my best. By the way, you asked me if I have doubts about leaving here, but you didn't wait to hear if I do."

"Do you?"

"About going to the Cape? No. About going with you?" Noah smiled at her. "What do you think?"

# XI

The cooler had been squeezed into the back of the car, in a space vacated by two boxes now wedged on the floor behind the front seats, so all that Noah had on his lap were the brown bags containing their lunch. He was doing his best to protect them from Melville with his arm. He'd flipped up the armrest to provide a bit more separation from Melville's drooling, but Melville kept pushing his face over the armrest and the cup holders. Something oozed out onto Noah's knee and covered his palm when he put his hand down.

"What the hell is this?"

Cassandra looked over. "Hand sanitizer. Useful when I do nature hikes with kids."

"I'm covered in it!"

"Good. Now you're sanitized."

"I just hope you'll like it on your sandwich."

"Did they include my pickle?"

"I have no idea."

The car swerved as Cassandra turned to investigate the lunch bags, and Noah cried, "For God's sake, Sandy. Keep your eyes on the road! I'll look for your damn pickle."

The pickle, it turned out, *was* included. It was in a leaky plastic bag, and the pickle juice had saturated the bottom of the paper bag, so the contents fell out of the bottom as Noah lifted it and deposited a puddle of pickle juice on his lap.

"Now I'm sticky *and* wet."

"There's a roll of paper towels under the seat. I keep them handy for when Melville gets carsick and barfs."

"Oh God," said Noah. "The slobber isn't enough?"

"Never!" said Cassandra.

When he was done mopping himself up, Noah glanced at the dashboard and noticed the gas light was on. "Sandy! Did you realize that the gas tank is close to empty?"

"No problem. I figured it's all downhill to the Cape, so we'll just roll there."

Noah was about to say something but caught her smile. "I don't find it funny to run out of gas."

"You didn't really think I forgot, did you?"

"Knowing you—"

"Come on!"

"Look, you're the same woman who told Barbara that my relatives were allergic to cats."

"The two are entirely unrelated," said Cassandra firmly.

"All right, maybe so. But do you have a plan for dealing with this empty tank?"

"There's a gas station on the way, not far from here. We'll stop, and you'll pump."

"Not far from here" turned out to be much farther than expected and not exactly on their route. They did manage to make it, though. Noah filled the tank, and Cassandra squirted hand sanitizer on his hands to clean off the smell of gasoline that he'd acquired from the pump handle.

When they were back on the road, Cassandra announced that she was ready for lunch. "I'm starving, and I don't drive well on an empty stomach."

"From what I've seen so far, you don't drive well under any circumstances," said Noah, but he dutifully unwrapped Cassandra's ham sandwich and held it in front of her mouth.

"You don't need to feed me."

"Since I'd like to get to the Cape in one piece, I'd prefer it if you keep both hands on your steering wheel."

When he was able to turn his attention to his own lunch, his sandwich—turkey breast on a bun—oozed mayonnaise onto his wrist. Melville quickly licked it off, and Noah had to eat with his back angled to keep Melville from licking the sandwich as well. He was afraid to take his eyes off the road.

"Who taught you to drive, anyway?"

"My daddy. He taught me everything: how to drive a stick shift, how to ice skate backwards, how to sex a box turtle, how to hold a dragonfly."

"Useful skills, for sure. Was he an entomologist too?"

"No, sadly for him—he was an attorney, but he was also an enthusiastic naturalist. He knew everything there was to know about amphibians, birds, and insects. When I was a kid, we'd leave my mother and sister at home and head off on excursions, nets in hand, binoculars around our necks."

"So you have a sister?"

"Technically, yes. Judy—Judith now—is four years older than me. We didn't really like each other when we were growing up—she was the pretty one, and I was the adventurous one—and we still don't. She always felt I got away with things."

"Did you?"

"Some of the time."

"Some?"

"Well, most of the time."

"Sounds about right."

"She 'found Jesus' when she was around twenty—not that he was ever 'lost,' since we were Congregationalists—and she became relentlessly moralistic and judgmental. She doesn't have a happy marriage, but she's sticking it out—just as my parents did. She didn't approve of me getting divorced the first time, so you can imagine her reaction to the second time."

"How did your parents feel about it?"

"My mother hadn't liked any of my husbands, but she claimed she was 'heartbroken' about my divorces. My dad told me that all he wanted was for me to be happy. He liked all my husbands, though he didn't live to see me actually marry Rob. I probably married Rob because my dad had died—Rob was quite paternalistic."

"I wouldn't have thought you'd like that."

"He was paternalistic in an endearing way."

There was some traffic on the interstate. Noah used to drive to the Cape in the middle of the night to avoid it. The road had an almost surreal loneliness to it, then. He glanced over at the speedometer. "You weren't kidding when you said you were happy 'speeding along the highway.' You know, this might not be the best time to be pulled over by a state trooper."

"You do want to arrive there before dusk, don't you?"

"That's several hours from now. I had been hoping to arrive there alive."

Cassandra turned to smile at him. "Not to worry," she said, and she patted his knee.

"Would you please keep your eyes on the road and your hands on the steering wheel."

"OK, I'll be good. But only if you tell me about *your* siblings. Or were you an only child?"

"Not much to tell. Two brothers."

"Younger, right?"

"Well, yes."

"You have that Firstborn confidence about you. I bet you were correcting their grammar when you were kids and are still doing it."

"My middle brother, Daniel, teaches computer science at Stanford and has never been concerned about the proprieties of language. We're not in touch very often. He's married but has no kids. In fact, my son, Larry, is the only child of the three of us. My youngest brother, Warren, died of a heart problem when he was thirty-four."

Cassandra turned to look at him again. "I'm so sorry, Noah. That's so young! Or at least it seems young now that I'm so old."

"Please, Sandy—keep your eyes on the road."

"Sorry!" She looked intently ahead of her. She was quiet for a while before she spoke again. "I've been meaning to ask, and maybe this isn't the best time to do it—what did your wife do?"

"Helene was a research librarian at Widener Library. We met when I was a grad student." He anticipated Cassandra's next question, so he continued, "She died of breast cancer. We'd thought she was in remission, but it came back again."

"That stinks," she said. "Rob died of prostate cancer. That stinks too." She was quiet again; then she added, "You'd think that having gone through all that nasty stuff with a person you love, you'd find other things less upsetting. But it doesn't seem to work that way, does it? People claim that surviving adversity makes you more resilient, but I don't think it's true—in my experience it just makes you feel more vulnerable."

Noah thought about this. "Maybe so."

"Well, I'm glad we got at least some of our sad backstories out of the way, aren't you?"

"What do you mean, 'some'?"

"You haven't really told me about your car accident."

"It's not relevant."

"No?"

"Sandy, we don't have to excavate everything, do we?"

"It depends on what kind of a relationship we want to have."

Suddenly Noah felt enormously tired. Cassandra had a way of confronting things head on, making him think about things that were exhausting to consider. And he hadn't gotten much sleep the night before because he'd started worrying about his cello, which he had packed in Cassandra's car. She'd covered it with a blanket—probably the one for the dog—and assured him it was safe, but he'd never done anything like leaving his cello in a car overnight before. Thinking about his cello had led to other worries that kept him up—the fact that he'd forgotten to get a refill for his high-blood-pressure medication, the fact that he had neglected to have his mail forwarded, the fact that his dentist had retired and he wasn't sure he trusted the young guy who'd taken over the practice. The worries had just kept unspooling.

He wondered if it was safe for him to lean back and close his eyes for a bit with Cassandra at the wheel. But he must have done so and dozed off, because he was suddenly jolted awake. The car had left the safe pavement of the highway and bumped along on the grass beyond the breakdown lane until it came to a stop.

"What the hell's going on?"

"Melville needs a bathroom break. Didn't you hear him whining?"

Noah hadn't. He massaged his temples and sat up straight. "You could have waited for a rest stop.'"

"I don't think you would have liked the consequences of waiting till we got to one."

Cassandra got out of the car and walked around to open the back door on the passenger side. She clipped the leash on Melville's collar and let him out. Noah had to admit that she may have been right, since Melville didn't go far from the car to lift his leg, and he held it up for a considerable length of time. Noah opened his door and climbed out of the car. It was always a good idea to stretch whenever he had the opportunity.

"Here, take him for a moment, would you." Cassandra thrust Melville's leash in his hand. "I've got to pee, too."

"Here?"

"Just look the other way."

"I can't believe this," said Noah, but he turned towards the road.

Cassandra was back quickly. She took the leash from Noah. "Your turn!"

"I don't think that—"

"Come on," she said. "No point in being shy. If we're going to be living together for a while, we're going to have to get past the fussiness."

"I'm not fussy!"

"I'm putting Melville back in the car, so go!" She shooed him off. But he got back into the car instead.


They hadn't yet gotten to the bridge to the Cape when there was a slowdown, and traffic started backing up. Noah checked on his cell phone.

"There's some kind of construction project. It looks like it's down to one lane. And the backup goes on for quite a while."

"But where did all these cars come from?" asked Cassandra. "I mean, where are these people all going?"

"Maybe there's a major exodus from senior living communities, and everyone's heading to cottages on Cape Cod."

"I hate sitting in traffic. Let's get out of here," said Cassandra, and she crossed quickly into the right lane, cutting in front of a pickup truck that honked furiously, and before Noah could stop her—though he had no idea how he possibly *could* stop her—she was tearing up the exit ramp.

"Where do you think you're going?" he cried.

"We'll figure it out."

There was no simple alternate route. Even with the help of the GPS, which Noah always had difficulty using, they followed back roads that seemed to lead nowhere. Miraculously—he thought—they eventually found their way back to the highway, not far from the entrance to the Bourne Bridge.

"It would have been faster if we just stayed on the highway."

"I doubt it. But in any case, wasn't it nicer exploring charming country roads than staring at the rear end of some truck?"

"We weren't exploring, Sandy, we were lost."

"Look, here we are, at the canal. So we were not lost!"

And then they were on the bridge, high in the air, with the sweep of the land and the canal far below, and Noah felt the exaltation he experienced every time he drove this way, undiminished year after year: the Cape lying in wait for him. The land and the sea and the summer stretching out before him, with their infinite possibilities. For the past three years, the exaltation had been coupled with the pain he felt going out to the cottage without Helene, but that had softened now—not gone away, but had just been relegated to a quiet corner of his heart.

"Cape Cod!" sang out Sandy, pointing to the ridiculous bushes in the center of the rotary that had been trimmed to spell out the words. She opened all the windows. Melville stirred from his slumber and stuck his head out. He and Noah inhaled the sea air.


They decided to stop at a supermarket in Orleans to pick up some groceries in addition to the food they'd brought, since there was only a small grocery store near the cottage. Cassandra found a parking spot partially shaded by a tree. She scribbled a list and handed it to Noah.

"Where are you planning to put all this stuff?"

"On the back seat, next to Melville. He likes sitting up. And on the floor there." She pointed to Noah's feet.

"You trust Melville with bags of food?"

"If it's fruit and vegetables, Melville won't be interested. You'll keep the meat and dairy up front."

"I don't know about that—"

"Take my credit card," Cassandra said, and she fumbled in her purse, which she'd stashed beside the seat.

"We're not going to worry about things like that now," said Noah. He got out of the car and was starting to head to the supermarket when Cassandra called him back.

"If you can't get organic apples, any apples are OK, but the celery and strawberries need to be organic. Celery and strawberries are the worst—they just soak up pesticides."

"I'll see what I can do."

It had been a while since Noah had been in a supermarket, and this one seemed to have ballooned since he had last been here. The aisles of food were separated by an acre of items that had no business in a grocery store: housewares, toys, greeting cards, and books (though not the kind of books he'd ever want to read). It was a long hike between the spinach and the bread. Noah consulted the list Cassandra had thrust at him and ran through the items on the list he'd compiled in his head. He secured a shopping cart and headed cautiously out onto the tarmac in the produce section.

He found some organic strawberries but was overwhelmed by the varieties of apples and ended up just tossing a bag of them in the cart. There didn't seem to be any organic celery, and he decided in the end it would be safer to do without celery than return to Cassandra with the pesticide-laced variety. He got porcini mushrooms, a quartet of Anjou pears, and a clump of fresh dill. The summer squash looked newly picked, so he filled a plastic bag with them, careful to select ones that weren't too phallic in shape.

On the Cape he usually subsisted on seafood, but he guessed Cassandra might appreciate some variety, so he got chicken and lamb. It had been a long time since he had shopped with anyone else in mind, a long time since he had thought about cooking for someone else. In gourmet foods he got stuffed grape leaves, fresh mozzarella, and olives and decided to splurge on caviar. He was in the dairy section studying the choices of brie and camembert when a young woman, her cart piled high with paper products, asked him if he needed any help. Did he look as if he was too old to decipher a cheese label?

"Thank you, no," he said politely. He refrained from pointing out that the toddler in the shopping cart baby seat was in the process of demolishing the lid of a not-yet-paid-for yogurt container, and its gooey contents were already decorating the side of the cart.

At the checkout counter, he was reprimanded for having more than twelve items in his cart, the limit for that particular line.

"You can use the self-checkout," the girl told him, pointing.

"Do I get a discount if I do?"

The girl looked confused. "No, sir. It's just that some people like it."

"Thank you," said Noah, and he scooted into another line just before that register closed.

In the parking lot, as he headed to Cassandra's packed car, she leaned out the window and waved to him. "You made it!" she cried.

She helped him get the cold things into the freezer chest and stuff the rest of the groceries on the floor of the front seat.

"No lemons?"

"I seem to have forgotten the lemons, but I did get some limes."

"That's a relief. At least we'll have our margaritas."

She drove out through the parking lot but stopped before she pulled out onto the road. She turned in her seat to look at him. "This is pretty crazy, right?"

"I'd say so."

She picked up his hand and gave it a squeeze. "At least we're off on this adventure together."

He reached for her face and touched the side of her chin. Then, before he could think about what he was doing, he leaned forward and kissed her. It was something he had been wanting to do for fifty-five years.

# XII

It was interesting the way places never turned out to look like the way she'd imagined them. When she was a kid and first visited relatives on Long Island, Cassandra had pictured a long, narrow island and was disappointed to discover there was nothing like an island about it, let alone a long one. When she got to see the actual Grand Canyon, she was amazed by how vast and deep it was—nothing like what she'd pictured based on a postcard a friend had sent her. Even Clarion Court, when she toured it in person, turned out to be quite different from what she imagined based on the online photos she'd seen. So it didn't surprise her that Noah's cottage wasn't at all like the place she'd been expecting.

The word "cottage" had summoned up something cute with dormers and small-paned windows complete with shutters and window boxes. But this "cottage" was low slung and asymmetrical, with additions poking out from the sides. The only cottage-y thing about it was that it was shingled. And its setting was all wrong too. Cassandra pictured it perched on a hill overlooking a beach with the sea in the distance. Instead, it was tucked in a hollow at the bottom of a steep dirt driveway. There was no visible beach, just marsh grass, and rather than lying at a respectable distance, the water was right there, practically lapping the deck. Nothing about Noah's place was true to the cottage she had conjured up in her imagination—it was its own self, entirely alien—but the smell, oh, that was exactly right, that familiar, insistent smell of the sea that always made her quiver with something like childhood joy.

Noah got out of the car before she even turned the engine off. If he had been forty years younger, she guessed, he would have "leaped" out of the car, but he was post-leaping now. He looked out towards the bay and flung his arms wide, as if greeting his domain. It was a most unlike-Noah gesture. Then he turned to her, clearly awaiting her approval. She stepped out of the car and took it all in. The sea beyond glimmered— not blue (when was it ever really blue?) but a dark gray-green.

"I got you here alive, just as I promised I would."

"Barely."

Cassandra opened the back car door, and Melville scrambled out and was off.

"No leash?"

"He got a whiff of the sea. But he won't go too far."

"Does he swim?"

"Watch him!"

"No wet dogs in the house!"

"Of course not," she said, and she laughed. She started walking towards the cottage. "You're so close to the water!"

"It's high tide. That's the closest it gets. Don't worry. This place was built in the thirties, and it hasn't washed away yet."

"I wasn't worried. I just wondered if I should sleep in my bathing suit."

"I'm glad to hear you brought a bathing suit. Some visitors think the water's too cold in March."

"Come, show me around!"

"Shouldn't we unpack first?"

"It'll wait." She turned back and caught the look on his face. "We're here, Noah. We made it! Even my tarantulas will wait."

The cottage was one main room, with a kitchen on the side and two small bedrooms, one with a double bed, the other just barely big enough for a single bed. The walls were paneled in age-darkened pine boards that ran vertically, ceiling to floor. There was a long, narrow screened porch and a small deck overlooking the sea. Outdoors, Noah showed her the old barn used for storing boats and an outbuilding that had built-in bunks, like on a ship, and pegs along the wall. Its low, wide window overlooked the water, and it felt more like a boat than a shed planted on land.

"My brothers and I came out to the Cape every summer when we were kids, and we slept out here," said Noah. He pointed to the initials carved into the wood-paneled wall. "I'd been hoping Larry's kids might enjoy the bunkhouse, too, but the one time Larry's family came out here, Elizabeth insisted they stay in the motel in town."

Although Cassandra thought the bunkhouse was a kids' dream, she could imagine how a daughter-in-law might balk at her children spending the night out here on their own. Instead, she said, "Children tend to disappoint their parents, don't they? And when they have families of their own, they rarely conform to our plans."

"Yours too?"

"I'd hung on to my old house with the hope my grandchildren would be coming to stay. I'd saved all my daughters' toys for them—the kitchen set and little chairs and table that I repainted for them—but they never came. I have to travel to New Zealand if I want to see them."

"Is that the reason you moved to Clarion?"

"One of the reasons." Cassandra sat down on a bunk bed. The wood on the edge had been rubbed smooth by kids' hands. She looked at Noah. "Actually, you're right. It was the main reason. It was a big house, and the empty rooms were a constant reminder of how I'd gone wrong in raising my daughters. Laurel deciding she didn't want to have kids, and Maggie not caring if her kids visited their grandmother."

"Not wrong!"

"Well, not right either. At least they thought so. I divorced their father and married someone much younger and entirely unsuited to be a stepfather. He was jealous of the time and attention I gave them. I finally came to my senses and got divorced from him."

"And he died after that?"

"Yup. Not exactly a nice, stable situation for teenage girls. By the time I married Rob, it was too late. They'd grown up and left home." Cassandra got to her feet. "Enough of this. Time to unpack the car."

Melville, wet, sandy, and slimy, bounded up to them, wagging his seaweed-festooned tail. He checked out the box Cassandra was carrying, which held the tarantulas, crickets, and stick insects, then dashed over to investigate the bags of groceries Noah was attempting to bring into the house.

"Off, beast!" cried Noah. Cassandra whistled, and Melville darted back to nuzzle her, then raced off again.

"He's happy to be here," said Cassandra.

"The feeling is not mutual. There's a hose around the side of the house. I trust you will make use of it."

Cassandra parked the box of cages and tanks on the low table in the living room and helped Noah with the food.

"I told Artie I was coming out," said Noah, "and he turned the electricity on, so the refrigerator should be working."

"Who's Artie?"

"He looks after this place for me. He and Bernice live in the house up by the road. His dad and I used to go out fishing together, just as his grandfather and my dad used to go out fishing together. Now he has a charter boat—takes landlubbers out fishing in the summer."

"And Bernice?"

"She's the town clerk, which is a good job because it's steady work year round—and there's not a lot of that. The first summer I was here alone after Helene died, Bernice kept bringing over food for me. Somehow she didn't think I could cook for myself. Dreadful stuff, but I couldn't say so, so she'd just bring me more. You'll like her, but don't get her started on the town select board—she'll talk your ear off."

The refrigerator capacity was not up to the quantity of food they'd brought, so they did triage and left the fruit and vegetables out on the counter.

"What should we have for dinner tonight?" Noah asked.

"Whatever the chef chooses."

"Lamb shanks?"

"Oh, dear. Sounds anatomical."

"You eat lamp chops, don't you?"

"Yes, but those come from plastic packages, not woolly little animals."

Noah scowled at her.

"OK. Sorry. I've been channeling my daughter Maggie. If you're willing to do the cooking, I shall happily eat whatever you prepare."

"Promise?"

"I promise to at least *try*."

Dealing with the food proved easier than dealing with the bedrooms. When Noah saw that Cassandra had put her suitcase in the smaller bedroom, he moved it into the larger one when she was out at the car.

"What did you do with my suitcase?" she asked when she returned.

Noah pointed to the larger bedroom. "I told you before we came here that I was giving you that bedroom and taking Larry's room."

"You should use your own bedroom. I'm fine with this one."

"It's not negotiable," said Noah. "There's not enough room for that dog of yours in Larry's room, and I have no intention of letting him sleep in the living room, since he has a propensity of laying claim to sofas."

It was a valid point, but Cassandra was sure the insistence on giving her the bigger bedroom was Noah being a generous host and Melville was just an excuse.

"But it's your bedroom, and I'm the mere guest."

"There's nothing 'mere' about you," said Noah. "And you're forgetting the rest of your menagerie." He pointed to the insects and tarantulas on the coffee table. "They can't stay there."

"Why not?"

"Because—oh, for God's sake, Sandy!"

They'd been joking, at least it seemed that way, but Cassandra felt the tone shift. Noah looked more aggravated than amused. She didn't want to push things, didn't want to irritate him. She was tired, and it was easier just to give in. When Noah went out to the car, she lifted the box of insects and tarantulas from the coffee table and dutifully carried it to the larger bedroom. Cassandra arranged the cage with the stick insects, the terrariums for the tarantulas, and the cage of crickets on the top of the bureau. The crickets chirped in their pleasantly monotonous way, blithely unaware of the fact that they were not there in the capacity of pets but as the tarantulas' future dinners.

Cassandra was relieved that there were only men's clothes in the dresser drawers and in the small closet. She didn't mind the fact that Noah had a dead wife whom he obviously still mourned—she understood such things all too well—but she didn't want reminders of Helene in the room where she was going to be sleeping. It was enough that she was going to be occupying the same bed. Clarion Court had been neutral ground. She and Noah had come there on their own. They'd never lived there with their now-deceased spouses. Unlike this cottage, Clarion Court was a ghost-free place.

There was a faded blue quilt on the bed, but when Cassandra lifted it, she found the mattress underneath was bare. The sight of the blue-and-white mattress ticking struck her. When Maggie, her baby, had gone off to college, she'd stripped her bed, and when Cassandra had returned home to her empty nest after dropping Maggie off, she was confronted by a bare mattress, and she'd flung herself down, arms out, and allowed herself to weep loudly and unrestrainedly after holding it in for hours.

Noah was carrying his cello into the house. He looked as if he were embracing an ungainly body. She watched him settle it lovingly in a corner of the living room. It was obviously the place where it always resided. A cello coming home.

"Are there any sheets?" she asked.

Noah came into the bedroom and dug in the back of the closet, behind the rack of clothes. He emerged, rear end first, carrying a large plastic bin.

"Trying to keep things from the mice."

"Do you notify them in advance of your return?"

"I do not confer with the mice. We have been at war for decades."

"Maybe you should have kept your cat."

"That was the sort of cat who would have *encouraged* the mice."

Cassandra threw the end of the sheet towards him. "Here, help me make this bed, and I'll help you make yours." She spoke playfully, but she felt suddenly embarrassed. It seemed too intimate to be handling sheets with Noah, to watch his hands smoothing the blue cotton where she would lay her body. She had not been able to decide about his kiss. She didn't ask what it meant—she didn't believe kisses necessarily meant anything—but she did wonder what had inspired it. As a scientist, she liked explanations, liked to understand the origins of things. Was it just the result of a need to connect with another human being? Or was it a kiss of desire that had been lying in wait for a while and simply found a good opportunity for release?

But, in the end, did it matter? It had happened; it was over. The real question was what would happen next. No, that wasn't a legitimate question. She retooled it: What did she *want* to happen? She told herself she didn't know, but that wasn't quite true.

"I could use your help carting out the Adirondack chairs to the deck," Noah said after the beds were made. "Then we can sit and watch the sunset."

The chairs had been wintering in the barn and were ridiculously heavy and ungainly, even when folded up. They'd lugged one down to the deck and were catching their breath before hefting the other one when two figures appeared coming down the driveway.

"Ah, Artie to the rescue!" said Noah. He set the chair down.

"Ahoy!" said Artie. "Can I give you a hand with that?"

"Did you hear me groaning all the way up at your place?"

"I should have set them up for you."

"You've done plenty," said Noah. He swept his hand from one to the other. "Artie, Bernice, this is Cassandra. Cassandra, my attentive neighbors, Artie and Bernice."

Artie was a head shorter than Noah and looked as if he was all muscle. His large head was planted directly on his torso without benefit of neck. His hair stood up straight on the top of his head, hedgehog style. His eyes were large and brown and unexpectedly gentle. It was the long eyelashes, Cassandra thought.

Bernice was taller than Artie and seemed permanently embarrassed about her height, as tall women sometimes were. Her long, limp pale hair was tucked ineffectively behind her ears.

"We were going to ask you if you'd like to join us for dinner tonight," she said, "but then I thought maybe seeing as you just arrived, you'd want a chance to settle in first."

"It was very kind of you to think of inviting us for dinner," said Noah. "We'll take a rain check."

"Sure thing. Artie will be bringing in stripers early May."

"Absolutely," said Noah. "We'll look forward to it."

It looked to Cassandra as if Artie could easily have carried not just one but both Adirondack chairs on his own, but he let Noah take one side. Cassandra and Bernice watched them carry it down towards the deck.

"That your dog out there?" Bernice pointed to the water.

"That's Melville," said Cassandra. "He's extremely happy to be here."

"Our dog, Luke, is out and around somewhere, but you'll see him soon enough."

"What kind of dog is he?"

"A yellow Lab. Artie's always had one. What's yours?"

"A Newfoundland."

"Sweet for Noah to have a dog around again."

"I didn't know he'd had a dog."

"It was Helene's dog, really—some kind of setter. Irish, maybe? But he loved that dog, too, though he wouldn't admit it. You know how he is."

"Yes," said Cassandra.

"He was so broken up when it died, not long after Helene passed. I think the dog felt guilty about leaving him alone but just went ahead and died anyway. It was about ten years old, so it had had a full enough life, right?"

"Right."

"Not like Helene. She did all the chemo and everything and was fine for, like, five years—let's see, Jed was in elementary school at the time. Jed's our son; he's fourteen now, going on fifteen—but then it came back. She had a double mastectomy and died anyway, which is terrible, just terrible, isn't it?"

"Oh, yes."

"Noah's been a lonely man. I'm so glad he's found someone." Bernice tilted her head sympathetically.

"I'm not—I mean, I'm just a friend—" Cassandra began, but she didn't have a chance to correct Bernice's assumption before Artie and Noah rejoined them.

"Let us know if you need anything," Artie said as he and Bernice started back up the hill.

"We're all set for now. Thank you," said Noah. He and Cassandra went down to the deck, and he put in wooden pegs that were stored in a cloth bag neatly tied to one chair arm. They were the kind of thing that Cassandra would surely have misplaced had the chairs been hers. Noah opened a bottle of wine, and they dusted the chairs off and sat down. Melville, delighted to have their company, settled nearby on the deck. It was a while before sunset, but the sea was calm and seemed to be cradling the sky.

"Helene and I would always sit out here soon as we unpacked the car," said Noah. "It became kind of a ritual."

Cassandra watched a tern balancing so perfectly on a buoy in front of them it looked like a carved wooden figure, a decoration on the buoy itself.

"Something the matter?" Noah asked after a while.

"I wasn't going to say anything, but if you want to know—"

"Of course I want to know!"

"That makes me uncomfortable. I don't really want to participate in your old rituals."

"Nothing wrong with rituals—"

"I don't want to be a stand-in for your dead wife."

"You're not a stand-in, Sandy. You're—"

"I'm what?"

"Entirely different. What did Bernice say to you?"

"She thought we were a couple."

"Oh."

"She's happy you 'found' someone."

"Very Bernice."

"I didn't have a chance to set her straight."

"Is that all right?"

"I don't know."

"Sandy, I don't want you to feel uncomfortable about Helene."

"I don't—it's not that." She stopped suddenly. Noah waited for her to continue. "OK, that's not true. When I was making the bed, it felt odd, which is why I wanted to sleep in the smaller bedroom: I thought, Noah slept in this bed with Helene. It's hard to be unambivalent about a bed that has a history."

"Almost everything in this house has a history."

"I still think we need to leave the past alone and not attempt to relive or replicate things we've done—let's let them remain intact."

"But some of the rituals—"

"Look, Noah, we both have a storehouse of memories, some of them actually quite nice. But we need to have some ground rules here if we're going to get along. While we're here together, we need to start from scratch."

"What are you talking about?"

"What we need to do is create some new rituals, a celebration of our leaving Clarion and our arriving here. Something neither of us has done before. Something that's unexpected, something fun."

"Fun is not who I am. That is entirely in your department."

Cassandra tapped his shoulder. "Take me seriously, Noah. Please."

"All right, then, what would your ritual be?"

"You start."

Noah sighed. He closed his eyes for a moment, and then he rose from his chair, pushing himself up with both arms. "All right, then. Sit where you are, and I'll be right back."

Cassandra turned and watched him go into the cottage. He took his cello and bow from its case, rosined his bow, tuned his cello, and carried it out onto the deck. He had to sit on the edge of the chair so he could bow.

"In honor of this occasion, I'm going to play a greeting to the sea. I know you think Bach is always boring and gloomy. I hope this gigue will help dispel that notion."

It was a short piece; cheerful, light. Cassandra could picture people dancing, fabric fluttering.

When he was done, he sat back in his chair. "So?" His face had an expression she hadn't seen before—he looked boyishly hopeful. Vulnerable. She hadn't expected he'd show her that.

She applauded.

"Is that what you had in mind?" he asked.

"Yes, I loved it. It says, 'Hello, we're here; we made it!'"

"And now, what's yours?"

"Put your cello away first."

When he returned, she said, "I want us to get our feet wet."

"You decided against a quick dip?"

"When I touched Melville and realized how cold the water is, I decided it would be prudent to avoid heart attacks."

There was a wooden seawall a few feet from the deck and a short set of stairs leading down towards the water. The tide had receded since they arrived, and they walked carefully, with winter-soft feet, over the wrack line. There was a band of small rocks, then pebbles, then coarse grainy sand, and then, just where the water touched, softer sand.

Cassandra stood beside Noah and looked out at the bay. Nothing moved out there. The wind had sunk to oblivion. They were side by side, not touching, but close enough so the backs of their hands almost grazed.

"How come you introduced me to Bernice and Artie as Cassandra and not Sandy?"

"Because Sandy is what I call you. Cassandra is for everyone else."

The cold water stung Cassandra's toes. She thought about everything—a blur of images and sounds: leaving Clarion, driving to the Cape, Noah kissing her, unpacking the car into the cottage, the cello singing out to the sea—and then she sank into the moment and let herself think about nothing. It had been so long since she'd been able to think about nothing. Nothing at all.

# XIII

"Enough wine, and any dinner tastes good," Noah told Cassandra, but he believed his cooking was accomplished enough not to require it. Tomato sauce with a generous addition of oregano for the lamb shanks, and they could imagine they were dining at one of those charming outdoor restaurants in the Plaka, Acropolis in sight. And Cointreau made the pears worthy of dessert status. Cointreau made *anything* dessert worthy. The cottage might be humble, but the liquor cabinet was well stocked.

Dinner was easy—they slipped back into their Clarion dinner pattern as if they were still there at the table Noah always favored. But how much better to be here, with the sea right beside them and candles on the table that dripped real wax, unlike those little teat-shaped LED things placed inside glass candleholders. Here there was no danger of having to fend off well-meaning Clarion residents like Jennifer, relentlessly trying to corral him into a game of Scrabble, though communal dining in "The Terrace" was temporarily on hold. His only concern at dinner now was the large beast eyeing his lamb shank. Not just large but redolent from the sea, since Cassandra had not hosed him down. (Though for perfectly good reasons: it had gotten late and dark, and the outside faucet didn't seem to be working yet, and the hose was still packed away in the barn.)

Dinner was relaxed and familiar, but Noah was worried the going-to-bed part of the evening would prove difficult. They had no experience with saying good night in these circumstances, and there was no play-book for "aged man and woman stranded together in romantic cottage." The possibilities for awkwardnesses were substantial. Possibly infinite.

When they were done eating, they continued sitting at the table for a while. The view towards the sea was just darkness—there were no lighted boats, no distant houses—but you could still sense its presence.

"When I was a kid, my dad would look at the dirty dishes on the table at the end of dinner and say, 'Maybe if we stare at them long enough, they'll disappear,'" Cassandra said. "I used to think that was hilarious, but my mother was never amused." She paused, then added, "My mother was rarely amused."

"Sounds like a charming marriage."

"But an enduring one, all the same. Forty-six years. Till death did them part."

"Should I feel sorry for your father?"

"No, he had me to appreciate all his jokes. And he was a funny man. He always saw the humor in situations. I wonder what he would make of the state of the world now."

"There's not much to joke about, is there? Unless you're into dark humor."

"I don't know—I think *we're* pretty funny, if you were an outsider looking at us: leaving a cushy senior living community to hang out in a 'rough'—your word!—cottage by the sea."

"I fail to see the humor in it. It seems like a perfectly reasonable thing to do."

"If you say so yourself!"

"I do."

Cassandra stood up and laid her silverware across her plate. "Come, let's make these disappear."

"That was one benefit of Clarion. They did the cleaning up."

"Ah, so you admit there was at least one benefit."

Noah followed her into the kitchen carrying the glasses. "I'm afraid there's no dishwasher."

"I rather like washing dishes by hand. I never used my dishwasher at Clarion. I mean I never used it for dishes."

"What did you use it for?"

"Storing boxes of dog treats. I took out the racks."

"What did you do with them?"

"Put them in the janitor's closet by the elevator."

"Sandy!"

"What? There was no place to store them in my apartment, was there?"

Noah shook his head.

Cassandra filled the sink and squirted in more dish soap than Noah would ever have used. He watched her plunge her hands into the water, the bubbles banding her wrists. She lifted a wet plate, rubbed its surface with the dishcloth, and rinsed it under the faucet. The clear water channeled down through the bubbles on her arms. She rinsed her forearms, one after the other, before she set the plate in the dish rack. Her wet skin glistened. He found a dish towel and reached for the plate. Their arms touched, wrist to elbow, then moved apart.

"Speaking of dog treats, I need to feed Melville. Do you have a bowl I could use?"

"What's that?" asked Noah, pointing to a bowl on the floor near the refrigerator.

"That's his water bowl. I used one of the mixing bowls I found in the cabinet."

"If you didn't ask then, why are you asking about a bowl for him now?"

"I'm being polite." Cassandra gave a large grin, showing lots of teeth. Cheshire Cat, thought Noah.

It had started getting cooler once the sun went down, and now it was definitely chillier in the living room. Melville, who preferred it that way, was stretched out on the floor by the door, where it was coldest.

"Time to heat up the woodstove?" Noah asked.

"That would be lovely!"

They carried in wood from a pile on the side of the cottage.

"Trust me with the fire?" Cassandra asked.

"Why not? I'm sure it's one of the many survival skills your father taught you. I'll sit back and relax while you get it going."

Cassandra opened the flue, rolled up some newspapers that had been stacked near the stove, and tied them in a knot. She placed several of the bunches along with some kindling in the stove, then laid several split logs on top. The match got the fire going on the second try.

"Why don't you leave the doors open," said Noah, "so we can enjoy the open fire, and I'll close them before we go to bed."

"Good. Flames are much less interesting when viewed behind glass. And by the way, it wasn't my dad who taught me about getting a fire going; it was Ethan, my first husband. We were into heating our house with a woodstove when we were first married—we cut and split our own firewood. We had lots of good intentions."

"But then?"

"But then we had a baby and had no energy for it, and like a lot of noble hippie-ish sorts of projects, it fell by the wayside."

"Your second husband was too young. Your third husband was too old. What was the problem with your first husband?"

"Age-wise, he was ideal, but that's about it. We'd gotten married because I had this old-fashioned notion that was a requirement for sex."

"It's not?"

Cassandra laughed. "I was busy with grad school; he was busy with law school. It was hard to find time to be together, and once we had kids, there was no time at all." She'd been kneeling by the front of the woodstove, studying the fire. She stood up. "After a while I realized that we didn't mind not spending time together. I felt marriage should be something more. I wanted to be with someone whom I couldn't bear to be apart from and who couldn't bear to be apart from me."

"And did you get that in marriage number two?"

Cassandra sat down in one of the armchairs in front of the wood-stove. She held out her hands to feel the warmth. "You do get to the heart of things, don't you?"

"Actually, that's what *you* do."

"Fair enough. We're two curious people who are stuck together for the moment, so it's bound to bring this out in us."

"You didn't answer my question."

"OK, the short answer is yes, initially. But it wasn't sustainable."

"You think passion isn't sustainable?"

"It requires ballast in order to last at all."

"Ballast! A nautical reference since we're by the sea?"

"Unintentional. I meant substance—and that was what was missing."

"And what does love require?"

"I'm not sure it requires anything. It just *happens*. Doesn't it?"

Noah leaned back in his chair. In so many of the works of literature he'd taught over his long career, it was issues about love that fueled the story. Yet in spite of all his reading, in spite of all his scholarly study, the subject remained elusive, and he was no wiser about it. It was one thing to love—and something quite different to understand its workings.

"Maybe so," is what he said. A safe answer. He was watching the fire in the woodstove. A real wood fire was satisfying in a way that the electric pseudofire in the fireplace in his Clarion apartment never could achieve. It wasn't just the comforting smell of the woodsmoke but the sounds too: the hiss of the fire, the thump of the logs settling in place.

"I promised my friend Mallory I'd call to let her know we made it here OK, but I don't really feel like it right now."

"You could text her."

"We don't text each other. We prefer to hear each other's voice."

"I should be calling my son, Larry, to let him know I'm here."

"But?"

"It can wait till tomorrow."

"It's rather nice to be here off the grid, isn't it? We could be any-where. Or nowhere. I feel I should be knitting or something while we're sitting in front of the fire."

"You knit?"

"No. But I could start."

"I can't picture you knitting."

"What can you picture me doing instead?"

Noah studied her.

"If you played the oboe, I'd picture you making reeds."

"Sorry, I'm oboe-less."

"So what that leaves me with is reading."

"I do read." She smiled at him. "Should we both get our reading glasses and a book now? We've certainly carted enough of them here. E-books are not allowed! It would ruin the ambiance."

"Of course. We could even read aloud to each other."

"That would be carrying the remote seaside cottage cliché a bit too far," said Cassandra, and she got up and walked towards a box of books and papers she'd brought, which had been left by the bedroom door.

"I never said remote, did I?"

"No, to be fair, you didn't. Perhaps you thought that 'remote' would scare me away."

"I would never take you for someone who would be scared off by something like that. And we're not remote—we're just down the hill from Artie and Bernice's house."

"A reassuring couple. Though I don't know about their son."

"Jed is less reassuring. I hope he'll outgrow it, but one never knows. He's not a happy teenager."

"Are teenagers supposed to be happy?"

"Probably not. But there's something unsettling about Jed. He's sulky and, I imagine, untrustworthy. In spite of having the most gen-erous parents in the world, he has a furtive streak."

"Should I consider that a warning?"

"Well—perhaps."

"One more reason, then, to be grateful for the presence of Melville."

"And the first reason?"

Cassandra pointed to the sleeping dog. "He's blocking the draft by the door."

Noah moved the two armchairs closer so the light from the standing lamp would be good for them both, then went off to fetch his book.

Cassandra plucked it out of his hand when he returned and looked it over. "I expected you to be reading something more erudite than a Dorothy Sayers mystery."

"This is more relaxing. Lord Peter Wimsey always sets everything right in the end. What have you got there?"

"A paper a friend of mine published." She handed the printout to him.

"'Effects of a biological control introduction on three nontarget native species of saturniid moths.' Really?"

"It's a study of the effect of the release of a parasitic fly, *Compsilura concinnata*, on the imperial moth, *Eacles imperialis*, a silk moth that had been wiped out on Cape Cod."

"I didn't know moths were your area of specialty."

"They're not my specialty. But in addition to tiger beetles, I did wasps. I studied foraging behavior in Vespidae, social wasps."

"And you find that interesting?"

"Oh, yes! You'll laugh, but before that I worked on scale insects—and there's nothing duller than that. The adults don't even move."

"Then why work on it?"

"Because you can get grant money. Insect research is all about the economics. There's money for studying insects that are considered 'pests,' that damage plants humans value—think of the potato bug—but it's harder to get money to study insects that are endangered, like some species of tiger beetle. The pleasure of being retired is I can study whatever excites me."

"Like those creepy stick insects you brought into my house." Noah pointed towards the bedroom door.

"I have those to show kids in nature classes to get them interested in bugs—get grown men interested too!"

"I'll take a pass on that, thank you."

"You do admire their skill at camouflage, don't you?"

"I may observe it, but that does not mean I admire it. Observation and admiration are not the same thing."

Cassandra got up and added two logs to the fire. Noah watched the embers come to life when she nudged them with the poker. She sat back down and picked up her article. Noah's eyes returned to his book, but he looked up again after a few paragraphs. Cassandra had a pen in hand and was making notes in the margins of the article. He hadn't seen her concentrating like this before, her mouth pinched, lower lip rolled in. The room was so quiet. It was never this quiet at Clarion. There was always background noise, including the drone of TVs, which he'd never quite accustomed himself to. And there was always this sense of being surrounded by people—old people—some sleeping, some trying to sleep, some giving up on trying. It felt as if he and Sandy had been here together for a long time. Had they really just come to the cottage today? Was it possible that she had never been here before?

There was only one bathroom in the cottage, and it was positioned next to the kitchen so that any sound produced behind the hollow-core door would be broadcast to whoever was sitting, ostensibly reading, in the living room beyond. Noah got to his feet and walked there as unobtrusively as possible. He shut the door carefully behind him. The sound of his urine hitting the water in the toilet bowl was astonishingly loud. There was nothing to be done about it.

When he emerged, Cassandra was looking up at him.

"Sorry about startling you," he said.

"No need to be embarrassed."

"I wasn't—"

"You were; I could tell. I remember a joke from when I was in high school. A girl was on a date somewhere with a guy she was interested in, and when she went to use the toilet, she ran the water in the sink first to camouflage the sound. When a friend later asked the guy what he'd thought about her, he said, 'She's great, but she pees like a horse.'"

"I did not run the water in the sink."

"I've been thinking that since this is a small place, we're going to become familiar with many intimate things about each other. There's a lot we don't know yet. For instance: Do you snore?"

"Possibly. Do you?"

"I don't know, but I guess we'll find out." She pointed to the bedroom. "Louvered doors aren't the best thing for soundproofing. But unlike you, I can blame any rude noises on Melville. Speaking of snoring, I think I'm ready to turn in."

"It's certainly been a consequential day. I'm sure you're tired after exploring all the back roads before we made it to the bridge."

"At least you got in some good nap time while I had to focus on getting us here. Which I did!"

Noah was about to parry with something clever about miracles but instead said, "You did."

"I need to give Melville a walk before I go to bed. Should I go up to the road, or am I in danger of encountering the furtive Jed?"

"Tide's low enough now to walk along the beach. I'll come."

Noah grabbed a flashlight but kept it in his pocket. He didn't see as well in the darkness as he did when he was young, but he could manage once his eyes got used to it. Cassandra was clearly someone who was comfortable walking in the dark.

"I'm putting Melville on a leash. He got dried off somewhat by the fire, and I know he'd want to swim some more. Did your dog like the water?"

"Not especially. She liked to chase shorebirds, so unfortunately she had to be tied up a lot of the time. How'd you know I had a dog? Oh, must have been Bernice."

"Yes."

"I hate to think what else she told you."

"She told me you were fond of your dog. I was happy to know that. It gives Melville hope."

"Melville should be discouraged from hoping," said Noah. But when Cassandra handed him the leash so she could zip her jacket, he took it and didn't hand it back to her when she was done. At a narrow place along the beach, she slipped her arm through his, and they walked that way towards the jetty, then all the way back to the house.

Noah added some more logs to the woodstove and closed the doors. The flames looked blurry behind the smoky glass. That soft pinkish red, the afterglow of a sunset.

"I think we need to establish how we'll say good night to each other," said Cassandra.

"I've been thinking about that too."

"You have?"

"Well, it's awkward, isn't it?"

"Yes. There's no precedent. I suppose we could just say good night and give each other a little wave and head to our respective bedrooms."

"Is that what you'd like to do?"

"No. Which is why it's a problem."

"How about shaking hands. Would that resolve the dilemma?"

Cassandra laughed. "You're confusing bedrooms with boardrooms."

"So how should we resolve this?"

"I think we can defuse the situation if we defined our relationship and established the parameters."

"So how would you describe our relationship?"

"Old friends who recently reconnected?" She paused, then said more softly, "Two old people confronting their mortality who find themselves living in close proximity?"

"In that case, I think a hug would be an appropriate parting gesture. Do you agree?"

She nodded.

They put their arms around each other cautiously and deliberately and hugged, just close and long enough so Noah could feel Cassandra's heartbeat against his.

"Good night," said Cassandra. "Come on, Melville."

"Sleep well," said Noah. He turned and went to the small bedroom. He'd never slept in this room before, and it made him think of his son, sleeping here alone. Later, when he was a teenager, Larry slept in the bunkhouse, but when he was a kid, he wanted to be close to his parents. Noah had slept in the bunkhouse from the time he was a young kid, but it was different for him because he'd had his brothers to keep him company.

At night, after Noah finished reading the good-night story (chapters from *The Wind in the Willows*, *The Trumpet of the Swan*, *The Sword in the Stone*) and turned off the bedside lamp, Larry would plead with him to stay with him until he fell asleep. And Noah usually did. He'd sit on the rug on the floor and lean against the bed frame, his head resting on the edge of the mattress. The room was dark except for a crack of light along the bottom of the door. He'd listen to Larry's soft breathing and the stirrings of the wind. Sometimes he'd fall asleep himself.

The child Larry was as vivid to Noah as the man Larry had gradually become, and though the residual affection for the child had endured, it had gotten complicated with other feelings as Larry grew up and moved off on his own. What came to Noah's mind now was Sandy's description of someone flapping their will and threatening to disown their offspring if they didn't measure up. Noah had insisted that it wasn't a question of whether they measured up, and what had she said? "Something more hurtful, then?"

If Sandy knew the whole story, she wouldn't see him as petty and punitive when it came to Larry. As unforgiving. But he had no intention of talking about this with her. He had no intention of thinking more about it either.

Noah returned to the mystery he'd been reading but struggled to get absorbed in it once again. After a while he reached up and flipped off the light. He lay in the darkness. The bed was much too small. He wondered if Cassandra had been able to fall asleep. He'd been so content while they were sitting in front of the fire, but now he felt incipient sadness. Being with Cassandra made him realize how much he craved tenderness, how long he'd gone without it.

# XIV

She awoke to darkness. The bed creaked as she rolled to her side, and there was the smell of old pine paneling. She was not in her bedroom at Clarion; she was at Noah's cottage on Cape Cod. The room was cold. It would soon be dawn, yet daylight seemed far away as a dream. She lay listening to Melville's slow breathing and the sound of wind stirring water, pushing waves against the shore, pulling them back again, combing and sifting the sand and pebbles. After she'd given up hope of falling asleep, she got to her feet slowly, testing the wooden floor with her toes. The bedside rug had been taken over by Melville. She had slept in leggings and a sweatshirt, her warmest sleepwear, and she was still cold. She put on the polar-fleece jacket she'd worn outside at night and opened the bedroom door. The woodstove was dark; no embers glowed. Noah's bedroom door was shut. She wondered if he was asleep or lying there as she had been, waiting for morning. There was just enough light for her to make her way to the bathroom. She was afraid that flushing would make enough noise to waken both dog and man—but decided to flush anyway.

She walked carefully across the living room and stood at the window. There was nothing to see. The sea was out there but perfectly hidden by darkness. She debated about starting a fire. When she touched the woodstove, it was barely warm. She squatted and opened the doors meticulously, slowly, so they made no sound, reached for a pile of newspapers, and began to roll some.

"Sandy?"

She flipped around to see Noah standing in the doorway of the small bedroom. He was wearing a T-shirt and plaid drawstring pants. College-boy clothes.

"You're up!"

"I was cold."

He crossed his arms and rubbed. "It *is* cold. Let's get this going." He knelt beside her in front of the woodstove, knotted the newspapers she'd rolled. He handed her kindling and stood up to get some logs from the stack. The chairs were too far from the fire, so once she got the fire going, she sat on the floor in front of the stove, her knees pulled up to her chest.

"Join me." She patted the space on the rug beside her.

"I'd be honored to, but I'm afraid I may not be able to get back up again."

"We'll haul each other up."

"Significantly easier to say than do," he said, but he lowered himself to the floor beside her. "Warmed up?"

"The front of me, but not the back of me." He put his arm around her, cupped her shoulder with his hand. "This better?"

"Yes." She wanted to squeeze closer against him. She wanted to lay her face on his chest, have his other arm come over her, encircle her. She closed her eyes and concentrated on the arm around her to dispel the wanting.

"Are you always an early riser?"

She opened her eyes. "Hardly! What about you?"

"Never was until old age laid claim to me."

"Please don't say that! We're not old."

"No?"

"No! At least not yet." She paused for a moment, then added, "I know people who believe it's virtuous to get up when it's barely morning, but I always viewed it as a discouragement to my dream time, which usually doesn't get into full swing until the sun is up. It's why I'm not much of a birder—you have to get up too early. I prefer odonates and butterflies, who have the decency to appear at a more civilized hour, later in the morning."

"Didn't you say something about going to watch a bird display while you were out here?"

"Yes, male woodcocks. But they do their stuff at dusk. We'll go in the evening, soon."

"We?"

"You don't want to miss out, do you?"

"I imagine you are expecting me to say that I wouldn't."

"I am." She turned her head to look at him. She spoke more seriously now. "I'm sorry, Noah. I just realized I must sound like our friend Jennifer, pushing you to join a Scrabble game."

He gave her shoulder a little shake. "You don't have to worry about that. You're not Jennifer."

They sat in the field of warmth of the woodstove, waiting for what? Waiting for the dawn. And eventually it came, as it does, even with no one waiting for it. The dawns she'd viewed had been more delicate, softer, more tentative than a sunset, but no less beautiful—but this was not much more than grayness giving way to some color. It took its time, but that didn't matter. They didn't have anything pressing to do; they didn't have anywhere to go. Eventually—but after a long while—what had counted as dawn yielded its frail display to morning.

"What would you like for breakfast?"

"Anything's OK."

"Anything?"

"Well, not the kind of cereal kids grab from the supermarket shelf, unless, of course, there's a great free prize inside."

"I believe there is oatmeal."

"As long as it's hot."

The oatmeal was hot. Cassandra anointed it with an overgenerous amount of maple syrup and dipped her finger into it for a lick. The brown sugar, which had aged in the cupboard for a year, was hard as the countertop, and Noah, who preferred sugar to maple syrup, had to hack away a chunk of it for his oatmeal. He produced a tin of what he called "antique" tea bags that turned out to be still viable.

After breakfast Noah got out his laptop and started looking at the *New York Times*. Cassandra glanced at the front page.

"Looking at the news doesn't improve it," she said.

"Don't you want to know what's going on in the world?"

"Wars, droughts, floods, fires, and famines—and the idiocy of politicians. Nothing new. We're here now. Couldn't we just be here?"

Noah put his laptop aside. "I'm going to call Larry, to get that over with," he said.

"I'm going to brave the shower," said Cassandra.

The bathroom was true to the rough cottage Noah had promised. The shower stall was steel-white with rust stains, and it bent alarmingly when she leaned against a side. It took a while for the hot water to kick in, and then it got so hot Cassandra had to jump out of the shower to escape being scalded. She adjusted it carefully before she tried it again. It was nicely warm for about two minutes, then went cold. The soap slithered out of the undersized soap dish, but the shower stall was too small for Cassandra to bend over to try to retrieve it. She hadn't intended to wash her hair—she hadn't brought shampoo to the bathroom with her—but it got wet anyway. The towel was bristly, no doubt having been line dried rather than fluffed in a clothes dryer. Bits of dried lavender that no longer smelled of lavender stuck to the nap.

From the bathroom she could hear some of Noah's conversation, and she imagined he was walking around, cell phone in hand, because his voice was clear one moment, inaudible the next. She didn't want to listen, but it was impossible not to pick up some of the words: "I have no intention of—" followed not long after by, "You can assure Elizabeth I did lock the—" Cassandra was about to come out of the bathroom when she heard, "Yes, she's still here." She waited for something more, but either the call had come to an abrupt end or Noah had walked farther away. When she felt it was safe to emerge from the bathroom, she found Noah, cell phone still in hand, staring out at the water.

"In a most unexpected turn of events, Larry has invited me to come and stay with them."

"That's nice, isn't it?"

Noah gave her a look.

"I meant his asking you."

"He's asking only because Elizabeth is afraid you're trying to seduce me."

"She's right," said Cassandra, and she laughed.

"That's what I remembered about you."

"Being right?"

Now Noah laughed too. "No, your laugh."


When Cassandra called Mallory later, Mallory said, "I've been waiting for you to call!" as soon as she heard Cassandra's voice. "How is it? How is Noah?"

"It's cold. And he's . . . well—"

"Well what?"

"I think we'll end up good friends."

"'Good friends' is nonsense," said Mallory.

"Not at our age."

"Especially at our age. 'Good friends' describes people who've been married for decades, like me and John, but not you and Noah, who barely know each other but who've run off together to a cottage on Cape Cod."

"We didn't run off."

"I don't know what else you'd call your exit from Clarion."

"A well-planned, strategic departure. And we don't 'barely know' each other. Actually I've been getting to know him and—"

"Oh good!" cried Mallory. "That's what I was hoping for!"

"No, not that!" cried Cassandra.

"Not *yet.*"

Cassandra didn't reply quickly enough, and Mallory pounced. "OK, I give it a day or two."

"I hate to disappoint you, Mal," said Cassandra, and her tone was more serious now. "But there are two things against it. First, neither of us is ready to start caring for someone again. And second, we've both worked hard to become emotionally independent. Neither of us wants to give that up, risk being vulnerable."

"But you already *are* vulnerable, aren't you?" said Mallory softly.

Cassandra thought about this. She didn't really want to talk about how she was feeling about Noah, even with Mallory, who was someone she usually didn't keep things from. "I'm not used to this getting old thing. I don't like the idea of facing the inevitable. I'm frightened, and part of me wants to cling to someone, but part of me needs to keep a safe distance to maintain my equilibrium. I imagine Noah's that way too."

Mallory was quiet.

"Mal? Something the matter?"

"Well—"

"What?"

"I wasn't going to say anything to you—"

"What happened?"

"One of John's clients died."

"Oh, Mallory! You should have told me right away!"

"He'd been seeing John for years—many years, and now he's—dead."

Cassandra thought about her joking that John's patients were with him until they died. It didn't seem amusing anymore.

"How old was he?"

"Our age."

"How's John?"

"Devastated and frightened. This man was in great shape, worked out at the gym every morning. Dropped dead jogging around the reservoir. John had seen him the day before, and he'd been just fine."

165

"I'm so sorry, Mallory. At least John's a psychiatrist, so he knows how to deal with this."

"John's very good at helping his clients," said Mallory, "but it's different when he's the one with a problem. He doesn't want to leave the house. He's scared, and I can't comfort him. Not that John is any good at *accepting* comfort. So I'm worried too. John seems so old and so frail."

"Oh, Mallory. This stinks. I was about to ask you what I can do to help, but I'm not sure there's anything I can do—"

"There is. You can listen to me—and you can tell me about your adventure there on the Cape."

"It's so unimportant! How can I talk about it when you have real things to worry about?"

"Please, Sandy, I want to know all about what you're doing out there. It's something to take my mind off my worries. Your adventure will keep me entertained!"

"My adventure so far was waking up before dawn because it was freezing cold in this cottage—the woodstove had gone out late at night—and later trying to take a shower in an ancient, rusty shower stall."

"Do you have warm clothing with you?"

"I didn't take much."

"I'll send you some of my winter clothes."

Cassandra smiled. "Just send me the pumpkin dress."

She and Mallory weren't exactly the same size, but in college they still borrowed clothes from each other, and once they'd bought a dress together. It was stylish, but it was orange and hadn't looked good on either of them.

"I probably still have it somewhere," said Mallory. And Cassandra guessed this might be true. She got rid of clothes when they were no longer useful or attractive. Mallory kept things on the chance they might be in style again. It was unlikely the pumpkin dress ever would.

"Check the children's dress-up box," said Cassandra.

Artie came down after lunch to see if Noah was planning to work on his boat soon. "Let me know if I can help in any way," he said. "Bernice is going to the supermarket later and can pick up anything you want."

"We stopped on our way here and stocked up on everything we need. As well as some things we don't need."

"Remember, we've always got plenty of eggs." He turned to Cassandra. "We'd have some chickens to eat, too, if Bernice wasn't so sentimental. Named every one of them."

"How many chickens?"

"More than I can count," said Artie. "And a rooster."

"I thought I heard one!" said Cassandra.

"Worse than the gulls." Artie turned back to Noah. "Bernice will keep asking about getting things for you. I told her you may be seventy-two, but you're tough and healthy, but she's convinced me I should be worried about you. She reminded me my dad was a year younger than you, and look what happened to him."

"I think I can manage just fine."

"Indulge her," said Artie. "It's easier that way. Let her bring you some groceries now and then. She needs to take care of people, and Jed's not a little boy anymore."

"How is Jed doing?"

"Don't get me started," said Artie. "I don't like the friends he's been hanging out with. They're lazy kids. Some of them have gotten into trouble. But he doesn't listen to me. Not much Bernice and I can do."

"Sorry about that. Kids do grow up."

"When I was his age—" Cassandra could guess what was coming, but Artie cut himself off and just shook his head. "I'll help you haul the boat out whenever you like. Though with the weather the way it is, you may want to work on it in the barn. I have an extra shop heater I can lend you. So just let me know and I'll bring it down."

"Speaking of heaters," Cassandra said, "aren't you cold?" She pointed to Artie's cargo shorts.

"Artie wears shorts even in the snow," said Noah.

"Keeps the circulation going," said Artie. He gave a wave, apparently his form of saying goodbye, and started back up the hill to his house. His legs were short and muscle heavy. The pockets of his shorts bulged with stuff, and a piece of rope dangled from a pocket down his thigh. He made Cassandra think of a donkey with packs on its sides.

"Want to go for a walk?" Cassandra asked Noah.

"I can be persuaded."

Cassandra called Melville, who came bounding towards them from somewhere, and they started along the beach. It was sunny out now but not that much warmer. The wind came across the bay, rustling the water, and the whitecaps glowed.

"Mallory told me that one of her husband's patients—someone who'd been in therapy with him for decades—just died. Our age. He'd been perfectly healthy, then dropped dead while jogging."

"One more good reason to avoid jogging."

They walked for a while longer, then Cassandra asked, "What happened to Artie's dad?"

"Lung cancer. Arthur was a heavy smoker. Said it was all there was to do out on his boat."

"Artie and Bernice like looking after you, don't they?"

"Unfortunately they do."

"It's sweet."

"It's unnecessary."

"Debatable, but in any case, I think you should be thankful."

"Artie is grateful to me because I helped his dad get the care he needed when his health started declining. But his dad was my best friend growing up. It's not like I deserve his gratitude. You just do these things."

"Not everybody does these things."

"Well, they should."

At night they gave each other a parting hug, quicker, somewhat more self-conscious, than they had the night before. Noah packed the woodstove with logs to last till morning. "It will be warmer in the bedroom if you keep the door open," he said. "I'll keep my door shut, so you won't worry about lack of privacy."

Cassandra laughed. "I'm long past worrying about lack of privacy, Noah! But aren't you afraid Melville might abandon the rug beside my bed for the comfort of the sofa?"

"I'll take that risk so you don't freeze."

"You are an obliging host," said Cassandra. "And with luck Melville will surprise you with his good manners. There's no reason for you not to keep your bedroom door open too. When I came on this adventure, I assumed you'd behave like a gentleman."

"Is that how you see me? A gentleman?"

"Of course, and a particularly distinguished one."

After six days of romping in the bay, Melville smelled like low tide, and scraps of seaweed had taken up residence in his fur. Noah found the hose in the barn for Cassandra and left her to set it up. She was working on attaching the hose to the spigot by the outdoor shower when a car came down the driveway. It was a silver SUV that looked as if it rarely encountered a dirt road. A man got out and looked Cassandra's car over before he started walking towards the house. He was carrying a shopping bag. Cassandra stood up, but the man didn't see her. Noah was down by the water getting his boat mooring ready, and Cassandra wondered if she should call him. The man approached the front door with a kind of familiarity, and there was enough about him that resembled Noah—his build, the shape of his head—that Cassandra guessed he might be Larry. Why was he here? Had Larry come to persuade—or somehow force—Noah to return with him? Then a worse thought occurred to her: that Noah might not have been honest with her about his phone conversation with Larry a few days earlier—or that she had grossly misunderstood. No, it was impossible that Noah was planning to trade his cottage for a guest room in his son's house—and equally impossible that she had misunderstood Noah's intentions. And with that certainty fixed in her head, she rallied and stepped forward.

"Hello!" she said, "I'm Cassandra, and I hope I'm correct in assuming you must be Larry."

The man wheeled around, his face such a combination of surprise and bewilderment that Cassandra almost felt sorry for him. His eyes were the same uncertain blue as Noah's, but just a few alterations in features, perhaps Helene's—a nose that was somewhat stubby and a chin that looked plump—and he missed out on being handsome.

Cassandra held out her hand. "Noah's told me all about you."

Larry, obviously well schooled in good manners, nodded graciously, and gave Cassandra's hand a perfunctory up-and-down shake, but his mouth remained half-open.

"I met your daughter, Cammie, when she was at Clarion. She's a delightful young person—so astute and interesting. You must be so proud of her!"

Larry blinked, but managed to utter a "yes."

"This is such a beautiful place," said Cassandra. "I gather you had a charmed-summer childhood here. You must have loved that bunkhouse!"

Larry looked where she pointed and nodded.

"How was your drive down?"

"Not bad."

"Would you like something to drink? I'm not exactly sure what there is, but I'm sure I can come up with something that you'd like."

"Thank you, but I don't really need anything."

Cassandra smiled at Larry. She reached to touch his arm. "I know things have been really stressful for you. Your dad's out by the water and should be up any minute, or I can go fetch him for you?" Cassandra laughed. "Wait! What am I thinking? It's been a long time since you've been here, hasn't it—let's go down to the beach. You're probably dying to put your toes in the water!"

Larry did not look like a man who was dying to put his toes in the water, but he followed Cassandra around the side of the house. They hadn't gotten far before Melville, roused from his sleep, trotted over to greet them. He wasn't too wet, but he smeared Larry's once-pristine chinos in his welcome.

"Melville clearly has taken to you. You must radiate that you're a dog person," said Cassandra.

Larry, who was probably not a dog person, forced a meek smile and tried to push Melville's muzzle away from his crotch.

"Larry?" Noah came up towards the house. He was wearing waders and a hat so battered it looked like a chew toy for Melville.

"Hi, Dad."

"Everything OK?"

"Yes, but—"

"How's the family?"

"All right, considering what's been going on with Elizabeth's job right now."

"What are you doing here?"

Larry looked as if he had forgotten whatever answer he might have prepared in advance.

"I just wanted to check in and see how you were doing and—"

"Elizabeth dispatched you to see if you could persuade me to abandon the cottage for a fold-out bed in your family room."

"Elizabeth is concerned about you. Out here."

"Yes, Larry. We know she's concerned. And why."

Larry handed the shopping bag to Noah.

"What's this?"

"It's from Elizabeth. Muffins."

Noah peered inside the bag. "She made these?"

"They're from Maple Hill Bakery."

"How nice," said Noah.

"The cranberry walnut ones are especially good. I ate one on my way here." Larry paused. "I didn't think you'd mind."

"There are a lot of muffins here," said Noah. "Why don't you take half of them back with you for the ride home?"

"I think I should leave you two to talk—" Cassandra began, but Noah clomped towards her in his waders and laid a hand on her shoulder. "You can assure Elizabeth that Sandy will take good care of me and there's nothing to be concerned about."

Cassandra laughed. "Don't believe a word of it," she said. "It's quite impossible to take care of your father. He's fiercely independent and does exactly what he wants." She patted Noah's hand on her shoulder and smiled up at him. "Right?" She turned back to Larry. "But don't worry; your father doesn't need taking care of—he's the most resilient man I know."

Larry didn't speak for a moment, but his face went through a contortion of emotions.

"You've done your duty, Larry." Noah's voice was softer now. "You can go home to Elizabeth and tell her you tried your best but your stubborn father refused to budge."

"Dad, it wasn't just Elizabeth's idea I should come. I wanted to make sure you were OK. I mean, it's fine with me if you want to live here with—"

"An old, old friend," said Noah.

"Didn't you just meet at Clarion?"

"When he says 'old, old,' he means old as in decrepit," said Cassandra, "as well as the fact that we've known each other for more than fifty years. My God, that's half a century!"

Larry looked puzzled.

"We were friends when we were in college," said Noah. "And were happy to find ourselves incarcerated in the same institution for the elderly."

"Dad, you can hardly call it incarcerated!"

"Your father's just a contrarian; don't let his semantics distress you," said Cassandra. "Clarion is fine for some people, but your father and I were misfits."

"I didn't realize you had already known each other," said Larry.

"Back when we were young and full of joie de vivre!" Cassandra flung out her arms.

"You still are," said Noah.

"Young? Please inform my knees of that."

Melville, who had been patiently waiting for the conversation to end, nudged Cassandra.

"I think this dog would like a walk," she said. "Larry, I trust you will join us for dinner. Your father is a true genius as a chef—he's managed to make gourmet meals even in this somewhat primitive kitchen."

"I think I need to get on the road and get home."

"We'll forego cocktails and have an early dinner, then. Larry, you can be his sous-chef while Melville and I get our much-needed exercise."

She didn't wait for a response but headed down towards the water. The tide was half out, and there was just enough beach for her to walk along the shore. She did not look back at the two men, father and son, whom she could picture standing there watching her walk away.

# XV

It was rare for Noah to have time with Larry without Elizabeth present. In recent years it was only when Larry had driven him to or from the Cape that that had been possible. Noah could have hired someone to drive him to the cottage, but he'd never suggested it, nor had Larry. Noah wasn't sure if Larry also appreciated this opportunity for them to have some time alone together or if he just did it to please his father. Larry had been almost annoyingly solicitous since Helene's death, and Noah's auto accident only confirmed Larry's view of his father—a view promoted by Elizabeth—as both incompetent and decrepit. At dinner, with Cassandra as his ally, Noah felt rejuvenated and was happy that Larry clearly noticed. Larry seemed surprised—even a bit bewildered—by the transformation. It was impossible to tell if he was pleased. Taciturn by nature, Larry was always more loquacious out of range of Elizabeth, and Cassandra succeeded in getting him to talk about his work (was she really interested in his engineering projects or just feigning interest?), something Noah (who was neither interested nor capable of pretending that he was) had never managed. While he talked, Noah watched Cassandra's face. She occasionally looked from Larry to Noah, as if she was studying what was going on between the two of them.

When it was time for Larry to leave, Cassandra suggested Noah walk him out to his car.

"I'm so happy I got a chance to meet you," she said to Larry. "Give my love to Cammie, and tell her I'm awaiting a list of names for the stick insects."

When Larry looked confused, she pointed towards the bedroom. "They traveled with me." She smiled at Larry and took his hand for a minute. "Have a safe trip home. And the next time you come, you should plan on staying longer. I'm sure Noah would like that." She did not look over at Noah for confirmation.

She went back to the kitchen, leaving Noah and Larry by the door.

Noah and Larry's usual gesture at parting was to clap each other on the shoulder. When was the last time they'd hugged each other? It was probably when Helene had died. Larry was built like Noah, but he'd never been an athlete, and Noah remembered how his back had felt soft against Noah's arms. Since then, when they parted, they were usually with the children, and Noah had found hugging them goodbye a satisfying substitution.

"Take care of yourself, Dad."

"No need to worry about me. I'll be just fine," said Noah. "You can tell Elizabeth that. And you can tell her that you fulfilled your duty and checked out Sandy."

"That wasn't the reason I came—" Larry began.

"Whatever." Noah held up his hands.

They stood without speaking for a moment. Then Larry said, "I liked her."

"I expected you would."

After Larry got into the car, Noah closed the door for him. His hand lingered on the door handle. Larry opened the window and shifted in his seat, and Noah thought Larry was about to reach out and grasp his hand. But before that might happen, Noah raised his hand and gave a little wave.

"Goodbye, Dad," said Larry, and he turned and started the car. Noah stepped out of the way while Larry backed around. He watched the car head up the driveway, raising eddies of dust, and he stood there still when it was out of sight, listening as it made its way up to the road, paused, then turned to the right and drove off towards town.


Cassandra didn't hear Noah come into the kitchen. The sink was on full force, and she was rinsing the dishes. He didn't want to startle her, so he stood by quietly while she put the last dish in the drying rack, turned off the water, and dried her hands and forearms with the dishcloth. When she turned around and saw him, she didn't say anything for a moment, then she reached up and laid her hand along the side of his cheek.

"It's always hard when they leave, isn't it?" she said.

He covered her hand with his and moved her hand so it was across his mouth. He closed his eyes and kissed her palm.

She slipped her fingers between his and gave his hand a playful shake. "We should get the fire going again, so we don't freeze tonight."

They worked on the fire, then pulled up the armchairs so they'd be close to the woodstove. Melville stretched out on the floor by the back door.

"Glass of wine?" Noah asked.

"Sure. Why not?"

Noah went back to the kitchen and returned with the bottle and glasses.

"You charmed my son," he said as he sat down.

"I'm happy I got to meet him," Cassandra said. She took a sip of the wine Noah had handed her. "I imagine it was difficult for him to see you with me—not that we're together. I mean to see a woman, not his mother, here with you in the cottage."

"I guess so."

"This was the first time, right?"

"I haven't been with anyone since Helene died, if that's what you mean."

"He's still a little intimidated by you."

"Intimidated?"

"He's obviously very smart, and he's apparently doing well as an engineer, but he still acts like someone who feels he hasn't quite achieved what you wanted for him."

Noah let this sink in. Then he said, "I wasn't a very easy father."

"There's something about English professors," said Cassandra. "They're not more intelligent than other people, but they act as if they are. I observed this at faculty meetings at the university. The English professors were so sure of themselves when they spoke. They'd grab the floor and they'd pontificate."

"I never pontificated!"

"Never never, or hardly ever?"

"Were you just quoting Gilbert and Sullivan?"

"Why not? I may not like music, but I love *Pinafore*. In fact, I was Buttercup in a high school production."

"You sing?"

"Poorly, but it's a comic role, and I got to wear a pillow under my costume. Do you sing?"

"I was a choirboy as a child. It solidified my dislike of organized religion as well as singing." Noah got up and added a log to the fire, watched it settle, then added a second one. After he sat down again, he poured them another glass of wine. They were both quiet for a while, watching the flames curl around the logs.

"We've been here just a week, and yet we seem like an old couple who've been sitting together in front of our fire night after night, year after year."

"Not an *old* couple, please," said Noah.

They were quiet again. Melville, who had been dozing, looked up, thumped his tail against the floor, then went back to dozing.

"I know you think Larry came out here at Elizabeth's bidding to reclaim you and keep you from being ensnared by me, but I got the sense he really came because he wanted to reassure himself that you were OK."

"Maybe that too."

"Why is it you dislike Elizabeth so much?"

"She's cold, arrogant, self-serving—"

Cassandra cut him off. "That's what you've said before, but there's more to it, isn't there?"

"That's not reason enough?"

"No. Larry is apologetic about her—as if he knows you have good reason not to like her."

"What is it about you, Sandy? You don't leave things alone. You're not satisfied unless you dig."

Cassandra shrugged. "It's probably the scientist in me. I like to understand things."

"But we're talking about people here, not science—"

"I like explanations."

"Do you do this with everyone?"

She shook her head, waited, then said softly, "No, just people I care about."

Noah's hand felt unsteady, and he set his wineglass on the floor beside his chair. He didn't take his eyes off Cassandra's face.

"All right, then. Since you want to know, I'll tell you. Elizabeth did something unforgivable."

"I thought that's what it might be. When our children do things that hurt us, we still love them, and we forgive them because they're our children. But it's different with our children-in-law. I know. I've been through that, too." She paused, then said, "If you're not yet ready to tell me what she did, it's all right. I understand." She laid her hand on his arm. "Is that the problem with you and Larry? That he sided with his wife, and so you haven't really forgiven him yet?"

Noah took in a breath. His whole body throbbed. He was going to say, "There is no problem with Larry," but as he looked at Cassandra, he couldn't.

Cassandra was uncharacteristically quiet. "I imagine Larry's been working all his life to earn your approval," she said at last. "And my guess is he finally achieved that. But seeking forgiveness from you—well, that's much harder."

"And you?" asked Noah. "What haven't you been able to forgive?"

"Laurel's husband, Drew, wouldn't come to Maggie's wedding. I was OK with that, but he kept Laurel from coming too. He said it would be condoning immoral behavior and offend the sanctity of their marriage. I am quoting him exactly here. As you can imagine that didn't endear him to me, nor did it help the already fraught relationship between my two daughters."

Melville rolled on his back, paws in the air, then got up and came over to nudge Cassandra's arm until she reached out to pat him.

"Maggie had persuaded Kathryn to have the wedding here in the US, in the garden behind my house, because she wanted her family to be able to attend. She delayed walking down the aisle—she kept watching for Laurel, hoping she'd come. But Laurel didn't come."

"And you've forgiven Laurel?"

"Oh, Noah!" Cassandra sighed. "I was going to say yes, but that's not totally true. I blame myself that Laurel's weak, since I'm the one who raised her. And I have to forgive her, because I've been weak, too."

"You?"

"Yes, moi."

In preparation for what Noah called "The Great Woodcock Folly," he submitted to a little lecture about *Scolopax minor*, the American woodcock. Cassandra insisted she was "not a birder," but she was more of an expert than anyone Noah knew, including some friends—not friends, really; more like acquaintances—who scurried around the globe adding to their life lists. Cassandra showed him photos of woodcocks on her laptop but refused to open any videos. "They ruin the experience. I want you to see things with fresh eyes when we're out there."

"On the other hand, we could experience the videos in the comfort of this living room rather than standing around on some windy beach—"

"We won't be on the beach. Although woodcocks are shorebirds, they prefer upland habitats—woodland clearings, fields."

Cassandra pointed to the photo on the screen. "Look at this marvelous long bill—perfect for hunting for worms, and the tip of it can open and close while it's in the soil."

"Admirable, I'm sure. What I'm struck by are those frog-like eyes. It looks like a bird with a thyroid condition."

"Its eyes are positioned high on its skull—over its ears, in fact, so it has three-hundred-and-sixty-degree vision—it can see what it's eating while it's watching for danger up in the sky."

Noah smiled at her.

"Oh, dear, I've been slipping into nature instructor mode, haven't I?"

"I'm rather enjoying it. Continue, please!"

"No, enough. But since you're a language buff, I think you'll enjoy knowing other names for a woodcock. It's called a bogsucker, a timberdoodle, a hokumpoke, and a Labrador twister."

"Delightful. It would be considered improper, I imagine, to comment on its common name, woodcock."

"Definitely improper." Cassandra turned off her laptop and flipped down the screen. "Time to go. Are we taking Melville or leaving him here?"

"You mean leave him alone in the cottage to tear up the kitchen before he reclines on the sofa?"

"It would make him happy."

"It would not make me happy. But if you bring him, won't he scare away the woodcocks and render the entire trip useless?"

"I'll leave him in the car. We have to hike out to the spot I have in mind."

"I don't believe you said anything about hiking. I thought we'd be sitting in lawn chairs, binoculars trained on the sky."

"You may bring your lawn chair, but you still have to hike to the spot."

Cassandra started towards the door, leash in hand. She turned around to face Noah. "This is supposed to be a fun adventure. If you feel the urge to complain, please resist as best as you can."

"I've already told you, Sandy: I leave the fun aspect to you."

"That's what you say, but I'm not giving up on you." Cassandra whistled for Melville, who roused himself—reluctantly, Noah thought—from his spot by the back door and trotted along as Cassandra left the house.

It had been only a week since Noah had last risked his life in the passenger seat of Cassandra's car, yet that trip, with her oversized dog in the back seat drooling on him, seemed like it was embedded so much farther away in the past. He'd rigged up a temporary clothesline across one end of the room near the woodstove (the cottage had a washing machine but no dryer), and the chorus line of her dangling bras and panties marked the days, but it felt as if Cassandra had been living with him much longer than that. He'd gotten used to her toothbrush leaning against his in the cup by the bathroom sink, her sweater draped over the arm of the chair.

"I feel like I'm on a school field trip," Noah said as they started to head north on the road towards Provincetown.

"Did you ever go on one of the Clarion excursions?"

"Surely you jest."

"To me, this feels more like going on a date. It's our first outing together since we came out here." Cassandra turned to smile at him, and Noah cried out, "Please, Sandy, keep your eyes on the road!"

"I got you to the Cape without mishap, didn't I?"

"Thanks to sheer good luck."

Melville was initially disconsolate on not being able to accompany them when they got there but was appeased with a chew toy in the car that smelled like a piece of old barbecued meat. Perhaps even *was* old barbecued meat. It was a longer hike to the woodcock observing spot Cassandra had in mind than Noah had anticipated, and halfway there he began to envy Melville relaxing in the car, gnawing on his redolent dog chew. Cassandra was not only a fast walker, but she was tireless, even though they'd just eaten a hefty dinner.

"I think here is good," she said at last. They were not far off a sand road that led to the ocean through a thicket of bayberries, *Rosa rugosa*, and gloating poison ivy. There was a field of long not-quite-green-yet grass in front of them. Behind them was a marsh, with an unrelenting din of spring peepers.

"The male woodcocks perform their courtship displays to impress the females—who may be around here, watching," said Cassandra. "They're very much into their performance, and some continue showing off even after they've nabbed their mate and even after the female has laid her eggs. Not surprisingly, they leave all the chick rearing to their mates."

"I apologize on their behalf," said Noah.

The sun had set rather modestly but left behind a lovely pink-hazed sky that was turning violet almost imperceptibly slowly. That was all that was happening. Nothing was moving. Cassandra, beside him, grew quiet and still, but he could tell she was watching hard, listening hard, her whole body on alert.

"There's a Chekhov story I teach called 'Misery,'" he said, "that begins with a sentence that is just one word: 'Twilight.' The second sentence is, 'The sky was the color of ever-changing violet.' That's this: ever-changing violet."

Cassandra squeezed his hand. There was the sound of a buzzer somewhere in the field. Again, and once again.

"That's our woodcock!" she cried.

"That doesn't sound like a bird."

"It's described as a 'peent.'"

"It's a crank in need of oil."

"He's on the ground now, but he'll be flying soon."

"Where?"

"He's perfectly camouflaged. Keep your eyes on the sky."

Noah didn't see anything, but then, when he was about to give up on the possibility, he spotted a dark bird shape against the violet. It rose, almost magically, straight up, in widening spirals, chirping, feathers whistling, and then tumbled straight down towards the ground. It was all over too quickly to make sense of. There was quiet, and then the whole exhibition began again. Noah tried to catch it on his binoculars, but he wasn't able to react in time. "You know the Yeats poem 'The Second Coming'?" he asked. "'Turning and turning in the widening gyre / The falcon cannot hear the falconer; / Things fall apart; the centre cannot hold; / Mere anarchy is loosed upon the world.'"

"Not now, Noah. Now is just being here."

"All right." He pushed the poem away and submitted himself to the background chorus of the peepers, the whirring of the woodcock wings, the smell of the marsh, the coming of night.

They didn't talk as they drove back to the cottage. But that was OK. It was dark when they got back. It felt as if they were coming home together. Noah had neglected to leave on the light over the door, but there was a small lamp on in the living room. It had an old yellowed silk shade that cast the room in a soft light. The base was a round glass jug that was filled with shells Noah and his brothers had gathered when they were kids.

There were just enough live embers in the woodstove to get a fire going again. Noah went into his bedroom and changed into the clothes he slept in; then he lowered himself into a chair in front of the woodstove. He listened to Cassandra's industrious brushing of teeth. When she came out of the bathroom, she sat beside him.

"I just need to warm up a little before I go to bed," she said.

"There's something I've been thinking of suggesting, but I'm not sure I should."

"Since I don't know what it is, I'm afraid I can't advise you, but in the meantime, tell me what you thought of our excursion."

"I was impressed by the agility of the male woodcock and the sheer extravagance of his display."

"Are you saying you're happy I dragged you along?"

"If that's what you'd like me to be saying, then I'll willingly comply."

"You were spellbound. I saw the look on your face."

"In the dark?"

"In the dusk. Now, what was it that you were hesitant about suggesting? That we go again tomorrow night?"

"Not exactly."

"What, then?"

"I was thinking that since you've been cold at night, if we shared a bed, it would be a way to address the situation."

"Oh."

"I wasn't suggesting something untoward; what I had in mind was a companionable being-in-bed-together."

"Then why were you worried about asking me?"

"I was afraid of upsetting what we have. Somehow we've worked out a comfortable accommodation living here in close proximity. I don't want to jeopardize it."

"You're thinking platonic bed-sharing, right?"

"That's what I intended. Will Melville mind?"

"Melville is a very acquiescent dog."

They went into the bedroom and got into the bed, one on each side, and turned out the light. Noah lay with his arms toy-soldier style, at his sides. It took him only a moment to be aware of the crickets chirping and something else. Was it the stick insects? He reached out and flipped on the light. The insect cages were lined up on the dresser top. The stick insects were silent, but the crickets were not just chirping but rustling around. One of the tarantulas, Petunia perhaps, was climbing up the side of her terrarium.

"Do you think we could relocate the menagerie to the living room so it would be possible for me to sleep?" he asked.

"Is the problem their noise or their presence?"

"Both. Neither is conducive to a good night's sleep."

"I think you'd get used to them," said Cassandra, but she got out of bed and helped Noah carry the cages out to the living room coffee table.

When they got back into bed, Noah could still hear the crickets, but the sound was distant enough that they could have been outdoors. He reached up and turned off the light again.

"My feet are cold," said Cassandra. "Would you mind moving yours closer?"

Noah turned partway on his side and slid his feet towards Cassandra's. "May I move my arm under you?" he asked.

"All right."

He slipped his arm under her back and around her. She turned on her side, too, and snuggled against him. "I've been sleeping alone for almost five years now," she said. "It feels good to be in bed with someone again. I'm not sure I'll be able to fall asleep, though."

But it wasn't long before her head lolled to the side and her arm dropped, and Noah realized she had fallen asleep. He wanted to stay awake all night, feeling the undulations of her breath; listening to the air move in through her nostrils; listening to her slow, even exhale. He wanted nothing more than this, to have the night go on forever, to be in his cottage, to smell the sea, to have Cassandra close beside him, but the monotonous choir of spring peepers had lodged in his head and mingled with the gentle din of crickets, and soon he fell asleep as well.

# XVI

In the gray of early morning, Cassandra, still dream-heavy, nestled in the warm crescent of bed next to Noah and began to pull herself from sleep. Noah was sleeping on his back, and after she was fully awake, she lay there studying him. There was something childlike about his partly open mouth and his vulnerable, pale eyelids. His almost-white hair hadn't been cut in a while, and it curled against his neck. She reached out a finger and touched it. It was soft as milkweed. She got up quietly and padded to the bathroom. She added some logs to the woodstove before returning to bed. She thought she'd just get back under the covers until she had warmed up again, but she realized she'd fallen asleep, because she awoke to discover she was alone in the bed, and there was a smell of something frying, something buttery and sweet.

"Do you like blueberry pancakes?" Noah asked when she made her way to the kitchen.

"Of course! What woman, man, or beast doesn't like blueberry pancakes?"

"This was the last of the flour. We'll have to get more at the market." Noah pointed at Melville, who had followed Cassandra from the bedroom. "Don't get your hopes up, beast," he said. "I am not making any for you."

"Don't worry, Melville," said Cassandra, "I'll give you some of mine." She dragged out the bag of dog food from the cupboard, filled Melville's dog bowl, and brought it outside on the deck for him. The view was shrouded by fog, and everything had blended together. You couldn't tell where the beach ended and the water began, or where the water ended and the sky began. She set the table, folding the cloth napkins so they were little temples. Noah had sliced an orange and laid it on a plate like an open flower. It was the brightest thing in the room. She placed it on the table between their two place settings and carried out their mugs of tea, and Noah followed with the pancakes.

"Where did you get the blueberries?"

"Bernice, the berry-picking champion of the Outer Cape. She picks gallons of berries—blueberries, blackberries, elderberries, juniper berries, cranberries, beach plums—and spends her nights making jams and jellies. I finally managed to convince her I didn't need any more jam—there are jars in the pantry dating back to the last century—but I'd be happy to be the beneficiary of berries that she'd frozen. She'd included several bags of blueberries for the freezer when she dropped off some provisions this morning."

"She was here?"

"She came by to bring us eggs and bread. You were still asleep."

"You didn't tell her that, did you?"

"I'm afraid I did. She wanted to ask you something about some bug she found in their basement."

"Oh, dear, I'm sure that just confirmed the wrong idea she has about us."

"Bernice is an unrepentant romantic," said Noah. "There's nothing that either of us can do or say that would dispel her fantasy of a passionate affair going on under this roof."

"She must be in cahoots with Mallory, who imagines that if we have not yet consummated our affair, consummation is imminent."

"How long does she give us?"

"When I talked to her after we got here, she gave us only a day or two—and that was more than a week ago!"

"In that case, we better get to work."

Cassandra laughed. "I'm going to take a long walk with Melville today. Want to come? I just have to get my stuff together, and then we'll be off!"

"I walked yesterday evening," said Noah.

"You barely walked at all. And, as you pointed out, that was yesterday."

"I have work to do."

"What sort of work?"

"I want to get my sailboat into the water soon as it's warm enough. Since it's a wooden boat, I have to touch up the paint and the varnish—a hundred other things."

"I thought sailboats were made out of fiberglass now."

Noah laid down his napkin on the table. "My dear Cassandra," he began, "there are sailboats made out of fiberglass. And there are people who sail them. But people like me prefer wooden boats, and there are boatbuilders who still make them."

"Kind of a cult thing."

"No! A *classic* thing. It's like the difference between reading an actual book with paper pages and reading a book on a Kindle."

"What color?"

Noah looked confused.

"Your boat."

"Dark green outside, white inside, mahogany trim. You can inspect it in person."

After they'd cleaned up from breakfast, Cassandra went out to the barn with Noah. His sailboat was on a boat trailer, and it looked perfectly content not to be in the water.

"*Sarabande*," she said, running her finger along the gold lettering.

"Bach's Suite no. 5."

"I thought as much." She hopped up on a crate and looked inside the boat. "No bathroom?"

"It's called the 'head.' And there is none. Men are adept at going over the side, and there's a pail for ladies, when you come."

"Do you imagine I'm going to risk my life going out on the high seas in a boat that doesn't even have a bathroom?"

"Low seas. And you already risked your life driving out here. I don't think you'd want to miss out on the chance to experience sailing."

"I can experience videos of sailing in the comfort of the living room," said Cassandra.

Noah walked back into the house with Cassandra.

"Sure you haven't changed your mind about coming with me?" she asked.

"I'm sure."

"Melville and I are going to hike far and wide. I'm bringing a sandwich, so don't expect me for lunch."

Cassandra made herself a peanut butter and jelly sandwich using the bread Bernice had dropped off, which looked home baked; peanut butter she dug out from the stash of food from her Clarion pantry; and some beach plum jelly she found on the shelf that was in an unopened jar that appeared botulism-free. She packed her backpack with her lunch, her Sibley bird guide, her notebook and pens, her camera, plastic bags for things she might collect, her water bottle, and a plastic container so she could give Melville drinks. She put on her polar-fleece jacket, tied her windbreaker around her waist, and hung her binoculars around her neck.

"If you're not back before dark, you're grounded," Noah said as she was leaving.

"If you keep yourself busy, you won't miss me too much." She waved goodbye and started for the door, then turned back towards him. "Please don't let me forget I'm doing FaceTime with Maggie tonight."

"I'll try to remember to remind you. And don't forget about the tide," he said. "You don't want to get stranded."

She smiled. "If I do, and the water gets too high, Melville will swim, and I'll ride on his back."

Cassandra headed towards the swath of land that was National Seashore. The fog was still cushioning the beach, and she was glad Melville instinctively stuck close to her so he wouldn't be obliterated. It was different from the fog at Clarion; it was moist and misty and smelled of the sea. It had no staying power, though, and she hadn't walked far before it began to thin. The near distance, then the farther distance, were restored bit by bit. Half an hour after she'd started, the fog was just a gauzy cousin to itself, and after an hour it had almost disappeared. There were no houses here; it was wild, beautiful, protected land. The wind picked up, ruffling the water and sending wisps of seaweed airborne. Cassandra put on her windbreaker before she started hiking again.

She walked the wrack line, the tide's highest reach, this untidy deposit of seaweed and shells, mermaid's purses, whelk egg cases, bits of wood and straw and feathers. Everything cast off by the sea. A bottle, a brick. A Mylar balloon, deadly to sea creatures that might mistake it for jellyfish, which she stamped on to get the air out of and tucked into her backpack. Part of someone's sea-ravaged dock. The remains of a skate, the skeleton of a gull.

The shoreline curved around the bay—made the cove a cove. She was familiar with the landscape because she'd been here one summer, years before, working on her research project on the Northeastern beach tiger beetle. She'd spent hours netting them to bring back for study in the lab. Of all the insects she studied, they were the fastest, the most interesting, the most misunderstood. It was too cold for them to be out now, but she knew the larvae were hidden in burrows in the sand all along the beach.

There was no one else out on the beach. She looked back now at Noah's cottage and tried to remember if she'd seen it when she'd been here in the past. Of course she must have seen it, because she'd certainly looked at the shoreline, but there was a difference between simply seeing something and noticing it. At that time, Noah's cottage had been just one of the houses along the coast, and she had no interest in man-made structures. She was interested in the natural world; she was focused on the habitat of the tiger beetles—caught up in their extraordinary leaps, the exquisite pattern on their backs, their skill in catching prey.

But now she was focused on Noah's cottage, a formerly ignored little building, wood-weathered shingles curled by the sun. Home of Noah. She was a creature in her own lab experiment: approach-avoidance. Getting close to him, shying away; longing for him, shaking herself loose of him. She sat down on the side of a low dune and lay back in the sunlight. She was happy to have time alone and was annoyed to realize that, in spite of that, she missed Noah. It had always been a conundrum in her life—her conflicting urge to be free and independent, and to stay close by the person she was intimate with. Although she didn't have a sexual relationship with Noah, it was certainly intimate—they shared a bed; they trusted each other enough to fall asleep together. Everything was happening so quickly—or was it not happening quickly enough?

Cassandra lifted her binoculars and trained them on Noah's property. There, in the driveway, was her own car, incontrovertible proof that she was connected to the place. She could not see any sign of Noah, and she wondered if he was in the barn working on his boat or if he had gone back to the cottage. She imagined him looking at her through his binoculars—that they would watch each other watching. And then, she had a wild thought that she would spot herself—see the tiny, distant Cassandra coming out on the deck.

She got up and dusted the sand off, gathered her things, and walked farther along the beach. It wasn't quite lunchtime yet, but she felt hungry, so she soon sat down to eat. She poured some water for Melville, who took a quick drink. Bernice's sourdough bread was made of a dozen different grains and was embedded with a myriad of seeds. It required considerable chewing. The beach plum jelly was chunky and sweet.

Melville had wandered off, and she spotted him farther down the beach. He was happily investigating some dark shape. She trained her binoculars on it—it was the carcass of a dolphin. She got up quickly and ran towards Melville.

"Melville, leave it!"

He looked up, surprised by the severity of her voice.

The dolphin's body had been there for a long time. Most of the flesh had rotted away, but the sand-logged bones were intact, the ribs perfectly symmetrical curves. She was always curious about marine animals, and ordinarily she would have studied this dolphin's remains. But there was something different now. There was nothing left of the dolphin that echoed its former grace and beauty. It was so irrevocably dead, and what was left of it was ugly: stripped bones and scraps of ragged flesh. She couldn't keep herself from thinking of David Sussman, dead now, the curve of his body under the blanket as he was wheeled out on a stretcher through the back exit of Clarion Court. And Mallory's husband, John, not wanting to leave his house, mourning the dead man who had confided in him for decades.

She hadn't wanted to think about death. She hadn't wanted to think about her own mortality. She'd been thinking about it as little as she could—as if by not thinking about it, she could keep herself immune from it. She had a sudden desire to be back at Noah's cottage, their safe little hideout; she wanted to lay her body against his, have his arms encircle her. She'd walked far enough on her own.

"Come on, Melville," she said, forcing brightness in her tone. "Let's go." She started running down the beach, her backpack thumping against her back. She did not look back at Melville but trusted he would follow her. When she was far enough from the dead dolphin, she slowed to a walk and turned to see that Melville was right behind her.


She found Noah in the barn when she returned.

"Ready to sail?" she asked, and she tapped the side of the boat.

"I haven't even started the painting yet," said Noah. "I've been puttering. The time-honored preamble to actual work." He took a longer look at her.

"Everything OK?"

"Yeah. I just forgot I'm too old for running."

"How was your excursion?"

"Good—"

"But?"

"There was a dead dolphin on the beach."

"I didn't think things like that upset you."

"They usually don't, but—I don't know. I found myself strangely emotional."

Noah waited, expecting her to continue, but this didn't feel like the right moment, so she just said, "I'll talk more about it later. Show me the product of your puttering."

"Puttering has no product," said Noah. "But there's something I found back here I want to consult with you about." He turned and started walking towards a dark corner of the barn. "I was looking for my sander, and I came across this." He pushed aside a crumpled tarp. There was a cardboard box that had been stowed underneath, and Noah lifted the flap of the box. Inside was a laptop and some other electronics. "I'm not sure what to make of it."

"It's not yours?"

"No."

"Then whose is it?"

"Good question, and why was it hidden in my barn?"

"Stolen stuff someone was storing here?"

"That's what occurred to me. There are a lot of summer houses around here that are easy to break into."

"You think whoever put it there will come back for it?"

"Good chance. They obviously didn't expect me to return to the cottage this early in the season."

"You think you know who it might be?"

"I have my suspicions." Cassandra saw him look up the hill towards Artie and Bernice's house.

"Jed?"

He nodded.

"I'm sure he panicked when he saw I was working out here today."

Noah covered the things with the tarp, just as it had been. They walked back to the house together and made tea and brought it outside. Noah dragged the Adirondack chairs towards the house, out of the wind, and they sat there in a sunny shelter, looking out at the bay. The tide was rising, but stealthily. You wouldn't catch it with your eye, but if you marked the edge of the dry shore with a stick, you'd have your proof.

"You're not going to call the police, are you?"

"I'm not sure."

"How old is Jed?"

"He's in high school. Fourteen, maybe fifteen? Too young to drive. Not that he doesn't drive, but too young to have a license."

"You really think he'd do something like this?"

"Not on his own. He's not a kid with a lot of initiative. My guess is he got dragged into this by someone else. And I bet he'll be coming around soon to retrieve the stuff. And then I'll catch him at it."

"And then what?"

"I don't know. What do you suggest?"

"Talk to Jed. See what he has to say for himself."

"You can't talk to a kid like Jed."

"Of course you can!"

Noah shook his head.

"If it *is* Jed, how do you think Artie will react?"

"Not well," said Noah. "If this cottage had a cellar, which it doesn't, I'd suggest hiding out there till the dust settles."

"Maybe it would be better to talk to Bernice first."

"Bernice? I can't really talk to Bernice."

"In that case," said Cassandra, "I'm just hoping it turns out that it's someone else and not Jed."

While Noah cooked dinner, Cassandra battled with FaceTime for a while and finally managed to connect with Maggie.

"Are you OK, Mom?" asked Maggie straight off.

"I'm fine, Dear. I'm out on Cape Cod, and everything's lovely. I just wanted to hear how you are. And I wanted to catch a glimpse of the darlings." She'd once called her grandchildren "my darlings," but Maggie had commented that Kathryn thought that sounded inappropriately possessive.

"They're just getting dressed," said Maggie, and the screen swerved so Cassandra got a view of the floor, then the side of the bed. In the background she heard a piercing cry—not a cry of pain, but a cry of outrage—from one of the twins, and then Maggie yelled, "Dahlia, put that down! Right now!" The screen showed only white ceiling.

"Sorry, Mom," said Maggie, whose face came into view again. "They've been up since five a.m., and I let them play in pajamas all morning." Maggie turned so Cassandra saw only the back of her head. "Odin! Dahlia! Come say hello to Grammy." The title "Grandma" had been snatched by Kathryn's mother before Cassandra could register a claim, and Cassandra had been offered the second-place titles of "Gran," "Granny," and the formidable "Grandmother." She had suggested "Gaga," but that had not been an approved option.

Odin got to say hello first, and he shoved his stuffed pink rabbit at the screen to show Cassandra. It had ridiculously large plastic eyes. He bounced the rabbit up and down in some grotesque re-creation of the bunny hop. Behind him Dahlia was screaming, "It's my turn! It's my turn." She was taller than her brother and considerably more assertive and articulate. She snatched the deplorable rabbit out of the way and pressed her own face against the screen. "Mama!" screamed Odin, and Dahlia turned to reprimand him and in her charming New Zealand accent informed him, "You're nothing but a baby," which produced a torrent of wails from her sibling.

"I'm sorry, Mom," said Maggie, who was back in view again. "This isn't a great time. We haven't eaten lunch yet. Everyone's hungry."

"I understand, Sweetheart," said Cassandra. "I just wanted to see how you were."

"We're all going crazy."

"I'm sorry, Maggie. I know this is a tough age, but it won't last forever."

"I wish you were here now!" Maggie cried. And although Cassandra would have loved to be with them in general, at this particular moment she was actually relieved to be on Cape Cod instead. "September will be here soon," she said brightly. "And I'll get to hug you all then."

"I've been worried about you, too, Mom. I was afraid you'd be miserable downsizing and living at a place like Clarion—you are, aren't you?—but at least when you're there, they look after you, or at least they're supposed to—"

"I haven't been *miserable*—"

"I can tell, Mom! And now you're off with some guy you barely know—"

"Maggie, I don't need looking after! And there's nothing to worry about. I'm in a lovely, safe place right now."

"Please, Mom, don't do anything rash!" Maggie had barely finished her sentence before Dahlia's face filled the screen and she cried, "Bye-bye, Grammy!" before the connection went dead.

After the FaceTime visit with Maggie, Cassandra was as tired as if she had been wrestling with the children in person. "It's exhausting being cheerful," she said to Noah as they sat down to eat.

"I wouldn't know," he said. "How is your daughter?"

"The kids are driving her crazy. I wish I could be there in person to help her out, hug my grandbabies. FaceTime is a torment. You can see them, but you can't *have* them. And Maggie's annoyingly worried about me. She'd been worried I'd be miserable moving into a place like Clarion, but at the same time she was secretly relieved I was somewhere 'safe,' and now that I'm out here on my own, she's worried about me again."

"You're not exactly 'on your own.'"

"That too."

After dinner, when they settled in the living room, Cassandra spent time looking through the books in the stuffed floor-to-ceiling bookcase. There was a whole section of books relating to Cape Cod, history books and guidebooks. She picked out a few to read when they sat by the fire.

"A guidebook on mollusks?" Noah asked. "I can't believe you'd choose that."

"I don't know much about mollusks. I think it's time I learned."

"Does that mean you might be sticking around here even after Clarion's renovations are complete?"

"I might consider it, if the landlord is willing."

"After a brief consultation, I can report, conclusively, that he is," said Noah, and he went back to his mystery. Cassandra looked up from her book when Noah got up. He added more logs to the fire, but he didn't sit back down.

"Here's what I've been thinking about," he said. "Do you have an interest in repeating the experiment of last night?"

"Experiment?"

"What would you call it, then?"

"A remedy for survival in a cottage lacking central heating."

"Is it a remedy you'd like to consider tonight as well?"

"I think so." Cassandra smiled at him. "You were expecting me to say that, weren't you?"

"Expecting? From you? No. I was merely submitting myself to hope."

"Are we going to have to go through this formality every night?"

"It would be nice if we could bypass it."

"Then let's just decide we've established a bedtime routine. And we'll continue with it until further notice. Agreed?"

"Agreed."

In bed they both lay on their backs, and Cassandra rested her neck on Noah's outstretched arm. She slid her feet close to his and pressed the soles of her feet against the top of his, arches over arches.

"When I took my walk today, I left everything behind," she said. "It was like years ago, just being on the beach on my own. But when I saw that dolphin—what was left of it—everything hit me. I'm not young anymore, and I never will be young again. I'm just going to get older and older—and that's if I'm lucky—and then I'll die. It's all happening too fast! I'm not ready to be old. And there's nothing I can do about it."

"I think there's something."

"What's that?"

"We can be not ready to be old together."

Cassandra turned and nuzzled against Noah's side. She let herself open up and cry.

# XVII

Noah decided to practice the cello in the morning. He had barely played since he arrived at the cottage two weeks before, and he felt apologetic towards his cello, almost as if he'd abandoned it for another woman. The other woman, at that moment, was going off on a mollusk-collecting mission that he had been invited to join but had naturally declined. He watched her setting off down the beach, Melville meandering along beside her. Now and then she squatted and poked at something on the sand. She seemed entirely engrossed in what she was doing, and he was disappointed that she didn't look back at the house. But then she did. He almost stepped back and pretended he hadn't been watching her but felt ridiculous doing that, especially when she waved at him. It was impossible for him to tell if she'd known that he'd been watching her, or if she'd just happened to look back at the house and been surprised to see him there. He guessed she probably knew. She seemed to know him well.

He'd been formulating a plan to deal with Jed and the items stashed in his barn but decided to wait on it and do his practicing first. He set up his chair and music stand in a sunny part of the living room and rosined his bow. His cello was dramatically out of tune, a protest against its neglect. When he had played cello decades before, he'd used a pitch pipe, but now he used an electronic tuner. It felt like cheating to rely on an electronic device rather than his ear to tell him whether a string was sharp or flat, but he'd decided one of the perks of being what qualified as an old man was that he was entitled to his conveniences. He had finally allowed himself to be, unapologetically, not quite the purist he once prided himself on being. He had a wooden sailboat, but he'd make use of an electric sander.

He wanted to start right off playing Bach but made himself do some vibrato exercises first. He'd never had a decent vibrato, and it was one of the things that Gertrude, his cello teacher, had been working on with him. Just a few days away from practicing and he felt out of shape. Playing an instrument was now a physical challenge as much as a musical one. His muscles—hand, wrist, arm, shoulder, neck, back—protested both during and after playing. Noah played longer than he should have, even though he expected he'd suffer aching body parts the next day, but it took considerable initial effort to get set up, and once he started playing, he didn't want to stop. He felt an acute kinship with Bach. He thought of Bach as being the same age as him, even though Bach had been sixty-five when he died, and here he was seven years older and not dead yet. Cassandra's crickets kept up a steady chirping while he played, as if they were his orchestral accompaniment, his continuo. He would have to tell Gertrude about that: the Cricket Continuo. It didn't look like he'd have a cello lesson with her for a while. Maybe they could attempt one on Zoom sometime? He hoped the bottle of single malt Scotch he'd given her at Christmas wasn't empty yet. They'd hold up their glasses to each other on the computer screen.

Cassandra returned with cold hands, a wet dog, and a pail full of shells. He went out on the deck to greet her.

"What are you going to do with all of them?"

"Lay them out so we can identify them."

"Wait a moment. I heard the 'we' word."

"We'll have fun, Noah."

"I was afraid of something like this."

Cassandra gave him a faux sweet smile. "Don't worry, I've done all the hard work, so there's no hiking required this time. You can enjoy this activity from the comfort of your dining room."

"You don't intend to bring that pail inside, do you?"

"It's getting chilly out there, Noah," said Cassandra as she did just that, "and I wouldn't want your hands to get cold too." Noah followed her into the kitchen, where she set the pail down on the counter and started lifting out the shells. She didn't seem concerned that they were sandy, and Noah decided he'd just wipe the counter off later.

"I discovered some cans of lentil soup in the cupboard," he said. "OK for lunch?"

"Are they post-Watergate?"

"The expiration date was too tiny for me to decipher, so we'll just take our chances if you're game."

"As long as you take the first spoonful."

After lunch Noah left Cassandra to her mollusks and went out to the barn to check out what he had in the way of paint supplies; then he hiked up the hill to Artie's house. Artie's property had a disjointed look. The front of the house, Bernice's domain, was tidy and photogenic, even in this scruffy early-spring season. The flagstone walkway had been swept of leaves, the plantings looked optimistic, and the wind chimes on the front porch—which had survived the battering of winter storms—tinkled in their mindless way. The back of the property, between house and garage, was Artie's domain, an obstacle course of boats in various stages of repair and disrepair, parts of boats, stacks of wood, lobster pots, buoys, moorings, anchors, ropes, sawhorses, crates, and debris. The chicken coop had been built by the side of the house, on neutral ground.

Artie and Jed were in the garage working on fishing tackle. "Ahoy!" sang out Artie, his usual tongue-in-cheek nautical greeting. "How are things doing down at the cottage?"

"We are holding up surprisingly well," said Noah. "How have you been, Jed?"

Jed looked up briefly. "OK." He was almost as tall as his father but had a puny look. His hair was long and dangled across half his face. He didn't bother to push it away.

"Any chance you'll be going to the marine supply place sometime in the near future?" Noah asked Artie.

"I might be stopping by there tomorrow afternoon. Let me know what you need, and I'll add it to my order."

"I could use some primer and maybe another can of varnish. I have one that's unopened, but it's been around a while."

"No point doing all the labor with crappy stuff," said Artie. "How are your brushes?"

"I'll take a look in the morning and let you know. I plan to clean out the back of the barn soon, and I'll see what I have. I promised Cassandra I wouldn't set foot in the barn today. She's gotten me involved in a project involving mollusks."

"Mollusks?"

"Apparently they're interesting if you put your mind to it."

Artie laughed. "I got to hand it to you, Noah—you've picked one unusual lady."

"I will pass the compliment on to her," said Noah. "And please thank Bernice for the eggs and the bread."

"Let her know if there's anything you need from the store. It's easy for her to grab some things for you while she's there—save you a trip."

"She doesn't really have to look after us, you know."

"Try telling Bernice that," said Artie.

"I have a strong suspicion that Jed will make an attempt to collect his haul from the barn tonight, once it's dark," Noah told Cassandra at dinner.

"You still think it's probably Jed?"

"As soon as I said something about cleaning out the barn soon, his face gave him away."

"Poor kid."

"Poor kid? He's the one who got himself into this trouble."

"Exactly."

Noah had left the barn door wide open, and once it was dark, he stood at the bedroom window, which looked out towards the barn, and waited there until he saw a speck of light move down the driveway and disappear into the barn.

"I'm heading out now to investigate," he told Cassandra.

"Would you like me to come along as backup?"

"I don't anticipate being in danger, if that's what you mean. I've known Jed since he was in diapers. He's sneaky and unreliable, but I don't think he's inclined to violence."

"If it *is* Jed," said Cassandra.

"If I'm not back by tomorrow, it would be kind of you to come investigate."

"My pleasure," said Cassandra. But she looked worried.

Noah got a flashlight from the kitchen and stuck it into his pocket. "I won't turn this on till I'm right there."

"Don't stumble in the dark and fall on your face," said Cassandra.

"I will do my utmost best to remain upright."

Noah crept up to the barn as cautiously as he could. He knew his way well enough, so he wasn't afraid of tripping even though his night vision wasn't good, but he moved slowly. He paused by the barn door. There was definitely someone in the barn, but they must have heard him coming and flipped off their flashlight. Noah waited a moment, listening. He aimed his flashlight inside the barn and was about to switch it on, but he wasn't fast enough. Whoever had been in the barn darted out and escaped into the darkness. Noah waved his beam of light back and forth, but it illuminated nothing more than some brambles and wind-stunted pines.

When he got back to the house, he found that Cassandra had been waiting for him by the door.

"No luck?" she asked.

"If what you mean by luck is did I get to catch Jed red-handed? No. But I'm now certain it was him."

"How so?"

"His dog gave him away. Jed must have climbed up the hillside to get back home rather than run up the driveway, and his dog started barking when he heard someone approaching the house through the bushes. He stopped barking when he saw it was Jed."

"Reading detective stories has served you well."

"I've always fancied myself an able sleuth. And you know, Sandy, there was really no need for you to be worried about me."

"While I'm here, anytime you head off into the dark of night to confront someone possibly engaged in criminal activity, I'll worry about you. After I leave, you can appoint someone else to take over."

Noah didn't say anything for a moment. He closed the door behind him and leaned back against it. "What do you mean by 'after I leave'?" he asked.

"Well, I've been here a lot longer than I'd originally planned, and I'll be leaving sometime, won't I?"

"Why?"

"Because this can't go on forever."

"Are you referring to extricating yourself from Clarion, or are you referring to us?"

Cassandra hesitated a moment, then said, "Both, I guess."

"You're right if you're talking about Clarion, but the 'us' part is an entirely different matter. There's no reason to conflate them."

"What did you want me to say?"

"That you have no intention of leaving."

"Ever?"

"That was the time frame I had in mind."

"Oh, Noah!" She shook her head sadly at him. "Next thing I know you'll be asking me to marry you!"

"Would that be so bad?"

She didn't answer him.

# XVIII

Noah was spending his day working on his boat, and Cassandra was spending her day studying mollusks. It seemed a fitting division of activities: she was involved with living creatures—or the shells of creatures that had once been living—and Noah was working on something man-made, not alive, but which the wind would imbue with life. Melville, partial to Cassandra but interested also in Noah's doings in the barn, navigated between the two of them with perfect canine neutrality. It was well into April now but still cool enough that Noah was making use of the shop heater Artie had lent him.

Although her colleagues who were malacologists would probably not agree, Cassandra considered mollusks, unlike insects, a relatively dull and limited field. And unlike live insects, most mollusks—bivalves at least—stayed put when you placed them on a table for study.

She had gathered dozens of shells, a variety of species. Live oysters and quahogs for dissection were stored in the refrigerator. She laid out some shells on the kitchen counter. They were winter-battered shells, and many were chipped or broken. Some were mere fragments, but she didn't care. She was interested in them for what they'd once housed. She remembered going on the beach with her family when she was a little girl, and her sister, Judy, had looked at the rough shells in her sand pail and said, "What on earth would you want those for?" Judy had collected only scallop shells and had discarded any that had even a broken edge. They were perfect shells, all the same size, but Cassandra hadn't found them interesting.

She lined the shells up now, the bivalves on one side: oyster, clam, razor clam, mussel, ark, false angel wing, scallop; and the cephalopods on the other: mud snail, moon snail, channeled whelk, knobbed whelk. It was a kind of graveyard. The quahog shell was still two hinged halves, a miracle of natural glue. The jingle shells, still glittery, were the most fragile, and yet several of them had survived intact.

Cassandra had been disappointed Noah had no interest in joining her in this mollusk project, but now she appreciated the solitude. She couldn't think properly about anything that involved Noah with him near her. Whenever she was dealing with intense matters with other people—children or spouses, lovers or friends—she was happy to be a scientist and have an orderly, objective world to immerse herself in. They hadn't talked more about it, but she was still thinking about what Noah had said: that he hoped she had no intention of ever leaving. She needed to think about what he wanted and what she wanted—that is, if she knew what she wanted. She'd come out here expecting to stay for a short time. Now more time had passed, and although she'd come to a conclusion about Clarion, that was an entirely separate matter and didn't help her clarify her feelings about staying here with Noah.

Cassandra poked at the shells on the kitchen counter, aligning them so their bottom edges were straight across, and decided to call Mallory before she got involved in her project. She'd meant to get in touch with her the day before, but other things had turned up.

"I've been hoping you'd call," said Mallory right off. "I'd call you, but I've been afraid I might call at the wrong moment and interrupt something—" Mallory hummed in place of the word.

"Please, Mallory! It's not like that."

"No?" Mallory spun out the word.

"No," said Cassandra firmly. "I'm calling to say hello and see how you are."

"We're no fun. I want to hear about you and Noah."

"Tell me how John's doing."

"John is impossible to live with. He's worried about dying. He doesn't want to go anywhere, not even to take a walk along the road. He doesn't enjoy spending time with the grandchildren. He's always been phobic about germs, as you know, and now he's concerned about salmonella in lettuce and bacteria in our drinking water and mold in the crevices of the Tupperware. He wants to sterilize everything!"

"Maybe that's not a bad idea—I mean, John did go to medical school; he knows something about pathogens."

"As you probably know, John chose psychiatry as a specialty so he wouldn't have to deal with real illness—physical illness, that is."

"At least he can read scientific studies," Cassandra said, "and figure out what's really worth taking precautions about."

"You think that's a good thing? He *obsesses* over them. And it's not just health issues; he obsesses over the news. He's all worked up about the state of the country—and the world. He devours the *Times* every morning and checks the news online all day. It's hard to get him to talk about anything else. And then he gets me all upset. My blood pressure is soaring."

"I'm sorry, Mal."

"Have you been following what's going on in the world?"

"Not really. Noah looks at the *Times*, but I haven't been paying close attention to the news these days. You think if you keep your eye on things you could help avert a catastrophe, but in fact you're helpless, utterly helpless, to do anything about it."

"And you don't like feeling helpless."

"Who does?"

Mallory laughed. "I wish I could have your perspective."

"It's because I'm out here. I've been kind of insulated from everything. But mostly I've been distracted, I guess. I'm just—"

"You're just in love," said Mallory cheerfully. "That's the best distraction in the world."

"No, nothing like that."

"San-dy!" Mallory elongated each syllable. "Now, it's time for an update. I want to hear the latest installment."

"We're not a soap opera!"

"Have you slept together yet?"

The suddenness and baldness of Mallory's question surprised Cassandra. When they were in college, "sleeping with someone" had meant having sex, but she and Noah had been sleeping together yet remained innocent. If the word "innocent" meant not having sex.

"We're just friends."

"Really?"

"Really."

She wasn't going to say anything more about it, but if she couldn't discuss things with Mallory, then there was no one. "The problem is that Noah is getting serious. He seems to want me to stay here—indefinitely."

"Why is that a problem?"

"I'm afraid he might eventually want to marry me."

"And what's wrong with that?"

"I can't marry him, Mallory. I can't marry anyone."

"Why not?"

"Because I've done it so many times before."

"So?"

"Mallory—I couldn't bear it. All that hope and promise! It's too much to contemplate. I don't have the stamina for it anymore. I'm too old."

There was uncharacteristic silence at the other end of the line. Finally Cassandra said, "Mal?"

"What about love?" asked Mallory. Her voice was somber. "If you're going to tell me you're too old for that, too, I don't want to hear it."

Cassandra sat down on a chair at the table by the window. She felt almost dizzy, the way she did when she was a passenger in a car and mistakenly looked down at something in her lap.

"I think I better get off the phone now, Mallory. I'm kind of—I don't know. I just need to sort it all out."

"OK," said Mallory, gently. "Call me when you can."

Cassandra said she would. She crossed her arms on the table, laid her head on her forearm, and closed her eyes. She wasn't sure what she was afraid of. She knew you were supposed to take deep breaths to calm yourself, and even though that had never seemed to work for her, she did it anyway: in through her nose, out through her mouth. She tried to concentrate on the feel of the air moving across the top of her hand. Out on the beach, an aggrieved gull, as if in perfect synchrony, let out a wrenching cry. She lifted her head to see it, but the gull was out of sight.

Cassandra got up and walked to the bedroom and looked out the window to the barn. Melville was lying across the concrete sill of the barn door, probably asleep. She couldn't see Noah, but she could see the bow of his boat, the "Sa" of *Sarabande*. She watched for a while, but Noah didn't appear. There was a sudden clattering, and Melville jumped up. Melville was a laid-back dog, but loud noises always startled him. He darted away from the barn, stopped to look back briefly, then ran to the house. He whined at the door.

"Hey, Baby," said Cassandra, and she let him in. He went over to what had become his spot by the back door, but he didn't stretch out again. Cassandra went back to the bedroom window and looked out at the barn. There was no sign of Noah. She wasn't worried, but she was curious. She slipped on her jacket and went out.

She didn't see Noah in the barn. Everything was still. The aluminum ladder that she remembered had been leaning against the edge of the loft was leaning back now against the stern of the boat. It must have fallen. That was the noise she'd heard. The barn was quiet now. She took this in and felt as if she had been struck. She stood, frozen, looking around.

"Noah?"

And then she saw him sprawled on the floor under the ladder.

She fell to her knees and reached to touch him. "My God!" she cried. "Oh my God!"

"I'm OK," he whispered, but he struggled to sit up.

"I'll call 911."

"I'm all right, Sandy," he said with difficulty. "Just got the wind knocked out of me."

She crouched beside him and placed her hand lightly on his shoulder. "What hurts?"

"Everything. But nothing feels broken."

"What happened?"

"The ladder toppled. I managed to hang on. Thankfully the ladder got caught on the boat as it fell."

It was concussions that were dangerous, she remembered. "Did you hit your head?" she asked.

"No. I landed on this." He pointed to the bunched-up tarp behind him.

She saw that one of the legs of his jeans had been ripped and he had a cut along his calf. "You're bleeding."

"Just a scrape. But I seem to be pinned here. Do you think you can pull the ladder off?"

"I'll try." She reached into her jacket pocket and pulled out some tissues. "Hold this on your leg." The ladder wasn't heavy, but it had gotten caught. Cassandra wrestled it free and managed to swing it so it was leaning against the side of the loft again. She sank down on the floor next to Noah.

"That's better," he said. He pulled himself more upright and rotated his shoulders, circled his neck.

"Are you sure you're all right?"

"I may be old, but apparently I'm built to last," he said. His voice sounded like his again. "Hey, you're not crying, are you?"

"Of course not."

He stroked her hair back off her forehead. "Thought you were going to get to see me carted out of here in a body bag?"

"Only for a moment."

"Poor you," he said.

"Poor *you*."

She put her hands on either side of his face and leaned down, placing her lips on his. Lips against lips, mouth against mouth.

"Our first kiss," she said.

"No. I kissed you in the supermarket parking lot."

"I was the recipient of that kiss, but not an actual participant. This was different." She laid her face against his chest, and his arms encircled her. She listened to the muffled but certain rhythm of his heart.

They stayed there on the floor of the barn until Cassandra said they should go in and take care of the cut on Noah's leg. She helped him to his feet, and they walked slowly back to the cottage.

"Sit down," she said. "I'll get something for that cut, but you better take off those jeans."

He slipped off his jeans and slowly seated himself on a chair by the table. She got a tube of antiseptic ointment and bandages from the bathroom medicine cabinet and knelt on the floor in front of him. She'd never seen his bare thighs before. There was no tape for the gauze pad, so she held it in place with three Band-Aids.

"How'd you tear the jeans?"

"Edge of the ladder. Now they're fashionably ripped, right?"

"I'm afraid there's nothing fashionable about them." She got to her feet. "I'm glad this didn't require a trip to the emergency room."

"I'd have to be in pretty bad shape to go near one."

"No more ladders!"

"Don't you do anything dangerous either." Noah looked over at Melville. "Did he come to you to summon help?"

"As much as I'd like Melville to endear himself to you, the truth is he came running to the house when the ladder fell because he was scared."

"That's a relief. I would hate to be beholden to him."

Noah stayed sitting in his chair while Cassandra put dinner together, heating up leftover mushroom risotto from the night before.

"This is the kind of cooking I enjoy," she said. "You make the dinner, and I serve it as if I'd been the chef."

Noah took a bite of risotto. "Your cooking skills are exemplary."

"How are you feeling?"

"I believe I've recovered."

"That's good. Then you can do the dishes."

As they were finishing dinner, Cassandra brought up the subject of Jed.

"Now that you've identified the suspect, where do we go from here?"

"We?"

"You don't want me to be involved?"

"I didn't mean that," Noah said quickly.

"That's good, because I believe I already *am* involved."

"In that case, we should discuss a plan. I expect Jed is eager to retrieve the stuff from the barn and will be coming around again at night when he feels it's safe to do. So we should set up a time he thinks will be safe, and when he turns up, I'll apprehend him, the stolen goods in hand."

"And then?"

"I'll haul him up to his house and turn him over to Artie."

Cassandra shook her head. "Uh-uh."

"You have a better idea?"

"We need to talk with Jed."

"There's no point in talking with Jed!"

"Oh, Noah! Someone has to talk with him, and from what you've said, Artie is not the person best suited to it."

"Why are you so concerned about Jed?"

"Because he's a kid, and he's in trouble. And because I think we can help him."

Noah studied her face for a moment. "I'm not convinced there's anything we can say or do that will have the slightest impact on him."

"You don't have to be convinced. But don't you think we should at least try?"

Noah sighed. "Sandy, if you feel compelled to take on the mission of rehabilitating Jed, I know it would be futile to try to dissuade you. But I hope you won't be discouraged by the outcome. And I trust you aren't expecting me to participate."

Cassandra got up from the table and kissed Noah on the top of his head before she carried the dishes to the kitchen.

"I don't promise this will work out. But I've done so badly when it comes to my own children, I might as well do badly when it comes to someone else's too."

"You haven't done so badly with your kids, Sandy. They still talk to you!"

"That's only because I'm willing to listen to them complain."

As they were getting into bed that night, Cassandra told Noah that while she'd been working with the mollusks earlier that day, she'd been thinking about how long she'd been here at the cottage and wondering when it would be time to leave.

"You're talking about leaving? Again?"

"Don't worry, Noah. I don't have plans to leave anytime soon."

"I guess I should be grateful to the tarantulas, then, for keeping you here."

"I'm not staying here because of them, Noah. I can always find someone to adopt them, even though they're insecta non grata at Clarion. I'm staying here because—"

"Because you're afraid I'll get into trouble on my own?"

"No, because I realized that if I leave, I might miss you too much."

"So I'm stuck with you for the foreseeable future?"

"Something like that."

They folded the quilt back, and Noah sat down on the side of the bed, then eased himself down. Cassandra got into bed beside him, reached down, and pulled the quilt up over them both.

"I would like very much to make love to you," he said, "and I wonder if the inclination to do so is mutual."

"It is, but do you think we should wait until you've had more time to recover?"

"I think that would be both unnecessary and undesirable."

"Good," she said. "But there's something I need to do beforehand."

"What?"

"Reality check. I want you to see me as I am now." She reached up and turned on the light. Then she got out of bed and took off her clothes and stood there for him to look at her seventy-two-year-old body: great legs, but flabby breasts, belly bulge, and fleshy arms.

"You crazy, beautiful woman," he said. He reached up and grabbed her wrist. He pulled her down towards the bed, and she climbed in next to him. She reached over and turned off the light.

# XIX

Noah woke before it was properly morning. Cassandra was still asleep beside him, and he would have been content to lie there watching her, but he didn't want to risk the consequences of ignoring his bladder. Everything hurt as he marshaled his limbs and made his way to the bathroom, but considering his gymnastics with the ladder, he was in better shape than he would have expected. He was always achy in the morning, a victim of what he was told was arthritis, the favorite complaint among the Clarion constituency. He refused to believe in the condition. When his doctor had ascribed the chronic discomfort in his left shoulder to arthritis and said in a comforting tone, "It's seventy-two years old; things wear out; it's to be expected," he'd pointed out that his right shoulder was the exact same age and suffered no ill effects.

During Noah's brief absence, Melville had relocated from the foot of the bed to the floor on Noah's side of the bed and sprawled in such a way that he blocked Noah's access. Noah had to climb into bed via the foot and woke Cassandra as he crawled towards his pillow.

She rolled from her side to her back, flung an arm back over the pillow, and wrinkled her nose as she yawned. "I was dreaming about periwinkles," she said sleepily. "*Littorina littorea.*"

This was not a good segue to the subject he'd wanted to talk about, so instead he said, "I'll take that as an augury that we should forage for our dinner today."

"Are periwinkles any good for eating?"

"If you're a Lilliputian, perhaps. We'll concentrate on quahogs and oysters. Low tide is at eleven."

"Good. That gives you time to prepare a sumptuous breakfast for me." She smiled at him. "Isn't that what's done? The male of the species pampers the female of the species after a night of satisfying revelry." She pulled herself up to a sitting position and stuffed the pillows behind her head.

"I'm gratified to hear that it qualified as satisfying."

"Not just that; it was a relief to get it over with."

"Get it over with?" Noah asked.

"I mean we've been living in a kind of suspense all these weeks, trying to figure out where things were going, eyeing each other for clues, testing the limits, and . . ."

"Courting the inevitable?"

"You thought it was inevitable?"

"No, I hoped it was. Fulfillment of a fantasy I've harbored since we were in college."

"I was afraid of that. That's why I decided to disrobe so unromantically last night. I wanted to be sure you had no illusions that I had miraculously preserved my nineteen-year-old body."

"I think I prefer the matured version."

"The *aged* version," said Cassandra.

Noah stood up. Then he lowered himself down again and sat sideways on the bed. He was going to start by saying, "There's something I've been wanting to discuss with you," but decided that such preambles were merely procrastinating, so he plunged ahead and asked, "Do you think it would be reasonable for us to explore the possibility of solidifying our relationship in an official way?"

"Before breakfast?"

"There is a three-day waiting period after you submit an application," said Noah. "So we would get rather hungry."

Cassandra pulled a pillow from behind her head and threw it at him. He caught it in one hand. "I realize it might seem a bit premature, but I thought it would be reasonable to broach the subject, given that—"

"Oh, Noah! You're so old fashioned! Sex and marriage have absolutely nothing to do with each other."

"I'm just saying that it's something I'd like you to consider." He paused, then added, "Eventually."

"That's sweet of you, Noah, but we're much too old for marriage!"

"There are people who think we're much too old for sex," said Noah. He placed the pillow on her feet and got up to make breakfast.


After lunch Noah went up to Artie's house to ask him if he would pick up a paintbrush for him in addition to the varnish. As he hoped, Jed was in the garage with Artie, still working on the fishing tackle. He greeted both Artie and Jed. Jed did not look up at him, but Noah guessed that the friendliness of his greeting confirmed Jed's hope that he had not been identified by Noah the night before.

"I checked out my brushes," Noah told Artie, "and I have some that are probably good enough, but if I'm inaugurating a new can of varnish, I think investing in a new brush might be in order."

"I thought you'd say that," said Artie, "and I was planning to pick one up for you even if you didn't think you needed one. It doesn't pay to work with crappy brushes. I'll drop the stuff off for you later."

"It can wait for tomorrow," said Noah. "If you bring it by later this afternoon, I might feel compelled to start work, but I'd rather put it off till tomorrow. And I promised Cassandra I'd take it easy tonight. Stay in the house and do nothing more strenuous than play the cello. By the way, I hope that sound doesn't travel up the hill very well, but should you ever find my practicing loathsome, I trust you will let me know."

This brought a round of chuckles from Artie. "Haven't heard you playing yet," he said, "but don't think I'd mind if I did. It's not like you're playing bagpipes!"

"I didn't know bagpipes were out of favor around here," said Noah.

"Sound like dying whales," said Artie. "Give me the creeps."

"You have my assurance that I will be sure to stick with the cello, then."

Noah related all this to Cassandra at dinner, and when they were done eating, he put on a CD of Bach suites for cello, turned the volume up higher than it should have been, and drew the curtains. Cassandra was reading by the woodstove and looked relatively content, in spite of Bach, inappropriately loud. Noah waited by the window in the dark bedroom, then crept out to the barn as soon as he spotted a flicker of light in the small barn window. This time he trapped Jed in the back of the barn and aimed his flashlight on him.

"Hi, Jed. What are you doing here?" he asked. He'd heard the expression "deer caught in headlights," and even though he'd never seen a deer in such an unenviable situation, that was what Jed resembled now. He dropped whatever he'd been lifting and froze, open mouthed, staring into the light.

"Can I help you find something?" Noah asked.

Jed didn't move.

"Come to the cottage with me, and let's talk about what's going on."

Jed looked around, clearly trying to figure out a way to escape, but Noah was standing in the middle of the doorway.

"OK, Jed, here's the deal. Either you come with me now, or I call the police."

Jed, sniveling and shaky, emerged from the back of the barn. He didn't look at Noah, but he walked along beside him to the cottage. Cassandra had turned on the outside light and was standing by the opened door. Bach had been silenced.

"Hi. You must be Jed," she said. "I'm Cassandra." She smiled at him. Melville came trotting over as they went inside, and she put her hand on his collar. "Don't worry about Melville," she said. "He's big, but he's a sweetie. Of course you're not afraid of dogs. You have one, don't you?"

"Yeah," Jed admitted. It was the first word out of his mouth.

"Let's go sit in the living room," said Cassandra, and she pointed to the chairs, which she'd angled so they now faced the sofa.

Jed entered the living room tentatively and looked around as if he expected someone else might be there, lying in wait for him. The crickets rustled in their cage, and Jed stood still when he saw them and the stick insects and the terrariums with the tarantulas.

"What are those?" he asked, pointing with his chin.

"Crickets and stick insects," said Cassandra brightly, "and a pinktoe tarantula and a Chilean rose hair tarantula."

"Why do you have bugs in the house?"

"They're pets," said Cassandra. "Come meet them." She stepped towards the cages, but Jed backed away.

"Maybe later. I know they seem a little alarming, but they're quite friendly. Noah was hesitant about them at first, but even he has warmed to them."

"I have accepted them," said Noah. "But it would be a stretch to say that I have warmed to them."

"I'm sure *you'll* warm to them," Cassandra said to Jed. "Now sit down, both of you. I've put water on to boil, and I'm making us some hot chocolate. I found a mix in the back recesses of the cupboard, Noah, and it doesn't look too old, so I imagine it won't poison us. You like hot chocolate, don't you?" she asked Jed.

Jed shrugged.

"My theory is whenever there's a difficult conversation that needs to take place, it's always best to have something to eat or drink. It helps make things more comfortable. I also unearthed some chocolate chip cookies. I'll get them."

She returned with a package and handed it to Jed. "Open these up, and tell me what you think. They got somewhat squashed in the car, but they should still be edible. A lot of things got squashed in the car when we drove here, and of course there was Melville. You love to squash things, don't you, Baby?" She put her arms around the dog and kissed the side of his head. "I'll go see to the hot chocolate. The water should have boiled by now. I didn't watch it, of course, since it never boils if you do."

While she was in the kitchen, Jed obediently opened the package of cookies. He looked inside and then looked up at Noah somewhat help-lessly. Cassandra must been watching, because she called out, "They're packaged with those frilly paper muffin cups, so if the cookies are bro-ken, we'll each take a muffin cup, and we can nibble on the pieces."

Noah shrugged. "Go ahead," he said to Jed. Jed awkwardly lifted out a muffin cup and handed the bag to Noah.

The cookies were, indeed, in pieces. Noah took out the remaining two muffin cups and set them on the coffee table. "They probably taste OK," he said, and he ate a piece of cookie. He looked over at Jed, who ate a piece also. Neither of them said anything until Cassandra returned from the kitchen. She carried a tray with three mugs of hot chocolate. It was a decorative antique tin tray—black with painted fruit—that had been on display against the wall over the counter and had never been put to use before. She set it down on the table. "No marshmallows, I'm afraid," she said. There was hot chocolate powder around the rims of all three mugs. Cassandra rubbed her finger around one of them. "These can probably use some more stirring," she said. She licked her finger. "Cookies OK?" she asked Jed.

"Yeah," said Jed.

"I hope the hot chocolate is OK. I'd give it a minute to cool, though."

They sat, rather solemnly, eating bits of cookie and stirring the hot chocolate. Noah was reluctant to have Cassandra introduce the business at hand and break the almost-companionable mood, but eventually the cookies would be gone and the hot chocolate would be drunk—if it was drinkable, that is—and they couldn't just sit in silence all night. He looked questioningly at Cassandra, and as if she had picked up his cue, she began, "So, Jed. Why don't you tell us what's going on."

"Nothing," said Jed after a moment.

"What were you doing in the barn?"

"Nothing," said Jed.

"Oh, dear," said Cassandra, "this isn't going well at all. I'd like to be able to get to bed sometime tonight, so we really do need to get to work and tackle the problem. Here's the thing, Jed. We found the items you hid in the back of the barn, and we know you came tonight to get them. They're obviously stolen property, and I can understand how worried you must have been to have us turn up this early—I know Noah doesn't usually open up the cottage before May."

Jed looked as if he might say something, but then changed his mind. "Noah wanted to go to the police," continued Cassandra, "but since you're a friend—practically like family—I persuaded him to give you a chance to explain yourself first. So please do! Where did these things come from? And what were you planning to do with them?"

Jed busied himself with a rip in the knee of his jeans.

"Jed, please, help me out here. If you don't, I can't keep Noah from going to the police."

Jed looked up. His face was almost defiant now. "So I was in the barn, but I was just poking around. The stuff in the barn isn't mine."

"That's the heart of the problem," said Noah. He had intended to leave this whole interview to Cassandra, but he couldn't help jumping in. "If that was your laptop and electronic equipment and you were just storing it in my barn, even without asking me first, it would not be a matter of significant concern. But it's not your equipment. You clearly appropriated it."

"Stole it," explained Cassandra.

"You can't prove it!"

"I probably can't," said Noah, "but the police can. I expect it has your fingerprints on it."

Jed's face crumpled. He didn't cry out loud, but his chin dropped to his chest, and his shoulders shook. Noah could see that Cassandra was fighting an urge to reach out and lay her hand on Jed's shoulder.

"What house did you take it from?" he asked.

"McNallys'."

Noah turned to Cassandra. "One of those new, so-called trophy houses up the road." He looked back at Jed. "Breaking and entering is a crime," he said, "even if you don't take anything." He wasn't sure if this was true, but Jed wouldn't know either.

"I didn't break in," said Jed quickly. "The slider from their outdoor shower goes right into that big bathroom on the first floor, and it's been unlocked since they were here in the summer."

"So you went in and helped yourself to their property."

"They've got so much," said Jed. "They won't even notice."

"Although I understand the moral distinction," said Noah, "the penalty for stealing from the rich is no different from the penalty of stealing from the poor. What were you going to do with the stuff? Is there someone who was going to sell it for you?"

Jed looked down again.

"I know you don't want to rat on your friends," said Cassandra, her voice was softer than Noah's, "and I respect that. But we can't resolve this if we don't know the real story. You really need to talk to us, Jed."

Jed didn't say anything.

"Please, Jed," said Cassandra. She got up from her chair and pulled over the footstool so she sat right in front of him. "Talk to me. I know you're not the kind of kid who usually steals things. Who came up with the idea?"

"Skylar."

"Who's she?"

"My friend Brendan's sister."

"Were you going to bring the things to her?" Cassandra asked.

"Yeah. She can drive."

"And she was going to sell them for you and give you a little of the money?"

"Half!" said Jed.

"What do you want the money for?"

"I'm saving up to buy a pickup."

Noah thought of pointing out the fact that it was more than a year before Jed would be old enough to drive but decided not to say anything.

Cassandra stood up. "OK, here's what I propose," she said. "First thing: your parents need to know, so you're going to tell your mom everything. I'll call her and tell her what we've decided, and she can explain it all to your dad. Second thing: you're going to take all the things and put them back in the McNallys' house, exactly where you found them. Third and final thing: you're not going to have anything more to do with Skylar or Brendan." She hadn't consulted Noah on any of this, but Noah realized there was no reason that she should have since he'd left this part of it all to her.

"They'll be expecting me to give them the stuff," said Jed.

"You can tell them it's been discovered and confiscated. And you can tell them that Noah may be contacting the police. I think that will encourage them to keep their distance. And you know, Jed, Brendan hasn't been a very good friend to you."

"Do you have to tell my mom?"

Cassandra looked over at Noah. "I don't think Noah would want to keep things from your parents, Jed. And neither should you."

# XX

Cassandra went into the kitchen to call Bernice from the land line. Cell phone reception was imperfect, and she wanted to be able to talk with Bernice without having to repeat anything if she hadn't been clearly heard. While she explained to Bernice what had been going on, she glanced back at Jed. He was drawing invisible circles on the armrest of his chair. She was afraid he might start crying again.

"I need to give Melville his nightly walk," she said to Jed when she came back into the living room, "so I'll accompany you up to your house, OK?"

Jed shrugged.

"But there's something we need to do before we leave." She went over to the cage of stick insects, carefully took one out, and brought it over to show Jed. The stick insect was perched on her hand, like a piece of oversized exotic jewelry. Jed pulled back in his chair.

"Don't worry. It doesn't bite or sting."

Jed looked over at Noah for help, but Noah had no intention of intervening.

"It won't hurt you, Jed," said Cassandra. "It's quite gentle. Here, let it walk on you." She bent close so the stick insect could step onto Jed's forearm.

It moved with exquisite slowness, lifting one impossibly thin leg after another.

"Cool!" Jed whispered.

"Would you like to meet one of the tarantulas now?"

"I dunno," said Jed.

Cassandra returned the stick insect to its cage, took one of the tarantulas out of its terrarium, and brought it over to Jed.

"This is Marigold," she said. "Not all types of tarantulas are good to handle, but Marigold is a Chilean rose and quite docile. She's a pro at school visits. You can touch her."

Jed tentatively extended his forefinger and moved it across Marigold's back.

"She's beautiful, isn't she?" said Cassandra. "I think you're ready to hold her. Hold out your hand." She placed the tarantula on Jed's palm.

"Get your phone, Noah," said Cassandra. "I want you to take a photo of Jed with Marigold."

Noah found his phone on the kitchen counter, and Jed posed with the tarantula. He was looking down at it, a goofy look of amazement—staged, but also real—on his face.

"Would you be interested in having a tarantula to keep as a pet sometime?"

"Sure!" said Jed. It was a burst of enthusiasm she guessed Noah had not believed him capable of.

Cassandra walked up the driveway to Jed's house with him, Melville between them. She left Noah standing by the door and guessed he was watching them, following the bobbing flicker of their two flashlights as they moved beyond the reach of the outside light.

Bernice was waiting for them. She grasped Cassandra's hand as she thanked her, then turned, plaintively, to Jed. "I've always felt that Brendan was a bad influence on you," she said. "Noah has been so kind—he could have gone straight to the police! I hope you'll work to regain his trust."

"Jeez, Mom," said Jed, and ran upstairs to his room.

Cassandra said a hasty goodbye and walked quickly back down the hill to the cottage. She turned off the outside light when she came inside and sat down next to Noah by the fire.

"That went well, don't you think?" she said.

"You seem to have worked your magic on him."

"I think we worked very well as a team. Good cop. Not so good cop."

"Hardly a team," said Noah. "This was entirely your show. How did things go with Bernice and Artie?"

"Artie was watching TV, and Bernice thought it would be better to talk to him in the morning."

"She knows Artie."

"Bernice was so grateful to us for being understanding she practically wept."

"I can imagine."

"I think she's one of those rare people who's actually as sweet as she appears to be."

"I'm afraid so," said Noah.

Cassandra turned around on her chair so she was facing Noah and tucked her legs up underneath her. "I have an idea—"

"Oh no!" said Noah.

"Before you start groaning, hear me out. Jed is interested in making money, and I thought there are some jobs around here we could hire him for."

"Like what?"

"You could use his help with the boat."

"I don't need anyone's help with the boat!"

"No?"

"No!"

"Even if that were true, which it's not, this has less to do with you needing help, Noah. This is about giving Jed something to do besides playing video games and checking out online porn sites."

"There's plenty for him to do up at his house."

Cassandra gave Noah a look. "Yeah, right, just what he wants. He's miserable, Noah. He can't drive, so he can't go anywhere on his own, and he's stuck with his parents and some chickens."

"So how would working here be any different?"

"Because we're not his parents. And because we'll be paying him. If you're feeling so possessive about your boat—"

"I'm not possessive!"

"I have something else in mind for him, but I think it would be best for him to be working with you rather than on his own."

"I do not believe he appreciates my company, and certainly would not after what happened."

"I think he likes you, Noah, in spite of yourself."

"Doubtful."

Cassandra got up and crouched down in front of the woodstove. She prodded the logs with the poker till a shaft of flame curled up between them, then she pumped the bellows so the gray embers glowed pink, then flamed. When she turned back to Noah, she waited a moment before she spoke.

"I have a feeling that all this isn't just about Jed."

"What are you talking about?"

"I'm talking about your attitude towards Jed. There's something more going on here."

"What do you mean, my 'attitude'?"

"You're so unforgiving. It's as if you've been just responding to what Jed did, but you're unwilling to look beyond it to understand the *why*."

"You see me as unforgiving?"

Cassandra thought about what she wanted to say, then decided to just go ahead and say it. "It's not just Jed."

"I think we've talked about this more than enough," said Noah, and he started to get up. But Cassandra put her hands on his shoulders and shoved him, so he sank back into the chair.

"No, we haven't. And if you insist that we have, then there's no hope for us."

"What is it with you?"

Cassandra sat down on the floor in front of Noah, her arms around her knees. She looked up at the ceiling, the rough boards, honey colored, mottled with dark knotholes. Then she looked at him. "I'm old, Noah. I don't want to waste the time I have left on a superficial relationship. It's not a good investment."

"What do you want me to be talking about?"

"Your son."

"I fail to see why the discussion about Jed bears any relevance to Larry."

Cassandra tilted her head, waiting for him to say something more. When he didn't, she asked, "What happened that you still aren't able to forgive Larry?"

"What makes you think I can't forgive him?"

"The fact that you're seventy-two years old and you're still holding back from settling your will."

"I've already explained the circumstances more than I intended to. Elizabeth did something unforgivable. And Larry was complicit."

"Complicit! That makes him sound like a criminal!"

"I'll rephrase it then: Larry allowed it to happen. So it should not surprise you that I'm just not ready to make everything over to them."

"But you didn't tell me what she did."

Noah took in a breath. He looked straight at Cassandra, but the soft flesh at the corner of his eye pulsed. "When Helene was in her final days, she wanted to see her grandchildren for a last time before she died. Elizabeth decided the hospital would be upsetting for Cammie and Richard, and she wouldn't let Larry bring them."

What was it about grief, its power to resurface, the way it moved from being simply a construct in the mind to something tangible, something that affected your entire body?

"How cruel that seems," she said gently. "Yet I can understand it, in a way. Elizabeth was protecting her children—at least she believed she was protecting them."

"Helene was dying."

"Even then, Elizabeth prioritized her children. That's what mothers do. That's what you should want the mother of your grandchildren to do."

"And Larry? You want me to forgive him for not standing up to her?"

"I see why it's hard for you: you feel he chose his wife over his mother." Cassandra reached up and laid her hand on top of Noah's. She gripped his hand, pressing his thumb close against his forefinger. "But might you have done the same? Sided with your wife?"

"Not if my mother was dying, stuck in a hospital bed, tethered to a battery of wires and tubes."

"Did Larry visit her in the hospital?"

"Of course."

"That must have been so upsetting for him. Seeing his mother reduced like that, and feeling helpless, unable to rescue her. I know how painful it is to witness what can happen to someone you love."

Cassandra loosened her hold of Noah's hand, pressed her palm against his palm, and slipped her fingers down so they were between his, rooted together.

"All these years you've been viewing this as a contest of allegiance. Larry, torn between the needs of his mother and the concerns of his wife, choosing his loyalty to his marriage over his ties to his childhood. But you haven't been thinking about Larry, himself. My guess is that Larry sympathized with Elizabeth because he'd been frightened by seeing his mother dying, and he wanted to spare his children from being frightened, too—and being in that hospital room, they would be, even if they were too young to understand what was going on." Cassandra shuddered. "Hospitals still frighten me! And I'm not a child anymore. Larry didn't want his children to remember his mother as she was at the end; he didn't want them always to associate her with the raw fear they'd felt when they were in the hospital."

"And what about Helene? What about what she wanted?"

"What the dying wish for counts, of course, but other people's wishes matter too. Larry was sad and frightened and vulnerable. There was no good choice, but he chose as he did not from a lack of caring for his mother, but from a love of his children. And surely, Noah, you should be able to forgive him that."

Cassandra raised Noah's hand to her face and kissed his knuckles. "Come," she said. "We've talked enough." She stood, and he let her draw him up from the chair. He closed the doors of the woodstove. They put their arms around each other as they walked to the bedroom. They walked slowly, as if they'd been invalids and were just testing out their first steps.

# XXI

Residents over the age of sixty-five got a greatly discounted rate for an annual shellfish permit, one of the few perks of being classifiable as a "senior" that Noah appreciated. He had sent away for the permit and gotten it in the mail before leaving Clarion, and he'd immediately put it in his cello case so he wouldn't forget to bring it with him to the Cape. It came in a plastic sleeve with a pin on the back, and when the weather started getting warmer and he felt ready to go out clamming, he attached it to his battered fishing hat.

"The shellfish warden has never paid a visit to this stretch of beach and is unlikely to venture out here now," Noah told Cassandra, "but we'll take just one clam basket and one clam rake, since you don't have a license."

"Do illegally harvested clams taste any better than legally harvested ones?"

"I have never eaten an illegally harvested clam, so I wouldn't know."

"Of course not!" said Cassandra. "Foolish me. Does that mean I'm just coming along to watch?"

"Hardly. I am counting on your full participation. Take a pail."

"Ah, a slight bending of the rules."

"I've been learning from you."

They went out to the barn together, and Noah dug out the clam rake and wire basket and put on his high black boots. Cassandra got her rubber boots from her car.

"You thought to bring those with you?"

"No, I just always leave them in the back of the car. Don't look so surprised, Noah. If you study odonates, you have to be prepared for wading in ponds and mucky places. What I could use, though, are some waterproof gloves. I'm leaving the clamming to you. I'll gather the oysters."

He was about to say that there must be some gloves somewhere that Helene had used but decided not to. Cassandra might feel awkward about wearing something of Helene's—even if he could find them—and maybe gloves were like a dead person's shoes. Instead he said, "Take mine."

They were old gloves with frayed cuffs and much too big for Cassandra's hands. She waggled her fingers at him. "What will you wear?"

"I have some work gloves that will suffice. I do not intend to get my hands wet."

As they set off to Noah's favorite clamming area, Melville followed along with them, wandering off now and then, sometimes by land, sometimes by sea. The tide was still going out, which is what Noah preferred. When he didn't manage to get out until after the tide had already turned, the water always seemed to rise too fast, and it undermined the serenity of clamming. Clamming wasn't about the clams but the enterprise of collecting them. If it was just the clams or oysters you wanted, you could buy them at the seafood market. They weren't that expensive out here and were readily available.

Noah waded out into calf-deep water and started raking. He fell into a natural rhythm. It took a while before he hit anything promising. He'd been clamming since he was a boy and was able to tell by feel alone whether the tines of his clam rake were prodding a quahog or just a rock or empty shell, as if the rake were an extension of his own arm, viscerally connected. Sympathy of man and rake, he thought. He found only an occasional cherrystone or littleneck, but after a while he struck a prolific spot for chowder clams. They were fine for clam sauce if he chopped them well. He leaned on the handle of his clam rake and watched Cassandra making her way along the edge of the water. Occasionally she nudged something with her foot—he guessed she was overturning oysters to see if they were viable or just shells—and sometimes she bent down, picked something up, and added it to her pail.

The sun had been allowing itself to be obscured by clouds now and then, but the day was pleasant. But after they'd been clamming for a while, the sun's showings were more infrequent and the sky was darkening, and Noah grew concerned about the weather. When he'd checked predictions before they left the cottage, there had been a 30 percent chance of rain showers or a stray thunderstorm. "Possibility of showers," it had said. What was the magic percentage when possible morphed into probable? He hated having to gamble about the weather. He just wanted to be informed definitively: rain or no rain. When his clam basket was two-thirds full, enough clams for sauce for dinner for two nights, he waded to shore and caught up with Cassandra.

"How have you been doing?"

She tilted her pail to show him. In addition to oysters, she'd collected shells, rocks, a corroded piece of iron that might have once been anything, and a brick that had come from God knows where and spent enough time in the sea its corners were rounded like a loaf of bread.

"Ready to head back soon?" he asked.

"I could be."

"It's looking like it might actually rain."

"OK, let's go then," said Cassandra. She turned and called out, "Melville, this way!" and they started back to the cottage. Noah reached to take her pail for her, but she held on to it.

They walked a while longer, and Noah debated how best to bring up again the subject he still had on his mind. Finally he just went ahead and braved it: "I wonder if you'd be amenable to telling me in advance any reasons you might come up with for turning me down if I asked you to marry me."

Cassandra set her pail down on the sand and turned to him. "Noah! You're thinking about that again?"

"I have been."

"You're not serious about this, are you?"

He put the clam basket down, too, and stuck the rake in the sand so the handle rested across the metal basket. "Why shouldn't I be?"

"Is that why you knew about the three-day waiting period? You researched it?"

"I thought I should be fully informed."

"Oh, dear," said Cassandra. "I was afraid of this. Are you interested in the practical reasons or the romantic reasons?"

"Both, I suppose, should there be any."

"All right, then, I'll tell you. Starting with the romantic, the reason would be that, in all this time, you've never even told me you loved me."

"Wouldn't that be implied when I asked you to marry me?"

"Not necessarily. It could be a marriage of convenience."

Noah laughed. "Sandy, with you, nothing is ever convenient. I'd call it a marriage of inconvenience!" He was relieved that she laughed too.

"OK, then. The practical reasons. Where shall I begin? Number one, the most obvious: I'm not a very good marriage bet. I've done it three times already with limited success."

"I'm aware of that, and I'm more than willing to take my chances. You could have been married a dozen times before, but you've never been married to *me*."

"All right, on to number two, then: it's unlikely our children would give their consent."

"We won't ask them. We'll inform them ex post facto."

Sandy took in a deep breath and exhaled slowly. "Number three: we haven't known each other for very long—only a few months."

"Not so. As you pointed out to Larry, we've known each other since we were in college more than fifty years ago."

"But that doesn't count."

"Of course it counts."

"OK, on to number four: it would be premature. We ended up thrown together here only because of some issues that arose at Clarion. If they were serving cordon bleu brown-bag suppers, we might still be back there, and we probably wouldn't even have held hands yet."

"Being here did accelerate the process of intimacy. It is, possibly, one of the most notable benefits my humble cottage provides."

It took Cassandra a moment before she continued. Finally she said: "Number five: there's no point in getting married. In the old days you got married in order to have sex, and obviously we bypassed that. Or you got married when the girl got knocked up, and you 'had' to. But if I got knocked up, it would be enough of a miracle I'd be a shoo-in for canonization once I'm dead, and even then we still wouldn't *have* to get married."

"I think there *is* a point in getting married," said Noah. "I wouldn't have proposed it if I didn't." He didn't feel up to talking about it anymore. He reached down and picked up the clam rake and slung it on his shoulder, picked up the clam basket, and started walking quickly back to the cottage again. Cassandra kept up with him.

"I'm sorry, Noah," she said. "I didn't realize you were serious about this. I thought you were just—"

He turned sharply towards her. "Just what?"

"Playing with the idea."

"Maybe that's what you were doing," he said, and he couldn't keep what probably sounded like anger out of his voice. "But I've been serious." He started walking again, but she came and stood right in front of him, blocking his way.

"Why?" she asked him. "Why would you want to marry me?"

"Because I want to be your husband. Because I want you to be my wife."

"Why can't we just continue to be together as we are?"

"Because we're seventy-two years old. We have what? Ten, fifteen decent years left—if we're lucky—and we should make the most of it before it's too late. Because there's no earthly reason to settle for anything less."

She stared at him and swayed a little before she said, "It's not that I wouldn't want to marry you; it's that I don't think I should get married again."

"*Should?* Since when were you ruled by 'should'?"

She didn't have a response. They were both done with talking. Suddenly all the aches of his body reasserted themselves, clamoring to be noticed because he'd been focused on other things and forgotten about them for a while. "Let's get back to the cottage before the rain," he said. He picked up the rake and the clam basket. Cassandra picked up her pail, and they walked side by side, pail and clam basket between them.

At the cottage Noah put the quahogs in a pot of water. He put the oysters in the sink and scrubbed them with a brush. "I thought I'd grill the oysters and we'll have them now, and I'll make clam sauce for dinner later."

"Don't you eat oysters raw on the half shell?"

"Grilling them opens them easily and kills some of the pathogens."

"Good old pathogens! I'll get us something to drink. Prosecco goes with oysters; shall I open a bottle?"

It seemed inappropriately celebratory to Noah, but he said, "If you like." He went outside and got the grill going and laid the oysters on it. He was glad when Cassandra came out with wineglasses for the prosecco. The champagne flutes would have been too festive.

"Have you seen Melville anywhere?" she asked.

"I don't believe I have."

"He must be around somewhere." She got up and walked around the cottage. He listened to her calling for him. When she returned she sat down in the Adirondack chair close to the grill.

"He'll turn up soon," she said. "He always does." She poured the prosecco into the glasses and took a sip of hers without toasting anything first. Noah placed the grilled oysters on a cookie sheet and set it on the table. He used his oyster knife to open the shells fully.

"These are yummy grilled," said Cassandra after she'd tried one.

"Somewhat overcooked," said Noah. It had begun to rain—so faintly that it was still possible to ignore it.

"You don't have to be like this."

"Like what?"

"Come on, Noah."

When he didn't respond, she went on. "I haven't left, have I? I'm here with you. We're here together."

He looked at her but still didn't say anything.

"I'd thought everything was nicely settled between us. I wish you felt that was enough."

He still didn't say anything. The rain was more obvious now. He watched dark spots appear on the table; first, each wet circle had an area of dry surface around it, but soon they multiplied and converged, and the wood was entirely darkened.

"Listen, Noah, I'm cautious about marriage, for good reason. But if it makes you happy, I'm willing to think about it, sometime—maybe—in the future. I promise you. But please, can't we just enjoy this time now?"

He sighed. "I'll try," he said. He took a sip of the prosecco. It was undeniably raining now. "We should move inside; no reason to get soaked." He took the tray of oysters, and she took the glasses and the bottle. They got inside just in time. Lightning suddenly whitened the sky, followed by thunder so loud it sounded as if the cottage had been bombed. Cassandra stood in the doorway, calling for Melville, but he didn't appear.

"When did you last see him?" she asked Noah.

"I don't remember. I thought he came with us when we started walking back here, but I can't be sure."

"That's just it. I know I called him, and he turned back our way, but I didn't check that he was following us. I just assumed he was. He's terrified of thunder, Noah. When there's a thunderstorm, he climbs onto the bed and burrows under the pillows."

She stuck her head out in the rain. "Melville!" she called him again, her voice plaintive as the cry of a gull.

"He'll turn up," said Noah, though as soon as he said it, he wasn't entirely sure this was true.

Cassandra started out the door, but Noah grabbed her arm. "You can't go out there now, Sandy."

"I've got to find him!"

"Just wait till the lightning passes."

"It's my fault. I should have made sure he returned with us."

"It's nobody's fault," said Noah. He was standing behind Cassandra, watching the rain hammering the deck where they had been sitting not that long before. He reached over and put his arm around her. "We'll go out looking for him soon as the storm's over."

Cassandra leaned around to face him.

"I didn't know you cared about Melville."

"I care about you."

It was already getting dark when the storm passed and the rain softened. They put on boots and raincoats and took flashlights with them. Cassandra searched around the property, calling for Melville, and Noah went to explore the barn. It seemed unlikely that a dog that big could have wedged the barn door open enough to get through, but Noah knew the determination of desperate animals. He flipped on the lights and looked all around, calling Melville's name, but there was no sign of him. He met up with Cassandra behind the bunkhouse. "I'll call Artie and Bernice. They may have seen him," he said.

"I'm going down the beach where we went clamming."

"I'll come with you."

"No, it's better you go up towards the road and look for him there."

"All right," he said. He started to give her a hug, but she was intent on leaving. As he watched her rush off, he felt a wave of misgivings and almost ran after her. She looked so small in the gray distance.

Jed was the one who answered the phone when Noah called Artie and Bernice's house. Noah was caught off guard by this. When Jed informed him that neither Artie nor Bernice were around and asked, "What's up?" Noah hesitated for a minute, then told him about Melville.

"Haven't seen him around here," Jed said. "How long has he been missing?"

"We're not sure, exactly," said Noah, and he felt a bit embarrassed about this. "Sometime before the storm hit. And he's afraid of thunder."

"Luke's like that. Any big noise and he hides wherever he can. He likes to dig under the old boathouse out towards the jetty. He's got a pit under there where he hangs out."

"Under the old boathouse?"

"Yeah. Want to take a look there? I'll show you."

It had not occurred to Noah to seek Jed's help at this time—or any time, for that matter. But he said, simply, "All right."

They met on the driveway. It was still drizzling, and Jed wasn't wearing a raincoat, just a sweatshirt. But that was the way kids were nowadays, Noah remembered, they were defiant of the weather. In the distance he could hear Luke barking in protest of having been left behind.

"Did you bring Melville's leash?" Jed asked.

Noah hadn't thought of this.

"Better grab some rope, then," Jed said, and as they passed the barn, Noah liberated a piece of rope from one of the kayaks. The tide was up, so as they walked down the beach, they stayed close to the dune edge. Noah had wondered about searching for dog prints, but if there had been any, they'd been obliterated by the rain.

The boathouse was ramshackle and probably hadn't been used to store boats for years. The roof had begun caving in, and the rain was abetting the process.

"Let's take a look," said Jed.

"Taking a look" involved Noah getting on his hands and knees in the wet sand and crawling along the boathouse, shining his flashlight where there were openings in the cinder block foundation. He was afraid that he might never be able to straighten out the curl of his back.

"Farther along here," called Jed, who was on his belly, squirming into a tunnel in the sand. Noah crawled towards him. Jed swept his flashlight around. Luke had certainly hollowed out an impressive lair for himself, a warren of tunnels through the sand. Cowering in the deepest pit was Melville.

"Melville," called Noah. "Come on out!"

Melville whimpered and thumped his tail but didn't seem to want to budge.

"Hey, Baby," said Noah, imitating Cassandra's voice, "we're here to take you home!"

"Did you bring any dog treats?" asked Jed.

"I'm afraid not," Noah admitted.

"I think I got something," said Jed. He twisted around so he could dig into his pocket. He extracted not a dog bone but a half-eaten power bar. Cassandra had told Noah that chocolate was toxic to dogs, but this, at least, was encrusted with nuts, and there wasn't that much chocolate. Melville was a very big dog, so it probably wouldn't hurt him. More to the point: there was no alternative.

"Here you go, Melville. Look what I got for you!" said Jed, and he slithered towards Melville, hand extended. When Melville nosed towards him to snatch the treat, Jed grabbed him by the collar. It was up to Noah to wriggle his way to them and secure Melville with the rope. He and Jed managed to drag out the wet, sandy dog. Had he thought to bring his cell phone with him, he would have texted the good news to Cassandra, but he was fairly certain she had neglected to carry her cell phone with her as well.

Dog and mistress had a wet and joyful reunion near the cottage. Noah wanted to thank Jed, but Jed started up the driveway before he could. Jed was soaked and sandy, and he looked like a young kid, holding his arms crossed over his chest to keep warm.

Noah did not protest when Cassandra used his favorite beach towel to attempt to dry Melville, or when she brought him inside so he could deposit sand and puddles wherever he walked. And after their very late dinner, he pretended not to notice when Melville settled beside Cassandra up on the sofa.

When they got into bed, Cassandra rubbed Noah's back. He didn't think it would have much effect on the pain he anticipated experiencing in the morning, but he loved the feel of her hands as they kneaded his shoulder blades, as they moved up and down his spine. The bedroom smelled of wet dog.

Cassandra kissed the back of his neck and sat up in bed beside him. He rolled to his side.

"I'm glad you've made your peace with Jed," she said. "You are a sweet, kind, loving man," she said, "in spite of your best attempts to disguise the fact. And if I were ever foolish enough to consider marrying anyone, I would probably choose you."

"But?"

"I didn't say 'but.'"

"You took in your breath at the end of your sentence, as if you were about to add a qualifying clause."

"All right, then. *But* I'm not there yet."

Noah pulled himself up so he was sitting beside her. "What is it you need to get there? Would it help if I slayed the Nemean lion? Cleaned the Augean stables?"

"I don't think so." Cassandra laughed. She snuggled down in the bed, and when he lay down beside her, she pressed close against him, the side of her face nestled in the warm space beneath his shoulder.

# XXII

Jed worked with Noah on the boat on weekends and on weekday afternoons when he came home from school. It stayed light so much later now, and sometimes Bernice would have to call to remind Jed it was time for dinner. Cassandra occasionally poked her head in the barn to watch them. They didn't talk much, but they worked harmoniously together. Jed seemed eager to please Noah, and Noah occasionally remembered Cassandra's advice to praise Jed anytime his work warranted it.

"How's school doing these days?" Cassandra asked Jed when she came by to see how the boat was coming along.

"It sucks," said Jed.

"That bad?"

"The teachers don't know what they're doing. Homework is a joke. Half the kids don't bother with it, but my parents make me do it. They're on my back all the time. They want me to be 'learning something.'" Jed attempted to imitate Bernice's voice.

"Well, aren't you?"

"Yeah, right. I'd rather be working here."

"How's it going?" Cassandra put the question to both Jed and Noah.

Jed's face brightened. "We could have her in the water tomorrow!" He looked to Noah.

"It's possible," said Noah.

"You coming out with us?" Jed asked Cassandra.

"I don't think so," said Cassandra. "I'm not really a sailor."

"It's a cool boat."

"So it is. But I can admire it from the shore."

Jed looked at her slyly. "Scared?"

"Maybe. A little. Sailboats tip."

"Yeah, well, they have to, don't they, if you want to get any speed going."

"Exactly," said Cassandra.

"Hey, it's like touching the tarantula. It's kind of scary at first, but then after you've done it a bit, it isn't scary anymore."

"An excellent observation," said Noah.

"It's quite different," said Cassandra. "No one gets seasick touching a tarantula."

With Artie's help, Noah and Jed launched *Sarabande* at high tide the next day. Cassandra kept Melville from following them when they rowed out in the dinghy, and she kept him by her side while she stood on shore and videoed the maiden voyage. *Sarabande* looked like a toy sailboat in the distance, moving smoothly out in the harbor, obedient to the wind. After *Sarabande* was back at its mooring and Jed had gone home, Cassandra and Noah sat in the Adirondack chairs, looking out at the water. The tide was going out, but *Sarabande* was still afloat, blithely unaware that in less than two hours she would be mired, ignominiously, on the flats.

"It looks like you've had a proper reward for all your hard work."

"There are still a few more things that could be done—"

"Noah, it's never going to be perfect. Just enjoy the fact that you managed to get the boat in the water today. Jed looked radiant. It's sweet that you've established this rapport with him. Did it remind you of working with Larry when he was a kid?"

"Larry wasn't as sullen as Jed. But he also wasn't as good with his hands."

"Jed does seem fairly capable, when he chooses to be."

"I wish you'd come out with us."

"I was quite content watching the two of you."

"Jed is right; I think you would like sailing if you gave it a chance."

"We don't have to do everything together, Noah. I just don't feel this draw towards sailboats that you do. And you're not particularly enthralled by insects. It's OK that we feel passionate about different things. Relationships thrive on differences."

"I hate that word."

"Passionate?"

"Relationship."

"What would you call what we have?"

Noah shrugged but didn't say anything.

Cassandra waited, and then decided to talk about something else. "Now that the *Sarabande* is happily launched, I can employ Jed for my little project."

Noah seemed happy to change the subject too. "That's right. You had something up your sleeve. What are your plans for corrupting our young friend?"

Cassandra smiled. "We're going to be growing vegetables."

"What? Here?" Noah pointed to the sandy hillside behind them and laughed. "You'd do better farming seaweed in the bay."

"That's next," Cassandra said. "But I'm going to rely on raised beds for now. I was going to surprise you with them, but come inside and I'll show you what I ordered."

Noah sighed and got up and followed her into the cottage. He put on his reading glasses and looked at the images on the website she showed him of wooden raised beds overflowing with green produce.

"Those are digitally enhanced photos," Noah said. "No one's garden turns out like that."

"Spoken like a true pessimist. I intend to produce enough to open a farm stand up by the road."

"I don't know why you had to spend all that money on fancy kits. There are some old boards in the barn you could have used."

"They're not cedar; I checked," said Cassandra. "And these are aesthetically pleasing raised beds."

Noah took off his glasses and looked at her. "Why are you doing this, Sandy?"

Cassandra sat down on the arm of the chair. "I guess I like the idea of growing our own food. It's like the satisfaction of foraging. If I grow enough spinach, we can subsist on oysters Rockefeller—minus the cheese. And growing things is supposed to be therapeutic, a way to deal with the stress of life."

"It sounds to me like a project you created to transform Jed from a fledgling felon into an organic gardener."

"That too," said Cassandra, and she patted Noah's arm.

"I'm sure Bernice and Artie are grateful."

"So grateful that Bernice has commissioned her entire band of chickens to produce fertilizer for me."

"I believe it's called a *flock* of chickens."

"I prefer 'band.' 'Flock' makes them seem religious. 'Band' is musical. I've ordered organic seeds online, and Bernice has a friend with a greenhouse who's giving me some flats of seedlings."

"Bernice is a treasure, and now that you've taken an interest in Jed's welfare, she will be indebted to you forever."

"That's good, right?"

"Wearing, perhaps, but certainly good. Where were you planning on putting this garden of yours?"

Cassandra walked across the room to the front of the cottage. She pointed out the window. "Right there. With your permission, of course."

"How about out by the bunkhouse?"

"Too far for the hose to reach."

"OK," said Noah. "This is your project. I'll do my best to stay out of it entirely."

What neither of them mentioned was the way gardening spoke to the future. If Cassandra invested in planting vegetables, it seemed to imply she'd stick around to harvest them, but she assured herself the project wasn't a commitment to staying: the lettuce would grow, Jed would water it, Noah would eat it, whether she was there or not. But she could tell that Noah felt reassured by her gardening and viewed it as her unspoken promise to stay through the growing season at least. But maybe the promise was to herself. Stay here, Sandy, she told herself, stay here and give this life a chance. She'd have to take the risk that the longer she stayed, the more involved she would become with Noah.

It took longer than Cassandra had hoped for the raised-bed kits that she'd ordered to arrive. Apparently everyone in the country had decided to grow vegetables, and raised beds were currently in style. The delivery truck wouldn't venture down the driveway, since they were afraid they wouldn't be able to get back up again, so the cardboard boxes were deposited up at the road in the morning. They sat there all day, and fortunately it didn't rain, so Jed didn't have to haul soggy boxes, just heavy ones. Flush with a sense of authority (Cassandra had used the word "manage" when she'd hired him), he'd insisted on lugging the boxes down to the cottage himself, though both Noah and Artie had offered to help.

The cedar boards for the raised beds were smooth and unblemished, and when Cassandra started opening the boxes, the smell was so evocative she sat down on one of the unopened boxes to let the memory work itself through. With startling clarity she remembered the cedar-paneled closet in her parents' bedroom in her childhood home. It was her favorite hiding place for games of hide-and-seek with her sister, Judy. She'd crouch in the dark closet between the garment bags that held her father's World War II uniform on one side and a strapless silk dress of her mother's on the other—her parents' love stuffed into that closet with the clothes that survived from when that love had been real. She'd try to keep absolutely still while she heard Judy on the stairs calling, "Here I come, ready or not!" Judy invariably discovered her hiding in the closet, and Cassandra suddenly realized that Judy had always known where to find her and had deliberately taken longer than necessary, looking in unlikely places, calling out, "Not here! Not here!" prolonging the game as a kindness to her little sister. It was unsettling to discover this about Judy all these years later.

Cassandra and Judy exchanged cards at Christmas and penned in brief updates at the bottom, but it had been close to a year since they'd spoken. Cassandra was always the one to call. She resented this but called periodically anyway. It was a good time to do it now, since the cedar boards offered an excuse to get in touch. Talking with Judy was always stressful—Cassandra had to be careful to avoid subjects that might stir up old issues—but she decided she'd make herself call that evening.

It was a relief to get up and work on assembling the raised beds with Jed. The cedar boards were well crafted. The six-foot-long boards dovetailed perfectly with the three-foot-long boards, and the frame fit together as neatly as a puzzle. The metal posts slipped down smoothly into the holes drilled at the corners to secure them.

"Hey, this is cool!" said Jed when they had completed the first rectangle and found that it was sturdy. "Bet this is how they make coffins." Jed lay down on the ground inside the bin.

Cassandra had a sudden image she'd once seen in the news of mourners keening over the coffin of a child who'd been a victim of gun violence.

"Get up, Jed," she said.

Jed closed his eyes and crossed his arms over his chest.

"Jed, cut it out!" she cried.

Jed sat up, surprised. "Hey, what's the problem?" he asked.

"Just get out of there."

Jed got to his feet and climbed out of the bin. "I was just fooling around."

She was going to say something about the inappropriateness of fooling around about something like this, but that wasn't all of it. She'd imagined her raised bins of vegetables as an optimistic investment in the future—she didn't want them to be contaminated by images of death. She didn't want to think about David Sussman and the man who had been in therapy with John for decades.

"There are already real people dying these days," she said. "I'd rather not be reminded of them."

"It was just a joke," said Jed. And he sullenly began work on the next bin.

The dump truck bringing the loam was initially more courageous than the delivery truck. It started backing down the driveway but lost heart at the steep curve and drove back up to the road. It dumped the loam where the boxes of cedar planks had once been. It took Jed many wheelbarrow loads to cart it all down. He shoveled it into the bins, and Cassandra saw that the minimum order of loam she'd had delivered was much more than they needed. She offered the rest to Bernice for her flower garden and incurred Bernice's typical outpouring of gratitude.

The soil was a dark brown and looked artificial compared with the sandy soil around it. It was soft and moist to the touch. Alien soil confined to wooden enclosures, it smelled of field rather than sea, and Cassandra wondered where it had been imported from.

"Doesn't it just look like it's awaiting its plants?" Cassandra asked Jed. Jed wrinkled his brow. "Whatever."

While Noah made dinner, Cassandra went into the bedroom to make her call. "I just wanted to say hello, Judith, and see how you are doing," she said when her sister answered the phone. She'd reminded herself to call her Judith, not Judy.

"How nice of you," said Judy. "We're both quite well. How are you?"

She never asked about the girls or the grandchildren, but Cassandra let that pass. "OK. We're all fine."

"That's good," said Judy.

There was a bit of silence, then Cassandra said, "I wanted you to know that I sold my house and moved to a senior living community."

"It's about time! You're younger than I am, Sandy, but you're not young anymore. Where is it?"

"Here, in Massachusetts."

"If you were going to move, you should have at least come to some-place warm, like Arizona," said Judy. Then she added, "We love it here," something she'd said countless times before.

"I've been hearing about the drought out there. How are things doing?"

"It's not anywhere around where we are. I don't know where the news outlets get their stories. They just want to get people to buy newspapers."

"I read that Arizona farmers are having a hard time, and some farms won't be able to survive because they can't get enough water."

"Oh, Sandy, you've always been so dramatic. Don't believe every-thing the fearmongers tell you! It may be a little dry now, but that's just the way it always is. Everything will be fine soon."

"I hope that's true, but I'm a biologist, Judith; I worry about things like climate change."

"Climate change! There you go again! Daddy's little scientist."

Cassandra sat down on the side of the bed. "Don't do this, Judith. Please. I just called to say hello, see how you were."

There was a pause on the other end of the call, then an audible sigh. "That was very nice of you."

"I'd been thinking about you because I was remembering us playing hide-and-seek when we were kids and how I used to hide upstairs in the cedar closet."

"Cedar closet? I don't remember any cedar closet."

"In Mom and Dad's bedroom, where they kept all the old clothes."

"I don't remember anything about it," said Judy.

"It was to the left of the door to the hall."

"As Mom often pointed out, you've always had an overactive imagination."

Noah called her for dinner, but it wasn't until he came to the door and tapped that Cassandra stood up.

"Everything all right?" he asked when she opened the door.

"I'm just battered from my call with Judy."

"Sisters!" said Noah. "Come and eat."

Artie had brought them striped bass, and Noah had grilled it outside. He kept looking at Cassandra, clearly eager for her response, and when she didn't say anything, he finally asked, "How did you like the fish?"

"It's good."

"That's it? Just 'good'?"

"It's the best bass I've ever eaten. How's that? Sorry, Noah, I'm still in recovery mode from my phone call." Cassandra put down her fork. "Judy thinks my worry about climate change is overly dramatic. It's like trying to talk to Laurel and her husband!"

"Unfortunately, they're not alone! There are a lot of people who don't share your worries about the environment."

"It's not just that. We don't ever have a conversation without her dredging up old grievances. It never changes. She's still resentful of me because she thinks Daddy loved me best."

"Why do you call her if she gets you upset each time?"

"Because she's my sister."

"And?"

"I feel an obligation to stay in touch with her."

"You shouldn't."

"It's not that easy."

"Be realistic, Sandy. Accept it for what it is, and move on."

"It's not like you and your brother."

"What do you mean?"

"You said you never call your brother. And he doesn't call you. But that doesn't seem to bother you."

"Sandy, my relationship with my brother is entirely different from your relationship with your sister. We have no unresolved childhood issues. We just don't feel a need to call each other."

"There are always some unresolved childhood issues with siblings!"

"Like your daughters?"

Cassandra sat back. She was about to say that the situation between Laurel and Maggie had no bearing on her situation with Judy. But maybe it did. But even if it did—or maybe *especially* if it did—Noah's remark stung.

"Would you like some dessert? There's still some of Bernice's pie left."

"No thanks."

Noah got up and started carrying the dishes to the kitchen.

Cassandra stayed at the table. "You haven't been particularly sympathetic. Talking with Judy is always tough for me."

Noah laid the dishes down on the counter and turned back to her. "What do you want me to say?"

"How about 'I'm sorry'?"

"I've been trying to be realistic."

"They are not mutually exclusive," said Cassandra, and she got up and went to the bedroom, leaving Noah to wash the dishes.

In bed that night she pulled away when Noah seemed to want to make love, but when she woke in the morning, she found she was snuggled against him. In her sleep she had either forgiven him or forgotten what she'd been angry about.

The next day Cassandra went to pick up the vegetable flats from Bernice's friend Julie, who lived near Provincetown. It was the first time Cassandra had driven anywhere by herself since they'd come to the Cape, the first time she'd been this far away from Noah. She felt vulnerable and strange, but she also felt liberated to be on her own. She rolled the window in the back partway down for Melville. He stuck his muzzle outside and lapped up the wind.

Julie's house was down a sandy road that wound through a forest of locust trees and pitch pines. There was a barn along the driveway, and two horses trotted to the fence and eyed the car warily. Cassandra pulled up close to the house. Julie had heard the car, and she came to the door to greet her. She was a tiny woman, her gray hair pulled back into a scraggly ponytail. She had a sweet, vague manner like Bernice's, and Cassandra could see why they would be friends. Julie pointed to the flats of vegetables she'd placed out on the steps.

"There are three kinds of lettuce," she said, "but the romaine will hold up the best. The rainbow chard doesn't look quite perky now, but it will come back fine. Do you prefer lacinato kale or russian?"

"I'm new to kale," said Cassandra.

"I've given you some of each," said Julie. "You'll have to let me know which you like."

Cassandra wanted to pay her for the vegetables, but Julie refused.

"We all help each other out! And Bernice has been giving me eggs for years. She'd like to give me chickens too," said Julie, "but I just can't get enthusiastic about them. Are you getting some?"

"Just eggs. My dog doesn't approve of chickens." Cassandra gestured back towards the car where Melville, nose out the window, panted amiably.

When she returned to Noah's cottage, Cassandra set the flats on top of the raised beds, but she didn't begin to plant them. Melville lumbered out of the car and headed down towards the bay. Noah was inside, practicing the cello. She stood outside for a while, listening. She'd gotten used to Bach, and some of the progressions of notes—she wouldn't call them melodies—had actually gotten embedded in her memory. When she went inside, Noah stopped at the end of a phrase, looked up, said a quick hello, and looked back at his music.

"Do you think we could talk?" she asked him.

He looked up again. "Now?"

"That would be nice."

"Let me just finish this piece."

She stayed there for a moment, watching him bent over his cello, engrossed in the music, then she turned and went out on the deck. She watched Melville digging for something in the wet sand. Eventually Noah appeared.

"You had something to tell me?" he asked.

"Could we sit down?" She pointed to the Adirondack chairs.

"Why not?" He was humming lines from what he had been playing, and once he'd made himself comfortable, he accompanied himself by tapping on the arm of the chair.

"Please stop that."

Noah looked surprised. "It's the Allegro movement. I was under the impression you liked it."

"What I'd like is to talk with you."

"Here I am."

"As I was driving to Provincetown, I was thinking about the problem that came up between us—"

"What problem?"

"Your lack of sympathy. What you said."

"I said a lot of things."

"About being 'realistic.'"

"Yes?"

"There was such a lack of understanding—a lack of compassion about what I had been going through. And then you made that comment about my girls."

"It was you who said that siblings always had unresolved issues from childhood. And so I was just referencing the situation between your daughters."

"You sounded critical of them, and it was hurtful."

"I don't see why it should be. After all, you're the one who's critical of Laurel for her treatment of Maggie."

"I talked openly with you about her, but Laurel's my daughter, and even though I've been critical of her, it was hard to hear it from you. You should understand that. Think about your brother."

"What about my brother?"

"The moment I suggested there might be any discord between you, you got testy and said, 'We have no unresolved childhood issues. We just don't feel a need to call each other.'"

"I don't believe you could characterize that remark as 'testy.'"

"It was the *tone*, Noah. But that's not the real problem. The real problem is that I've been talking honestly about my difficulties with my family, but you clam up when it comes to talking about your family. Your family is off limits. You and your brother might be out of touch for decades, yet you insist everything is absolutely perfect between you."

"Maybe I just don't feel a need to dissect everything the way you do."

"Maybe you just don't want to confide in me."

"What's really going on here, Sandy?"

"I need more from you."

"More what?"

"More communication. More openness. More empathy."

"I may not be demonstrative, Sandy, but that doesn't mean I'm not empathetic."

"Saying you're 'not demonstrative' is a cop-out, Noah. It's an excuse to avoid having to put yourself out, an excuse to not fully commit to the other person. It's emotional laziness."

"Maybe it's just who I am."

"It's not who you are; it's what you've chosen to be. What you've been *allowed* to be."

"Whoa!" Noah held his hands up in front of him. "You know, Sandy, I think we've talked about this enough, don't you?"

"No! I think we were just getting to something important."

"I believe I'm done for now. This conversation is not productive."

"This is exactly what I mean," said Cassandra. "As soon as we confront anything, you shut down and refuse to talk about it. In order for our relationship to work, I need you to engage fully with me."

"Why are you being so demanding?"

"I guess I have to be. It's obvious you're not used to being in a relationship where the other person makes demands on you, where you have to put in any emotional work."

"What are you saying?"

"I think you had it easy in your marriage. My guess is that Helene didn't ask much of you. She spoiled you."

"Leave Helene out of this!"

"But she's part of this, Noah."

"I am not going to talk with you about my dead wife."

Noah started walking away, but Cassandra snatched his sleeve.

"That's exactly what I've been unhappy about! Your unwillingness to talk with me."

Noah spun back towards her. "I have experienced loss and grief. I ask you to respect that."

"We've both experienced loss and grief, Noah. You lost your wife, and I lost my husband."

"Helene and I were married for forty-one years."

"And that gives you a corner on suffering? Rob and I didn't have that much time, but I don't feel his loss less deeply."

"Helene was my only wife."

"So that makes your grief morally superior?"

"I was merely stating a fact."

"The fact that I've been married three times doesn't invalidate my grief; in fact, it triples it. I grieved when my marriage to Ethan ended—I'd been young and full of hope when I married him—and even though I was no longer his wife, I still cared about him, and I grieved when he died. He got MS when the girls were teenagers, and it was horrible for Laurel and Maggie, so I had their grief to deal with in addition to my own. My marriage to Denny may have been a mistake, but that didn't mean I didn't love him. He was crazy and irresponsible, and his death was tragic and probably avoidable, so in addition to my grief, I felt guilty that I'd abandoned him. So if there's a competition of who's experienced more grief, it's not clear that you've won."

"I don't see this as a competition," Noah said. "Are you done?"

If Noah had said he was sorry, if he had made any gesture of affection, she would have been done. But things were spinning out of control, and she just let them take her.

"You'd said you wanted me to stay here—you even said you wanted to marry me—but that's clearly impossible now. I'd been OK living alone—it took me a long time to get there after Rob's death—and then I started getting involved with you. I started falling in love with you. I can't do this to myself. If you can't give me what I need, I've got to take care of myself. I've got to get out of here."

"If that's what you want to do."

"It's not what I want to do. It's what I have to do."

"Where will you go?"

"I'll figure it out. I haven't stayed here just because I had no alternatives."

There was a short space of time when he could have reached towards her, when he could have tried to repair things. But if he intended to, he didn't act quickly enough. She started towards the bedroom. She wanted him to come after her, to put his arms around her, to say, "Please, let's try to work this out."

"I guess you want me to spend the night in Larry's room," is what he said.

She didn't answer him. She closed the door behind her.

# XXIII

At night, in Larry's small room, in Larry's small bed, Noah tried, unsuccessfully, not to think about Cassandra. He didn't understand what had happened, how everything had changed. He didn't know what he might have done that had turned her against him. Was there anything at all he might have said, or was it completely out of his control? He couldn't figure it out; he'd hit a brick wall.

Larry's narrow bed sagged in the wrong place, and his back ached. Noah rolled onto his side but didn't feel any better. He'd gotten used to sleeping with two pillows, but there was only one on this bed; his second was in the bed he'd been sharing with Cassandra. It had gotten warm enough now that the woodstove was no longer in use, but his feet were cold. He pressed them together, left one on top of right one, then right one on top of left, but he couldn't warm them.

What he couldn't understand was why Cassandra was so angry at him. He was just the way he'd always been, but something had provoked her—some small act or words she found insensitive—and brought out grievances she'd never articulated before. Was it some perceived failure of his she hadn't been aware of in the past, or did she feel he had changed? He went over their argument in his mind, searched for clues but found none.

Noah sat up, shook out his pillow, then lay down again. If Cassandra insisted on being unreasonable, then it was a good thing that she was leaving. He certainly wasn't going to ask her to reconsider and stay.

He didn't need to be with someone who thought him unsympathetic when he was just being realistic, someone who accused him of lacking empathy, someone who found him incapable of openness. They'd been alone together in this small cottage for a long time. They both needed to move apart.

Filled with certainty and resolve, Noah rolled onto his back again and tried to fall asleep. He felt sorry for himself for having been misjudged, especially by someone he had thought understood him so well. The night seemed interminable, but eventually he did fall asleep. When he awoke, he reached, instinctively, for Cassandra's shoulder, and touching only sheet, not skin, he slowly began to make sense of where he was and what had happened. He sat up in bed and set his feet on the floor. It was already daylight. He listened for sounds—of Cassandra, of Melville—and hearing nothing, got up and went to the bathroom, then he went back to the bedroom and got dressed.

The kitchen hadn't been touched since the night before. Noah put on the kettle to heat water and looked out the window. Cassandra was walking with Melville down the beach. She walked in a straight path, and Melville ran back and forth in front of her, from dune to water, from water to dune. Noah made himself tea and had a bowl of cereal. He watched them until they turned back towards the cottage. When Cassandra returned, she went straight to the bedroom. He heard her talking on the phone. He didn't want to listen to her making plans. He took his cello outside on the deck. He sat on the front edge of the Adirondack chair to play, as he had that first night when they had come here and he'd played the gigue for her, establishing a new ritual. He played it now, got tangled halfway through, and started from the beginning again. He played it more slowly this time, letting the notes settle into the air around him. After a while he looked back into the house and saw that Cassandra was in the kitchen, getting herself breakfast. He carried in the cello and set it gently in its place in the corner. He turned to Cassandra and waited for her to look up at him. He wanted her to smile and ask him to forget everything that had happened. He wanted her to say that she'd just been upset about her call with her sister, and her response to him had been unfortunate, hyperbolic. He wanted her to come to him and put her arms around him and say she wasn't going to leave. Instead she looked at him with sorrow, and when she finally spoke, she said only, "I'm giving Marigold to Jed. Would you hold the door open for me while I carry the terrarium out?"

He nodded. He wondered if she was hoping he would say something, ask her not to leave. He wondered if she was waiting for him to make some gesture of reconciliation. But he was waiting for a gesture from her, and so they were trapped by each other's silence.

He held the door while she brought out the terrarium with Marigold. He watched her carry it up the driveway towards Bernice and Artie's house. She was gone for a long time, and he imagined that Bernice would be distressed and bewildered and would try to talk her out of leaving.

When Cassandra came back down to the cottage, he decided he wasn't going to be the one who spoke first, but when she came inside and he saw that she had been crying, he blurted out, "Where are you going?"

"Back to my apartment at Clarion for now. I won't be staying at Clarion, but I'll park there for the moment."

"And the insects and the other tarantula?"

"A friend at my old lab at the university will babysit them for a while."

"Can I help you carry things out to your car?"

"Thank you, but I think I can manage by myself."

"I guess I'll go out on the boat, then," said Noah. "So, goodbye."

It would be excruciating to shake hands, like the conclusion of a business deal, but if she had held out her hand, he would have taken it. But she didn't hold out her hand.

"I'm not good at this," she said, and she turned from him quickly and ran to the bedroom. She swung the door hard to shut it, but it hit the doorframe and swung back, leaving it still open a few inches. He stood for a moment, looking into the bedroom. He could have slipped his fingers around the side of the door, swung it open fully, stopped her from lifting the pile of clothes from the dresser drawer and dropping them into the suitcase that was lying open on the bed. But instead he left the house and walked down to the beach. He flipped the dinghy over, pushed the oars into the oarlocks, and dragged the dinghy to the water. He rowed out to *Sarabande*, tied the dinghy to the mooring, and climbed aboard the boat. It was faster if there were two people working to get the boat ready, but he was practiced at doing it himself. He put on his life jacket, lowered the centerboard, hoisted the sails, and cast off. The wind was coming from the west, and he knew that while it would be easy sailing going out, it would be challenging to get back. But he was in no hurry. He didn't want to return to the cottage while Cassandra was still there. Noah settled down in *Sarabande* and let the wind do its work.

It was a weekday morning, and there were no other sailboats out in the harbor. Noah looked out towards the open bay. A dragger was making its slow, monotonous circles, scraping the same poor patch of sea again and again. Noah wondered how there could be any clams left there to find. A few fishing boats were heading out in the boat channel. Artie was probably already far out in the bay by now.

Noah looked back towards the cottage. He didn't spot Cassandra. She was probably inside, packing up the last of her things. Collecting her toothbrush from the bathroom, her bathrobe from the hook on the back of the bedroom door. She'd said that Helene didn't ask much of him, that she'd spoiled him. But Helene was like that. She hadn't worshipped him, but she'd accepted him as he was, made no attempt to change him. Maybe he had gotten more self-involved, self-indulgent, less able to compromise. That was the trouble with living on your own: you got stuck in your ways. But that's how it was. If Cassandra had been disappointed, that was unfortunate. But it was too late to do anything about it now.

There were commercial oyster farms along the harbor, close to shore. It was safe enough to sail over their grants at high tide, but Noah still steered around them. He'd once ripped the hull of his boat on some abandoned gear. A tern was balanced on a buoy marking the corner of one of the grants. It flapped its wings as Noah sailed close but didn't abandon its perch. A group of cormorants, close together on what was the last bit of a rock not yet covered with water by the tide, was alarmed by Noah's approach, and when the most nervous of them flew off, the others followed.

Noah looked back at the cottage. He grabbed the binoculars he stowed in the bow, and, holding them in one hand, he trained them on the cottage, then on the driveway by the barn. He had to turn the boat and let the sail luff so he could get a steady view through the binoculars. The rear door of Cassandra's station wagon was up, and she emerged from the cottage, carrying a liquor-store box that looked heavy. Probably her books. She set the box down on the edge of the trunk and shoved it farther in. Then she climbed up into the back and rearranged some things that were already there. She sat for a moment at the back of the open trunk, legs dangling, then pushed herself off. She left the rear door open and started walking back to the cottage. When she disappeared inside, everything was bare and still. Noah kept his binoculars focused on the cottage, but there was no sign of her. He lowered the binoculars and turned around to look out towards the bay. There were no boats in the channel now, and nothing moved except the dragger, making its languorous orbit around an invisible sun. The water was an unrelenting gray.

Noah turned back and focused the binoculars on the cottage again. He tried to spot any movement inside, any sign of Cassandra. But he couldn't see anything through the windows. Thinking of her not being there when he returned, not being there ever, suddenly hurt him so much he dropped the binoculars onto the seat. He couldn't do anything about it—it was a pain that was unexpected and total. His life without her—all the days ahead—seemed joyless. She'd said she'd fallen in love with him. Yes, she'd said that. She wanted him to engage more with her, she wanted him to share everything, she wanted him to *feel*.

He didn't think now. He just fell to the handling of the boat with speed and certainty, as if he were battling a squall. Everything he did—the way he moved his arms, the way he shifted his weight—was automatic, tutored by the past. He pulled in the sail to catch the wind again, then he pushed the tiller hard and turned the boat. Once he regained his proper course, his thoughts flooded his mind. He'd sail back to the cottage and plead with Sandy to stay. He'd tell her that he'd listen, he'd try, he'd do whatever she needed him to do. He'd ask for her forgiveness for his host of failings, for even what he didn't understand.

But the wind was against him. It came straight at him, pushing him as if it were keeping him away. It was impossible to sail directly back to the cottage. He started tacking, back and forth, but he didn't make much progress. It would take him a long time to get back to his mooring. He'd never make it before she left.

He felt helpless, almost dizzy with the fear of loss. He needed to try something else. But he couldn't think of what else to do. Then, suddenly, he caught a glimmer of an idea, and seized it. He shoved the tiller so the bow swung around and he was headed east again. The wind filled the sail, and *Sarabande* flew across the bay. Noah steered past the jetty and towards the town beach by the marina. He didn't have time to tie up at the public dock, so he aimed for shore, pulled up the centerboard, and ran the boat right up on the sand. He leaped out into the shallow water and dragged the boat up on the beach. There wasn't time to lower the sail, so he pushed the bow so it was aimed windward and let the sail luff. Then he ran.

He ran across the beach and up to the road. Cassandra would have to drive this way to get to the main road when she left. He wasn't sure if she'd already passed by, but there was nothing he could do but wait. He stood, panting, by the side of the road and tried to catch his breath. A gull waddled across the parking lot near the harbormaster's shack. It snatched something from the boat ramp and flew off. Three bikers, hunched over their handlebars, came around the bend in the road and slowed down at the crossroads. The first rider signaled left, and they turned in unison, like a flock of birds, their bikes tipping so close to the road they almost brushed the pavement. Noah leaned back against a telephone pole and kept his eye on the spot in the distance, down the road. He thought he must have missed Cassandra, but then he saw her car coming. He dashed to the middle of the road and stood there, legs apart, arms in the air. He held his hands out towards her, as if he could stop her car by the sheer force of his love, alone.

# XXIV

The spinach and the swiss chard were wilting, but the kale survived the day of neglect with no visible effects. Although Noah declined to get involved in the gardening project, he sat on a campstool by the raised beds and watched Cassandra plant the seedlings.

"I don't do dirt," he said when she offered him a trowel.

Cassandra laughed. "It's soil, Noah, not dirt. And if I hadn't returned, would you have just left these innocent plants out here to die?"

"Bernice would have come to their rescue, I'm sure. And there's nothing innocent about kale."

Cassandra gardened without gloves so she could feel the soil and the texture of the plants. The leaves were young and delicate, and she handled them tenderly. She filled one raised bed with the different varieties of lettuce, spacing them closer together than they probably should have been. She planted the kale and chard in another bin, with parsley along the side. That left just one bin for the spinach, not to mention three varieties of radish seeds and two varieties of peas.

She sat up on her knees and brushed off her hands. "I think we need another raised bed," she said, "or maybe two."

"The spinach looks like it might not be worth planting. Then you'll have plenty of room."

"I intend to revive it."

"Then it will just have to share its bed with the peas."

Cassandra tucked the roots of the limp spinach plants into holes in the soil and planted the peas in the rows behind them. She squeezed a row of radish seeds in between the kale and the chard. She handed the hose nozzle to Noah.

"This doesn't count as gardening, so you're safe," she said, and she went to turn on the water at the spigot by the outdoor shower.

When she came back, she stood behind Noah and rested her hands on his shoulders. "You know, we haven't been to the ocean beach since we came to the Cape. Why don't we go tomorrow?"

He leaned around to look at her. "Where did this come from?"

"It's sunny out, and I just thought it would be a nice thing to do."

"All right, but you're not planning on surfing, are you?"

"I've never surfed, but maybe it's something worth trying."

"How about trying to go out on the sailboat?" He turned off the hose nozzle and waited.

"If you really want me to. But it has to be a day when there's no wind."

There were only a few cars in the parking lot when Cassandra and Noah got to the ocean beach. It was a cool day, and sand had swept across the pavement, covering most of the black asphalt and obscuring the white lines for the parking spaces. The summer season hadn't started yet, and the cinder block bathrooms had padlocks on the plywood doors, as if there was something inside worth stealing. On the pavement next to the side labeled "WOMEN," a wooden lifeguard chair lay on its side, legs splayed in the air like a dead four-legged insect.

Cassandra parked close to the edge of the dune. Chunks of asphalt had broken off the end of the parking lot and lay scattered on the dune below; some of it probably had made it all the way down to the beach and been gobbled up by the ocean. The town had shoveled out two paths down to the water.

Cassandra had left Melville back at the cottage because she didn't want him pulling on the leash as they walked along the beach, and she didn't trust him if she let him loose. He'd been content with a frozen marrow bone as they'd left, but she guessed he'd become aware of the treachery of her abandonment when he heard the sound of the departing car and was now probably howling by the door.

"I'm leaving my shoes up here," she said. She didn't expect Noah would take off his shoes, too, but he surprised her and did. She ran down the path, and when she was close enough to the bottom, she jumped off the side of the dune onto the beach below. Just as she landed in the soft sand, she caught an image from years past, when she took Laurel and Maggie to the ocean and they ran halfway down the dune, then leaped off, flinging out their arms and whooping as they sailed off into space, Maggie's pigtails up in the air above her head. Cassandra had gone on that trip to the Cape with just the girls, after she was divorced from Ethan and before she married Denny, that short space of time when she'd been single. There had been only a short space of time, too, after she was divorced from Denny and before she married Rob, and she realized that the years since Rob died was the longest space of time she'd ever been on her own. She'd not only gotten used to it, she'd come to feel empowered by it and appreciate it, just the way all those self-help books she'd never read had promised. If she married Noah, at least she knew it wouldn't be because of her base need to be with someone, a need that no doubt had something to do with the loss of her father, not that she had (or ever would have) consulted with a therapist to help her illuminate this realization.

"Which way are we going?" Noah asked when he'd made his way down the path and joined her.

"If we walk to the right, we'll have the wind in our faces as we go and at our backs as we return. It will push us along." Cassandra held out her arms and spun around, the loose sleeves of her jacket flapping, her hair blowing into her face.

"How far are we going to hike?" he asked.

"As far as you like."

"This is your outing. I am coming along only to keep you from dashing out into the waves."

"It's *our* outing," she corrected him. She took his hand.

The tide was going out now, but occasionally a defiant wave rose high on the beach, and Cassandra and Noah raced up closer to the dune. They stood still for a while, looking out over the ocean.

"I always liked to picture what was far away on the opposite shore," Cassandra said, "as if you could see the whole globe with Europe— Spain, Italy, France—all right there." She pointed to a small gray spot, a distant container ship moving steadily along the horizon. "Do you ever feel guilty that we're this lucky compared with so many people?"

"Guilty? No. I just feel relieved. Why would you feel guilty?"

"Because I don't know that I deserve to be this lucky."

"You're a seventy-two-year-old widow. Your children are far away, and you've been living in a rough cottage without central heating. I don't think you have anything to feel guilty about."

"But I do get to live in that rough cottage with a kindly old man, who happens to be a gourmet chef," said Cassandra. She squeezed his hand, then let go. "The thing about the ocean is it forces you to confront your mortality."

"That doesn't sound like you!" said Noah, and he laughed.

"Too pompous?"

"Too grim. But useful if contemplation of your mortality enhances the chances of my proposal."

"You know you didn't actually propose to me, Noah."

"I most certainly did!"

"No, you asked me to list the reasons I might turn you down if you proposed."

"It was just a circuitous phrasing, perhaps, but—"

"But not an actual proposal."

"So would you answer in the affirmative if I did a conventional down-on-one-knee, 'Will you marry me?' proposal?"

"Not necessarily."

Cassandra rolled up the cuffs of her jeans and stepped towards the edge of the water. An oncoming wave stopped just short of her toes. She took a step closer, and the next wave reached farther, burying her feet in foam.

She turned back to Noah. "It's not that cold," she said.

He sat down on the side of the dune. "I'm quite happy up here on dry land, observing you."

"I'll come sit with you for a bit," she said. She climbed up the beach and settled beside him. She pointed to the side of the dune where there were circles engraved in the sand.

"Look, the artistry of the wind."

"What are they?"

"They're called scratch circles." She bent a long, slender piece of sea-grass so it lay flat across the sand. "It's rooted here," she said, touching the base of the stem. "The wind blows it back and forth, and it draws a curve, and when the wind blows it all around, it inscribes a circle."

"You are a fount of information," said Noah.

"Some of it useful, I hope."

"Possibly." Noah drew a circle in the sand beside him using his forefinger. Then a smaller one inside it. He turned to Cassandra.

"What more do you want from me?" he asked. "What more do you need before you can say 'yes' to my proposal?"

"It's nothing simple—"

"With you? I'd never suggest that it was."

"I'd like to know more about your car accident."

"That! Why?"

"Because I feel you may not have told me the whole story. And it worries me that you're withholding something."

"I'm not withholding anything! There's no reason you should be worried about it."

"Then why are you unwilling to talk about it? I don't want us to keep secrets from each other."

"There's no secret. I was in the supermarket parking lot, ready to drive home, and I backed out of the parking space without looking behind me. I slammed into a car that was driving past."

"When did it happen?"

"Three years ago."

"Before Helene died?"

"No, after."

"Soon after?"

"A few days after. It was the first time I'd left the house."

"Oh, I'm so sorry, Noah." She laid her hand on his knee. "You can hardly blame yourself for the accident."

"Of course I blame myself! I should have been more careful."

"You were upset. You were in pain. Things like that happen. It's expected."

"What are you, some sort of amateur psychologist?"

"Actually, I'd describe myself as a semiprofessional. I've had lots of experience analyzing people."

"Whether they asked for it or not."

Cassandra laughed. "Maybe so. But you know, Noah, it wouldn't hurt if you allowed yourself to acknowledge your feelings. When you lose someone you love, it's OK to feel the full force of grief—in fact, you're *supposed* to."

"I don't need anyone to tell me how I'm supposed to feel."

"That's true. Sorry. But I do think you need someone to remind you when it's time to forgive yourself."

"You wanted me to forgive Jed. And you wanted me to forgive Larry. And now you want me to forgive myself?"

"That's always the hardest one, isn't it?"

"Why does it matter whether I forgive myself or not?"

"Because if you can't forgive yourself, Noah, I'll worry that you won't be able to forgive me."

"And do you forgive yourself for everything?"

"I'm working on it."

Cassandra got herself up and walked back down towards the water. She didn't turn back to see if Noah was following her. She guessed he wasn't, but that was OK too. She reached down and rolled her jeans higher up on her legs. She gazed out at the waves. A gray seal poked its head up not far out from shore, looked with curiosity at Cassandra, then submerged again. Now that the weather was warmer, the great white sharks were back, and the seals needed to be wary. In the water, they'd be safe from people on the beach, but they'd have to haul themselves out on the sandbars to be safe from the sharks. She saw the curve of the seal's black back out farther among the waves; then it was gone for so long she gave up looking for it, until she spotted it farther down the beach, before it dove again.

Then there were just the waves, going about their business, untouched. Their pattern was predictable—the rush of the water, the suck of the undertow—but there was endless variation. Cassandra took another step farther out. A wave crested over her ankles and pulled back, dragging sand and pebbles with it, digging out the sand around Cassandra's feet so her heels sank in. The next wave was higher, and the spray wet her cuffs. It invariably did.

The bay was beautiful, but the ocean had bite to it. It made Cassandra feel suitably insignificant, put everything in its place. She looked back at Noah, sitting up on the beach, arms propped on his knees. He was squinting in the sun but watching her. She'd been hoping for something that would help with the decision she had to make, and finally an idea began to take shape in her mind: something she would ask of him that would give her the confirmation she needed. The only problem was she didn't know what she'd do if he refused.

She turned from the water and walked up the beach towards him. "Ready to head back now?"

He got to his feet. "I am." He pointed to her cuffs and laughed. "I didn't think you'd escape unscathed."

"No comment," she said. The wind was behind them as they walked back, nudging them along. She thought about the ocean's indifference to the concerns of humans. All their fears, all their troubles, were just swept away, like everything else, by the wind. She slipped her arm through Noah's. It was just the two of them now. She fingered the key ring in her pocket as she climbed the path up the dune ahead of him. She knew everything by touch: the key to the car, the key to her apartment at Clarion, the key to her old house, which she hadn't gotten around to taking off the ring, and a bronze cicada that dangled from the ring, a gift from one of her old graduate students.

They climbed up the dune and put on their shoes when they got up to the parking lot. Cassandra's car was the only one left there now. The film of sand on the pavement turned the parking lot into a flat, deserted beach bordered by banks of *Rosa rugosa*, beach plum, and wind-stunted pines. Cassandra unlocked the car; then she handed the keys to Noah.

"Why are you giving these to me?" he asked.

"I want you to drive me back."

"You know I don't drive."

"You may not have driven for a while, but you *do* drive." She opened the door on the passenger side of the car and climbed in. She settled in the seat.

Noah put his hand on the edge of the car roof and leaned down towards her. "What are you doing, Sandy?"

"I'm giving you a chance to get past something that happened three years ago."

"Why?"

"So I can marry you."

"What is this, some kind of a test?"

"I suppose it is. I guess I've just been needing to know that you're really ready to marry me."

"And what about you? What are you going to do to demonstrate that you're really ready to marry me?"

"I'm trusting you to drive my car."

Noah took his hand off the car roof and straightened up carefully. He shook his head at her. "What am I going to do with you?" he asked.

"You're going to take me back to the cottage." She smiled up at him. He shut the car door and walked slowly around the front of the car. He opened the door on the driver's side and took his time getting into the seat and closing the door. He studied the wad of keys she'd handed him, flipped the cicada to the side, and inserted the car key into the ignition.

"I'm not sure I can do this," he said.

"You can. The parking lot is empty, so drive around a bit to get used to it again."

"My driver's license is expired."

"I know. But you'll get it renewed soon."

"So I'll be driving illegally now."

"It's not that far to the cottage, Noah. And you're not going to be stopped as long as you aren't speeding. And even if you were speeding a little, they don't stop old people driving old Volvo wagons."

"You know that for a fact?"

"Of course."

He turned on the ignition; then he placed his hands on the steering wheel. She wanted to bend down and kiss his hands, kiss his fingers one by one, but she decided to wait until they'd gotten back to the cottage.

She shut her eyes for a moment, then looked at Noah. "I'm right here beside you," she whispered. "I'm right here."

Noah stepped on the gas, and the car started up. They drove slowly around in a circle in the parking lot. The tires etched the sand, marked their trail behind them. They drove to the entrance of the parking lot, paused for a moment, and then headed out together on the road towards home.

# ACKNOWLEDGMENTS

My thanks to my intuitive and supportive agent, Jennifer Weltz, whose wisdom guided me from the first moment she met Noah and Cassandra, and to my superb editor at Lake Union, Alicia Clancy, who enthusiastically championed their story. Thank you also to Ariana Philips and the team at Jean V. Naggar Literary Agency, to my writing group, the cheering section behind so many of my books: Barbara Diamond Goldin, Patricia MacLachlan, Leslea Newman, Ruth Sanderson, Ann Turner, Ellen Wittlinger, and Jane Yolen, and to numerous friends, including John Clayton, Sharon Dunn, Betsy Hartmann, Nick Picariello, and Amy Timberlake.

I'm indebted to Jeff Boettner and other biologists at the University of Massachusetts, along with naturalists at the Hitchcock Center for the Environment and Mass Audubon Arcadia Wildlife Sanctuary, who sparked my interest in entomology. My thanks to Gail Howe Trenholm, Melissa Lowe, Bob Prescott, Barbara Brennessel, and all the inspiring mentors at Mass Audubon Wellfleet Bay Wildlife Sanctuary, who fostered my love of the natural world of Cape Cod.

I'm endlessly grateful to my generous manuscript readers—family and friends—whose insights enriched this novel and whose encouragement nurtured me while I was writing: Austin Bliss, Artemis Demas Roehrig, Carol Baim, Joseph Baim, Elaine von Bruns, Valerie Martin, Carole Adler, and most especially, Matthew Roehrig.

# ABOUT THE AUTHOR

*Photo © Matthew Roehrig*

Corinne Demas is the award-winning author of thirty-seven books, including five novels (among them *The Writing Circle* and *Returning to Shore*), two short story collections, a memoir (*Eleven Stories High: Growing Up in Stuyvesant Town, 1948–1968*), a poetry chapbook (*The Donkeys Postpone Gratification*), a play, and numerous books for children (including *Saying Goodbye to Lulu*, *The Littlest Matryoshka*, and *The Disappearing Island*). Her short stories have appeared in more than fifty publications. She is also the editor of *Great American Short Stories: From Hawthorne to Hemingway*.

Corinne is a professor emerita of English at Mount Holyoke College and a fiction editor for the *Massachusetts Review*. She divides her time between Western Massachusetts and Cape Cod. Visit Corinne's website at www.CorinneDemas.com, or find her on Twitter @corinnedemas.